Glimpses of the Dreamwood

Brian Ligouri

*For those who carry invisible scars the world cannot see,
and still find the strength to keep going.
This is for you.*

"To live in hearts we leave behind is not to die."

— **Thomas Campbell**

Chapter 1
Cracks in the Shelter

The air in the subway bunker tasted of rust. The sound had been part of their lives for so long that, when it wasn't there, the silence felt wrong. Elias pressed his back against the cold concrete wall, his arms wrapped tight around Mira, who buried her face in his chest. At eleven years old, he was the big brother now; the one who had to hold it together. But his heart hammered like the artillery's merciless pulse, a distant thunder rolling over Nova City, each boom a reminder that the world above was tearing itself apart.

It was 2045, and World War 3 had turned their home into a graveyard of steel and smoke. Nova City, once the shining jewel of the post-2020s world, built on a coastal peninsula where grand bridges linked continents in promises of peace and trade, now buckled under siege. The invaders, faceless superpowers locked in a brutal scramble for dominance, had zeroed in on the city like vultures on a decaying carcass. Those bridges, symbols of unity, were now twisted wreckage, destroyed to block any hope of escape or rescue. The city's ports, meant to feed the world with oil and grain, were blockaded by enemy fleets, starving everyone inside. Elias didn't understand all of it, not really. But he felt it, deep in his bones, the way the ground trembled and the sky screamed when fighter planes zipped by.

Their father was gone. Just two weeks ago, a factory raid had turned the sky black with fire and smoke from the refinery. Elias had been at school, or what was left of it, lessons squeezed into a basement, when the alarms wailed. By the time he and Mira got home, their mother was already sobbing, clutching a crumpled notice from the defense council. "He was fixing the generators," she'd whispered, her voice breaking as she read the letter. The superpowers had targeted the refinery factories to cripple the city. Elias hadn't cried then. He couldn't. Mira, though, at seven years old, her small body shaking like a leaf in the wind; she couldn't help but cry. She had already felt the grief of war. She carried herself like someone who'd already learned disappointment: careful, quiet, quick to read fear in a grown-up's face. Now, in the bunker, she clung to Elias as if he could stop the next bomb from falling.

The shelter was a forgotten stretch of the old subway line, sealed off with metal doors and sandbags. The old posters along the subway walls had faded; faces of smiling travelers on a beach under reflected blue sunlight, words promising things like *progress through connection for a better tomorrow*. The letters cracked and flaked whenever the ceiling shook. Dozens of families crammed in with them: elders with hollow eyes, children too scared to speak, mothers doling out meager rations from dented cans. The air was thick with the smell of unwashed bodies and sulfur. Flickering lanterns cast long shadows on the walls, making the cracks in the concrete look like veins pulsing with bad blood as water seeped through. Above Mira's head, a crack spread through the concrete. Elias stared at it, imagining it widening, splitting the whole bunker open.

Boom! The ground buckled from an explosion above, and screams ripped through the dim space. Dust sifted from the ceiling like gray snow. Mira whimpered, her fingers digging into Elias's shirt. "Is it over?" she asked, her voice muffled against him. "Not yet," he whispered, though he had no idea. His mind raced ahead, faster than the fear could grab him. He couldn't stay here, trapped in this shaking tomb. He needed somewhere safe, somewhere green and alive, where the bombs hadn't charred everything around him.

It started in his head, a secret place he'd built long before the war, back when Nova City still buzzed with lights and laughter. It was a forest without end, tall trees with leaves that glowed like fireflies at dusk. Sunlight filtered through the canopy in golden shafts, warming the mossy ground. No bombs fell there. No soldiers marched. Elias was the guardian, a boy with a wooden staff carved from an ancient oak, patrolling paths that wound through whispering ferns and babbling brooks. There, he was strong. There, he could protect Mira and keep the shadows at bay.

"Hey," he nudged her as she hid her face against his chest. "Close your eyes. Let's try a game." Mira lifted her head, her eyes wide and red-rimmed. She was small for seven, all sharp angles and tangled brown hair, but her gaze held a spark that the war hadn't snuffed out completely. "A game?" she asked, her voice a fragile and soft. "Yeah. Trust me, close your eyes." Mira blinked slowly, then closed her eyes. Elias painted the picture in words, soft and steady, like how their father used to tell bedtime stories. "There's a path that starts right here, under that crack in the wall. See it? It opens up, and when we walk along it, we're no longer here. The air smells like rain falling off green leaves, and the ground is soft under our feet. No more shaking. Just us."

She nodded, squeezing her eyes shut, and for a moment, the bunker faded. In Elias's mind, they stepped onto a carpet of emerald moss, the trees rising like silent giants around them. A breeze rustled the branches, carrying the faint melody of wind chimes hidden in the bark. Elias led the way, his staff tapping the earth, Mira's hand warm in his as she tried to see. Elias talked about passing a clearing where deer with silver antlers grazed, unafraid. Elias was piecing this together from scraps of memory and emotion, from picnics in the city's parks before the war, and from stories their brother Theo used to read to them. Theo. Elias shoved the thought down. Not now.

But the real world clawed back. Their mother shifted beside them, her face pale in the lantern light. She was thirty-two, but the war had aged her a decade, lines etched deep around her eyes. "Elias," she said, her voice low, almost lost in the chatter of other refugees hiding in the bunker. "Keep her close. It's getting worse up there."

He opened his eyes, the sanctuary dissolving like mist. Mira blinked too, disappointment flickering across her face. "What was that place?" she whispered. "It was pretty, I could see the trees." "The Dreamwood," he whispered back, the first thing that had come to his mind, though he'd never thought of naming the escape.

Their mother pulled them closer, her arm a frail barrier against the chaos. After all that mess in the '20s with the pandemics and the divides, wars happening across the world, Nova City was supposed to be different. Built on a peninsula to link the world with grand bridges, connecting Europe to the Americas, and Asia to everywhere else. A place for talks and trade, for peace. Neutral ground. But the superpowers couldn't stand not being in control.

Elias had heard bits and pieces from school videos before the raids shut them down. How Nova City rose as a beacon, its multicultural districts buzzing with diplomats and merchants. Offshore oil rigs and deep harbors made it a lifeline, feeding global supply chains. Leaders of smaller nations would meet to break bread and find common ground, avoiding conflict. But in this war, Nova City was the prize. The superpowers, locked in their endless grudge matches, saw the city's fall as a victory. Propaganda broadcasts blared from stolen airwaves. "Nova falls, unity dies." Elias didn't care about the politics of it all. He just wanted the bombs to stop.

A low rumble built overhead, vibrating through the tracks beneath them. The lanterns swung wildly. "Artillery!" someone shouted from the far end of the bunker. Panic rippled through the crowd. Parents grabbed children, elders stumbled to their feet, and the metal doors groaned as city guards yanked them open, barking orders. "Everyone evacuate! Surface team's signaling breach! Debris is falling everywhere!"

Elias's stomach cramped. The Dreamwood, as it's now known, felt miles away, fragile as his sister. He scooped Mira up, her legs wrapping around his waist. She was light, too skinny from the skipped meals, but she held on like a lifeline. Their mother stood, wincing. Elias caught a glimpse of the fresh scar on her thigh, a shrapnel wound received a week ago on a scavenging run that was still healing. She took Elias's free hand. "Stay together," she said, her grip iron despite the fear in her eyes.

They surged with the crowd into the dim stairwell which led to the streets above, the air growing thicker with smoke and dust as they climbed. The rumble escalated into a deafening roar, the ceiling shuddering as if the whole city were collapsing. Elias's mind raced, unspoken fears rushing in: What if this was it? What if the next blast took Mira, or their mother? He'd be alone, just like after Father. No more stories. No more safety. Just endless dark.

A crack split the air. Too close. Too real. Chunks of concrete rained down, one grazing Elias's shoulder, drawing a sharp sting. Mira screamed, burying her face again. He ran, legs burning, pushing through the press of bodies toward the surface. The Dreamwood flickered in his thoughts, a desperate anchor keeping him moving. "Hold on," he told himself, and her, amidst the chaos. "The trees are still there, we'll get back."

They burst into the ruined street above the tunnel, the night sky a hellish orange from flares and fires. Nova City's skyline, once a forest of gleaming towers, was now jagged stumps silhouetted against the bombardment. Enemy bombers droned overhead, their shadows blacker than the smoke rising all around. Debris littered the ground. Hunks of twisted rebar and broken glass blanketed the streets. Cars were split like eggshells. Elias set Mira down but kept her hand locked in his, their mother limping right beside them. Elias spotted the remnants of a shop across the street; its window was spiderwebbed with cracks. Through it, though, he spotted a glimpse of a time before the war: a mannequin wearing a sundress, ready for the beach. He wished Mira had seen it, but she kept her face to the ground as they passed broken shells of what used to be cars, now tombs to those still inside.

"Over there!" A guard waved them toward a cluster of sandbagged barricades, temporary cover in what had once been a thriving plaza. They ducked in, panting, as another barrage lit the horizon. Explosions bloomed like deadly flowers, reaching to the sky and shaking the earth. Elias pulled Mira onto his lap and rocked her gently. His shoulder throbbed, blood warm under his shirt, but he ignored it. Instead, he whispered, "There are deer running now, Mira. Fast, through the trees. We're right behind them."

She nodded and squeezed her eyes shut, but tears leaked out anyway. Their mother leaned against the sandbags, breathing hard. "We can't stay here long," she said, scanning the sky. The invasion had ramped up; the invaders pushed harder to cut off supply routes and claim the city's oil. The attacks and air strikes intensified from what they were a week ago.

Elias nodded, but inside, the isolation clawed at him. The city that promised connection had become a cage, trapping them as it sank like the destroyed ships in the harbor. He glanced at Mira, her small chest rising and falling rapidly with each breath. In the Dreamwood, he could protect her. Out here, he wasn't sure. The bombs fell on, cracking the night, and Elias wondered how many more pieces of their world he could lose before there was nothing left to imagine.

"There are smooth stones on the path, Mira, step on those as you walk through, to not hurt your feet." Mira's forehead wrinkled as she concentrated on Elias's words, trying to picture it. Her breath steadied, and tears stopped. "I guess I can see the stones," she whispered through a halfway smile, the first Elias had seen in weeks from her. This is how he'd protect her; he just needed to focus.

The evacuation dragged on through the rubble-strewn streets, the family weaving between collapsed buildings and smoldering craters. Guards shouted directions, herding survivors toward a secondary bunker deeper into the subway network. Elias's arms ached from carrying Mira partway, but he didn't complain. It was his duty now... now that his father and Theo were gone.

As they descended again, the air cooler and humid, Elias's thoughts turned inward. The Dreamwood called to him, a pull stronger than fear. Sharing it with Mira made it real... fragile. What if the cracks spread there, too? He pushed the thought away, focusing on the path ahead. For now, survival meant one step, one whisper, one imagined tree at a time.

In the new shelter, quieter but no less crowded, they claimed a corner. Mira curled up on a threadbare blanket, asleep at last, exhausted from the day. Elias heard the elders mumble next to them, "Heard the scouts... tanks rolling in... targeting the grid..." He didn't understand them, but then again, why should he? Their mother bandaged Elias's shoulder with strips from her scarf, her hands steady despite the tremor in her voice. "You did good today," she said softly. "Keeping her calm. That was very nice, that's what matters. Your father would be so proud of you."

Elias managed a nod, but his mind was already drifting. The Dreamwood waited. Tomorrow, he'd take Mira deeper. Build walls of vines against the noise. Out here, the cracks were everywhere: in the walls, in their family, in the city itself. In there, he could mend them. He had to. Elias curled up next to his sister, closing his eyes, picturing a stream running through trees. For the first time in a long while, the sleep came easier, though it was more of a half-sleep, the kind where your body is still awake, ready to react to the slightest noise or action, the kind that only leaves you half-rested.

As they slept, a hum grew in the distance. The surface rattled, metal scraping on concrete, the budding rumble of treads more consistent than thunder.

Chapter 2
Whispers in the Dark

The hum from the surface grew into a grinding roar that shook the new bunker's walls, pulling Elias from his half-sleep like a hand yanking him back to reality. Mira stirred beside him, her small hand clutching the edge of the blanket, but she didn't wake. Their mother sat up slowly, her bandaged hands pressing against the concrete floor as if testing its stability. The lanterns still flickered, casting jittery light over the huddled families, but the air felt heavier now, charged with something worse than dust.

Elias rubbed his eyes; the sting from his shoulder wound a dull reminder of the evacuation. The elders' words lingered in his head... "tanks rolling in... targeting the grid" ... nonsensical fragments that painted pictures he didn't want to see. He glanced at the group nearby, two old men with gray-stubbled faces leaning close, their voices low but carrying in the cramped space. "Heard it from the scouts before we sealed up," one muttered, his voice rough and raspy.

"Enemy's got armor divisions pushing from the eastern docks. Not just probing this time, aiming straight for the power stations."

The other nodded, his eyes darting to the children nearby as if weighing whether to keep going. "No power means no comms, no pumps for the water reserves. We'll be sitting ducks in the dark."

Elias shifted closer, pretending to adjust Mira's blanket, but his ears strained. He knew bits about the city from faded school lessons, projected on cracked screens before the raids turned classrooms to rubble. Nova City had been designed as a lifeline after the pandemics fractured the world; a sprawling megacity on the coast, its districts a mosaic of cultures where diplomats from fractured alliances once haggled over resources under glass-domed halls. The power grid was its beating heart, drawing from wind farms along the cliffs and deep-sea cables that fed energy to half the globe. But the war had twisted it all. The blockades choked the supply ships, and now the tanks, the massive, tread-crushing machines Elias had only seen in grainy propaganda videos, were coming to rip out the veins of the city.

A deeper tremor ran through the floor, followed by a sharp crackle overhead, like lightning striking the ground. The lanterns sputtered, their flames dancing wildly before one by one, they dimmed to nothing. Gasps rippled through the bunker as darkness swallowed the space, thick and absolute, broken only by the faint glow of emergency chem-lights some families pulled from their packs.

Elias's heart jumped; his hand finding Mira's in the black. She woke with a jolt, her voice small and sharp, "Eli? Why's it dark?"

Their mother fumbled for him, her fingers cold against his arm. "Stay put." Her voice held an edge of resignation, as if she'd expected this. In the low voices around them, the panic built as mothers soothed crying babies. A father cursed under his breath about "those bastards starving us out." The air grew more stale without the fans humming, the smell of sweat and sulfur pressing in like another layer of walls.

Elias pulled Mira onto his lap, her body tense against his. The darkness made everything worse; sounds sharper, shadows in every corner. He could hear the elders still talking, their words weaving through the murmurs. "The grid was never built for this." Elias blocked it out, focusing on Mira's ragged breaths. She was shaking again, the blackout stripping away the illusion of safety the light had provided.

"It's okay," he whispered, though his own voice wavered. "Remember the woods? The path with soft ground and the stones?" The Dreamwood tugged at him, a faint pull in the void; a place where light came from within the trees themselves, not fickle wires. But sharing it now, in this total black, felt harder. Mira had glimpsed it earlier, seen the trees and stones, but the war kept dragging her back, her mind too tangled in fear to hold on.

She nodded against his chest, but her grip tightened. "It's too dark here. I can't see the path." Her words came out choked, like the shadows were already clawing at her. Elias closed his eyes, willing the image to form despite the chaos. "You don't need to see it with your eyes. Feel it. The moss is under your feet right now, cool and springy. The trees are close, their branches brushing your arms like a hug." He spoke low, adding details to pull her in, building on what he'd started before. The world unfolded in his mind: not just the glowing leaves, but hidden glades where fireflies gathered at night, their lights pulsing like tiny heartbeats. Paths forked into tunnels of vines, heavy with blossoms that released a scent like roses after rain.

Mira whimpered, shifting. "But the rumbling, I hear the rumbling, they're coming for us." The ground vibrated again, a grind that matched her words, sending dust scattering from the ceiling.

"They're not," Elias said firmly, though the doubt troubled him. In the Dreamwood, sounds transformed. The rumble became the low call of a distant waterfall, steady and alive, not destructive. "Listen, that's the brook now, rushing over smooth rocks. We can follow it, you and me. The water's clear, and there are fish jumping, silver flashes in the glow from the leaves." He painted it vividly, drawing from memories of the city's old aquarium, before the bombs shattered its domes. The brook wound through the forest, its banks lined with ferns that curled protectively, shielding them from any noise that tried to follow.

For a heartbeat, Mira's breathing slowed and her body eased. "The fish... do they have colors?" Her question was tentative, a probe reaching out, but the darkness pressed, and she tensed again as another tremor shook the bunker. Whispers turned to urgent mutters around them. "Rations will go bad without the coolers," someone said.

Elias pushed on, his voice a steady anchor in the blackness. "Yeah, the fish are blue and gold, moving like shooting stars under the water. We can sit by the brook, dip our hands in, feel the current flowing gently." But even as he spoke, the real world intruded. A child's cry pierced the black, followed by her mother's sharp hushing. The elders' talk drifted back. "Grid down means the whole eastern district's blind. They will use it, sneak in under cover, pick off the ports one by one."

Mira pulled away slightly, her face invisible but her voice small. "I can't see anymore." The Dreamwood felt thin to Elias, too, stretched by the blackout's weight. He held her closer, whispering more about berries along the bank, sweet and bursting, but the roar outside swelled, metal on metal, drowning out his words.

The blackout stretched on, turning minutes into an endless stretch where time lost its edge. Elias's throat grew dry from talking, his stories about the brook fading against the persistent grind above. Mira had relaxed a fraction at first, her questions about the fish sparking a flicker of curiosity, but now she huddled silent, her head heavy on his shoulder. The chem-lights glowed faintly, painting faces in a sickly green, revealing the strain: a woman rocking her toddler with bloodshot, hollow eyes, an elder staring at the ceiling as if willing it to hold.

Their mother squeezed Elias's arm in the dark. "Food," she said quietly, rummaging in their pack. The rations were meager: a shared tin of preserved beans, cold and metallic, divided with a bent spoon. Elias took a small portion first, chewing mechanically, the taste like wet earth. He passed the rest to Mira, who poked at it with her finger. "It's slimy," she whispered, her nose wrinkling. "Eat it anyway," their mother urged, her voice soft but firm. "We need the strength."

Elias nodded towards Mira, though she couldn't see it. He remembered the harbor district from before. Vast piers lined with colorful stalls, thick with spices and salt, families strolling under the strings of colorful lights. It had been a place of movement, bridges arching to distant shores, diplomats sealing deals over steaming bowls. Food was plentiful and delicious. But the war had frozen it. Enemy submarines lurked below, aircraft carriers blotted the sea, and drones buzzed like angry wasps. The blockades and shelling had ruined it, and the only food left had to be foraged from crumbled stores and kiosks.

Mira managed a few bites, then pushed the tin away. "Tastes bad. Like it smells in here." Her words lingered, upsetting Elias. She was trying, he could tell. Earlier, by the brook, she'd almost added to the story, asking about the fish's colors like she wanted to shape it herself. But the fear restricted her, making the Dreamwood feel too distant, a place she glimpsed but couldn't grasp fully.

"Let's go back," Elias said, wiping her mouth with his sleeve. "To the woods. The brook's still there." He closed his eyes again, drawing her in with a welcoming tone. The darkness helped this time, forcing them to rely solely on words. "We're walking along the bank now, the water trickling beside us. The ferns brush our legs, soft like blankets. Up ahead, the path widens into a grove. The trees are circling a patch of grass where the ground glows faintly, lit by the moon. Do you see it?"

Mira shifted, her breath hitching. "The moon? Is it behind the trees?" There it was, her question, a step closer. She wasn't just listening; she was probing, wanting to understand.

"Exactly, the moon is shining through the trees," Elias said. He quickly built on it, expanding the Dreamwood to hold her. The grove was new, inspired by the city's lost parks; wide lawns where families picnicked under perpetual twilight lamps. Here, the grass shimmered with dew that caught the leaf-glow, creating a soft carpet that warmed their feet. "We can lie down in it, Mira. Feel it cushion us, like the old swings in the park before... You know. And above, the branches form a roof, keeping any rumbles out."

She was quiet for a moment, but then spoke out: "Can I touch the ferns?" Her voice held a hint of wonder, fragile but real. Elias felt a spark of hope, progress. Her mind was reaching instead of retreating.

"Yeah," he whispered. "Reach out, feel the leaves, velvety and soft. They're taller than you are, waving like they're glad to see you." In his mind, the ferns unfurled taller, their tips brushing Mira's hair, releasing a scent of earth and hidden flowers. The grove deepened: a central tree with bark like woven rope, perfect for climbing. Its roots formed natural seats. No hum there, no slimy food tins… just the quiet buzz of the forest, drowning the bunker's murmurs.

But the real world wouldn't stay quiet. A cough echoed from across the shelter, followed by a child's wailing. The elders picked up again, their voices threading through the dark like smoke. "Those tanks will roll right over the grid stations. Remember the old fusion plant on the cliffs? Probably headed straight for it. Without that, Nova's just a dark spot on the map."

Their mother shushed them gently, nodding that there were kids listening, but Elias heard the fear in her tone. She leaned in, her breath warm against the side of his face, "Ignore them, Elias. Keep going. It's helping her." She passed out the last of their water from a bottle in the pack, the liquid precious now that the purification pumps were offline.

Mira's hand found Elias's in the dark. "The tree... can we climb it?" She was leaning in, her body less rigid, but a fresh tremor from above made her flinch. The grind of treads vibrated through the ceiling, down the walls, and across the floor. It was closer now, and the earth felt like it was groaning.

Elias nodded, unseen in the dark. "We can. The bark's rough but kind, no splinters. Up we go, branch by branch, until we're high enough to see the whole Dreamwood stretched out." He described the view: endless green rolling to misty horizons, silver brooks snaking through the trees, distant glades where animals gathered without fear. It was his way of making Nova City's vastness his own; the peninsula's cliffs turned to forested edges, harbors to serene lakes.

Mira's questions kept coming, hesitant at first, then more inviting. "What do the branches feel like?" Her imagination flickered to life amid the rationed bites she chewed on and whispered fears of the elders around them.

Yet the blackout wore on them. Mira's energy drained as the tin emptied, her head dropping. "I'm tired," she murmured, the grove slipping from her grasp. Elias kept talking, adding fireflies to the branches for light, but the elders' words intruded. "Grid down... starvation's their weapon now."

Elias held her as she dozed fitfully, the Dreamwood a half-formed shield in the unrelenting dark, which, good for nothing else, seemed to help her to sleep.

Time dragged on, the bunker's air decaying as bodies shifted and sighed. Elias's arms ached from holding Mira, but he didn't move, his mind weaving the Dreamwood like a net to catch her drifting thoughts. She mumbled in her sleep, murmuring about the climbing tree, her fingers twitching as if gripping bark. It was the closest she'd come so far, not just hearing his words, but touching them in her sleep, starting to claim the place as hers.

Their mother dozed beside them, her breathing uneven and shallow, the scar on her thigh a reminder of how close the war had already come. Elias stared into the black as the chem-lights faded. Hunger pinched him sharper now, the rations barely touching it, and thirst made his tongue and saliva thick.

Just as Elias started to fade, a sudden jolt rocked the shelter, sharper than before, not thunderous, but mechanical. Shouts erupted: "They're through! Grid's gone!" Panic surged, bodies colliding in the dark as people fumbled for their packs. Elias clutched Mira tighter, her eyes snapping open with a gasp. "What's happening?"

"Nothing," he lied, his voice steady by force. But the roar outside intensified, a blend of engines and shouts filtering down through the vents. Tanks breached the surface barriers, their treads pulverized the streets. The bunker doors rattled, city guards barking orders in the gloom. "Hold position! Reinforcements enroute! Don't let them through!"

Their mother woke fully, pulling them close. "We move if we have to. Stick together." But the chaos built: a family scrambling for their pack, knocking over a lantern that sparked briefly before dying. In that flash, Elias saw faces twisted in fear. Mira buried her face in his chest, her body stiff and trembling. "The tanks... they're loud. Like monsters."

Elias's mind raced. "Close your eyes," he urged, his words cutting through the panic building around them. "We're back in the grove, high in the tree. The branches hold us safe, strong as the old bridges." He desperately expanded it, making the tree a lookout; trunk wide as a house, limbs forming a platform where they could watch the forest without fear. From there, the Dreamwood revealed more: meadows dotted with wildflowers, swaying in a breeze that carried hints of the sea, suggesting Nova's lost coastal paths near where they lived before the invasion sealed them in this subway.

Mira resisted at first, her breaths quick. "I can't... the noise is too big." But Elias persisted, his voice low and insistent. "Feel the bark under your hands. Rough, but steady. Look out... see the meadow? Flowers in reds and yellows, tall as you are, bending but not breaking." He drew from the city's pre-war vibrancy, the flower markets in the diplomatic quarter. Here, the flowers whispered welcomes, their stems weaving a barrier against any rumble.

Slowly, Mira's trembling eased. "The flowers... do they smell nice?" Her question came softer, curiosity piercing the fear, a sign she was latching on, piecing the world with him.

"Like summer," Elias said, relief flooding him. "Sweet and warm. We can pick some, weave them into crowns." In his mind, they descended the tree into the meadow, petals brushing their legs, the ground firm and alive. The tanks' roar twisted into the wind's rush through the grass, distant and harmless. Mira added haltingly, "Can the flowers sing too?"

Elias's heart swelled. She was reaching, struggling, but starting to shape it, her innocence fighting back. "They can. A soft tune, joining the brook and the chimes." The meadow bloomed fuller: butterflies with wings like stained glass flitting between blooms, landing on their shoulders without startle. It was a step toward sharing, her ideas molding into his.

That's when the raid hit. Sharp cracks above, not bombs, but gunfire, shouts echoing down. The bunker erupted: "They're raiding supplies! Soldiers breached the outer seals!" Families surged toward the doors as guards fired shots into the dark. Their mother yanked Elias up. "We go, now!" Chaos swallowed them, bodies pressing, Mira's hand slipping in his sweat-slick grip.

He pulled her along, whispering fragments of the meadow to keep her steady. "The butterflies are flying out with us," but the dark tore at it, the raid scattering their fragile peace. They burst into a side tunnel, the family separated in the stampede, gunfire popping closer. Mira cried out, lost in the black press, her voice cutting through: "Eli! The flowers, I can't see them!"

He lunged toward the sound, heart pounding, as the tunnel shook with the weight of invading boots overhead. The Dreamwood vanished. Elias's fingers brushed Mira's hand in the chaos, yanking her back just as a guard's flashlight beam swept the crowd, revealing snarling faces and scattered belongings. "This way," their mother called from ahead, her voice strained. But the troops were closing in, their shouts in a foreign tongue mixing with the guard's barking orders.

Mira clung to him now, her nails digging in, but in her panic, she gasped out, "The butterflies... they are leading us out." It was small, but it was hers, a piece of the Dreamwood she'd held onto amid the terror. Elias nodded, breathless, guiding them toward their mother's silhouette. The image steadied him, too, the meadow's brightness a faint counter to the gunfire's snaps in the dark.

They squeezed through a narrowing gap in the tunnel, the walls closing like jaws, until they spilled into a dimmer chamber lined with crates, the raided supplies, half-torn open by looters.

Their mother hauled them behind a stack of boxes, panting. "Quiet. They're right above us," she said, pointing up towards the ceiling and pressing her finger over her lips to signal a hush. Footsteps thundered overhead, then faded slightly as the raid splintered the crowd further. Mira whimpered, curling into Elias, her addition to the story hanging between them like a promise. For the first time, the Dreamwood felt shared, not just his gift but something growing between them, still fragile, but growing.

As the gunfire lulled into sporadic bursts, the soldiers seemed to withdraw. The tunnel fell silent, except for the drip of water from cracked pipes and the ragged breaths of the survivors huddled together, waiting for what might come next. Their mother pulled a thin blanket from the scattered crates, wrapping it around the three of them as they pressed close, sharing what warmth they had. Elias kept one arm around Mira, his free hand finding their mother's, the family's silent grip a fragile anchor against the endless black.

Chapter 3
The First Shared Glimpse

Air raid sirens started as a low wail, cutting through the thin morning haze that clung to Nova City's ruins. Elias froze mid-step, his hand tightening around Mira's as the sound built into a piercing howl, the kind that drilled into your skull and set your teeth on edge. They had been out scavenging since dawn, their mother leading the way through the shattered streets, picking over debris for anything usable: a can of preserved fruit missed by looters, a scrap of cloth to patch their blankets, maybe even a forgotten bottle of clean water. But the sirens changed everything. They meant the skies were alive and planes were coming.

"Down!" their mother hissed, yanking them toward the nearest cover: the gutted shell of what used to be a market stall, its walls crumbled to jagged piles of brick and rebar. The three of them squeezed into the tight space, backs pressed against the rough stone, the ground beneath them littered with shards of glass that crunched underfoot. Elias pulled Mira close, her small frame and shallow breathing wedged between him and their mother. The sirens kept screaming, a relentless wail that made the air feel heavier, as if the sky itself were pressing down on them.

Nova City sprawled around them in broken pieces, a maze of toppled buildings and cratered roads that stretched toward the distant coastline. From their hiding spot, Elias could see the remnants of the multicultural districts. Blocks where diplomats from every corner of the world once gathered, their summits held in grand halls lined with murals of linked hands and shared horizons. He remembered school lessons about it, fuzzy now but sharper in moments like this. Teachers had shown videos of the city's founding, how it rose as a neutral ground, its districts designed like a patchwork quilt of cultures: Asian markets spilling into European cafés, African art galleries bumping up against American tech hubs. Those summits had brokered deals that kept the peace for a while, turning the peninsula into common ground where rival powers talked rather than fought. But that's what made it a target. The superpowers saw it as a threat, a place that mocked their divisions, preventing them from seizing difference and creating proxy wars. Now, in the grip of World War 3, they wanted it crushed, its strategic coastal position seized to control the flow of ships and supplies. Elias's mind turned over those old facts, a bitter taste building in his throat like the dust coating his tongue. What good was all that history if it just led to this, hiding in rubble while the world burned?

The sirens faded to a distant moan, but the tension didn't break. Their mother peered out, her face drawn tight, scanning the empty street. She was thinner than ever, her cheeks hollow from the constant skimping on food, but her eyes held a fierce glint. "We can't stay here, we're too exposed," she said in a low, unwavering voice. "

Mira whimpered, burrowing deeper into Elias's side. She was starting to understand more than he wanted her to, like the way the sirens meant death dropping from above, or soldiers sweeping through with rifles ready. Her fingers twisted in his shirt, pulling at the frayed threads. "Elias, it's too loud. Make it stop."

He wrapped an arm around her, feeling the rapid flutter of her heart against his ribs. The ruins offered little comfort. Dust hung thick in the air, stirred by every faint breeze, and the smell of charred wood, metal, and gunpowder lingered from last night's fires. Shadows danced across the walls, twisted shapes that looked like figures lurking just out of sight. Elias's own pulse raced, a steady drum that matched the growing rumble in the distance. Not thunder, but something mechanical. Heavy. Tanks, maybe, grinding over the pavement on the outskirts. The war never let up; it just shifted forms, from bombs to blockades to boots on the ground.

"I can't stop it, Mira," he said softly, brushing a strand of hair from her forehead. "But we can go somewhere else. Remember the Dreamwood? From the blackout? Let's try it again. Let's explore together."

Her eyes lit up a fraction, curiosity cutting through the fear. She nodded, shifting to sit cross-legged in front of him, her knees touching his in the cramped space. Their mother gave a small, approving glance but stayed vigilant, her gaze fixed on the street. Elias took a deep breath, pushing down his own unease. He felt the weight of being the one trying to hold things together, especially since Theo and Father were gone. The Dreamwood had started as his private escape, a place to hide from the noise, but sharing it with Mira made it feel more solid, like it could actually push back against the chaos. He just had to make it real, for her.

"Okay," he began, keeping his voice steady and low, as if the words were a bridge pulling them away from the ruins. "Close your eyes. We're not here anymore. The sirens are far off, like a storm that's already passed. Instead, feel the ground change under you, soft dirt, not this hard stone. It's the edge of the Dreamwood, where the trees start thick and tall, their branches reaching out like arms welcoming us in."

Mira squeezed her eyes shut, her face scrunching in concentration. Elias closed his, too, letting the image build in his mind. He described it step by step, painting with words to draw her along. "The path is right here, wide enough for both of us to walk side by side. Leaves crunch under our feet, dry and crisp, but not sharp. The air smells clean, like after rain, with a hint of something sweet, the berries growing wild on bushes along the path. You hear birds, Mira? Not loud, just soft calls, like they're saying hello?"

She tilted her head, as if listening. "I hear them," she whispered, a small smile tugging at her lips. "And the path... It's going up a little hill?" A breeze drifted through the crumbled market stall from outside.

"Yes, exactly." Elias felt a spark of relief; she was grabbing onto it, adding her own touches. In his head, the ruins dissolved, replaced by the forest's embrace. The sirens became a faint hum, drowned out by the rustle of wind through leaves. "We're climbing the hill now. That breeze makes it feel nice and cool. It's easy, not steep. At the top, it opens up into a clearing, big and round, with grass so green it looks painted. Sunlight pours in from above, warm on our skin, chasing away the cold."

In the shared space of their imaginations, they stepped into the clearing. Elias guided the adventure, keeping it simple, nothing too wild yet. "Look around. There's a big rock in the middle, flat on top like a table. We can sit there. Flowers in the grass, yellow ones, like little suns. And purple ones that sway when you walk by. No bombs here, Mira. No sirens. Just quiet, and us."

She leaned forward in the real world, her body relaxing a bit. "Can we pick the flowers? Make a chain or something?"

"Sure," he said, smiling even with his eyes closed. "You start with the yellow ones. They're soft, stems bend easy. I'll find some vines to tie them together. We'll make crowns, put them on our heads. We'll be the king and queen of the woods!"

The picture sharpened for Elias as they built it together. In the clearing, the sunlight filtered through a canopy, letting in patches of blue sky. A gentle breeze stirred the grass, carrying the scent of wildflowers. They sat on the rock, legs dangling, weaving their crowns with careful fingers. Mira laughed in the vision; a light, cheerful sound Elias hadn't heard from her in weeks. He added a nearby stream trickling, its water clear and inviting with small fish darting in the shallows. "We can dip our feet in," he narrated. "The water's cool, but not too cold. It tickles."

Mira giggled softly, the sound muffled in the ruins but real enough to warm Elias's chest. For a moment, the war felt distant, like a bad dream they could wake from. He deepened the scene, letting her lead a little. "What do you see over there, by the trees?" he asked. "Animals," she said after a pause. "Rabbits! Hopping! Fluffy tails, they're not scared of us."

"You're right. They come close, sniffing at our crowns. One even lets you pet it. Its soft white fur is warm under your fingers." Elias let the adventure unfold, a simple loop of exploration: wandering the clearing's edges, finding hidden spots like a cluster of berry bushes where the fruit tasted sweet and juicy, staining their fingers red. No threats, no interruptions. Just peace, the kind Nova

City was supposed to have before the superpowers turned it into a battlefield.

But Elias's thoughts wandered even as he narrated. Hiding here, in the bombed-out husk of a stall, brought back those school memories in sharper detail. The teachers were proud, showing maps of the districts: how the coastal position made Nova City perfect for summits, with its harbors open to all flags, no questions asked. Leaders from warring sides would meet there, shake hands over tables laden with food from every culture, forging pacts that held the world together. It was a thorn in the superpowers' sides, a place that proved unity could work without their control. That's why they sieged it; they wanted to erase that example and claim the peninsula's resources for themselves. Oil from the rigs, grain from the inland fields, all funneled through those ports. Controlling it meant choking the resistance, tipping the war in their favor. Elias felt a budding sense of how pointless it all seemed. Why build something this beautiful just to watch it get torn down? The despair settled in him like dust in the ruins, making the Dreamwood feel like a fragile lie against the truth of the world. But he must carry on, for now, for her.

Their mother shifted suddenly, breaking the spell. "Quiet," she whispered urgently. The rumble Elias noticed earlier grew louder, vibrating through the ground like a giant's footsteps. Tanks. Approaching from up the road, their treads grinding over rubble, engines growling. The sirens kicked up again, sharper now, mixed with shouts from distant defenders scrambling to positions.

Elias's eyes snapped open, the peaceful clearing shattering in his mind like glass under a boot. Mira blinked too, confusion washing over her face, followed by terror as the noise hit her full force. "No," she said, voice rising. "We were there! The rabbits..."

"Shh," Elias pulled her down, flattening them both against the ground. The tanks were close. Massive machines painted in camouflage, cannons swiveling like predators searching for their next meal. Soldiers flanked them on each side, rifles at the ready, scanning the ruins for movement. One tank rolled past their hiding spot, close enough that Elias could smell the diesel exhaust and feel the heat from its engine. Debris crumbled under its weight, and a loose brick tumbled from the wall above them, landing inches from Mira's head.

She clamped a hand over her mouth, eyes wide with panic, but Elias saw the hook in her, the way she clung to the remnants of the Dreamwood even as fear gripped her. "It was real," she mouthed, tears welling. "But now... what if they find us?"

Their mother lay still, barely breathing, until the convoy passed, the rumble fading into the distance. Only then did she exhale, sitting up slowly. "We need to move now, back to the bunker before more come."

Elias nodded, but his mind churned. The interruption had yanked them out so brutally, leaving Mira hooked on the escape but terrified of how unpredictable the war made everything. One moment, safe in a sun-lit clearing, the next, tanks bearing down like monsters from a nightmare. He helped Mira to her feet, her hand trembling in his. "We'll go back," he promised quietly. "Deeper next time. Make it stronger."

As they crept out of the ruins, weaving through the bombed streets under the fading sirens, Elias's thoughts darkened further. He spotted a faded mural of linked hands from every nation in the rubble. The siege was about more than land; it was about breaking the idea of unity, claiming the ports to starve out anyone who resisted. Elias felt the weight of it pressing on him, a despair that made him question if anything ever really lasted. He was starting to see the patterns in the world: build, thrive, destroy, repeat. It deepened the isolation in him, the sense that the war wasn't just outside, but burrowing into his core, making even the Dreamwood feel like a temporary fix. He wondered what Theo would think of it all. But he just as quickly stopped that thought. He couldn't do it right now.

They reached the bunker entrance by midday, slipping underground into the familiar damp and dim. Their mother bartered a few scraps they'd found for a shared meal: stale bread and a watery soup that barely filled the emptiness. Mira ate in silence, her eyes distant, but when they settled into their corner, she tugged at Elias's sleeve. "The clearing was nice," she said softly. "Even if the tanks ruined it. Can we try again later? More animals, maybe?"

He managed a nod, feeling the weight of the day. She was hooked, drawn to the refuge, but the war's unpredictability terrified her, and him. The rumble of those tanks lingered in his bones, a reminder that no mental forest could fully block the real world. Still, he had to try. For her. For both of them.

As the day wore on, the bunker filled with the usual murmurs. People traded stories of the latest raids, and elders lamented the city's lost glory. Elias listened half-heartedly, drowning it out. His mind drifted back to the clearing. He added details in his head: taller trees around the edges, a hidden cave for shelter. But the despair from earlier stuck, constantly lingering in his mind. He pushed the thoughts down, focusing on Mira curled beside him. The Dreamwood was their weapon, fragile as it was. He'd guide her back, make the adventure stick. Out here, in the unpredictable grip of siege and loss, it was all they had to hold onto.

The afternoon dragged, marked by sporadic booms from distant artillery that shook the bunker walls. Their mother dozed first, exhausted from the morning's tension, while Mira fidgeted, drawing aimless patterns in the dust with her finger; circles that might have been the clearing, lines that could be paths. Elias watched her, feeling the pull to dive back in. But he waited until the lights dimmed and the bunker settled into evening hush.

"Ready?" he asked, voice barely above a whisper. Mira nodded eagerly, though her eyes still held a shadow of fear. They closed their eyes together, and Elias began again. "Back to the edge. The path is waiting..."

This time, the clearing came quicker, the details sharper from their earlier visit. They explored further, discovering a cluster of glowing mushrooms at the base of a tree, their caps pulsing with soft light like the bioluminescent displays in the old science hall. Mira suggested a bird's nest high up, eggs speckled like jewels. Elias let her lead the narration for a bit, her voice gaining confidence as she described chasing fireflies that danced in the air.

Even in their mental space, Elias felt the war's shadow creeping. A faint rumble echoed in his thoughts, not real yet, but a warning. He ignored it, advancing the adventure. "See that hill beyond the clearing? Let's climb it. From the top, we can probably see the whole Dreamwood filled with endless trees and rivers winding like ribbon."

Mira agreed, her imagined steps light and nimble. They reached the summit, the view unfolding: a vast forest under a twilight sky, safe and untouched. For a brief stretch, it held. No interruptions, just the two of them, king and queen of their wooded refuge.

The quiet didn't last long, though. Outside, a real rumble started; another patrol, or perhaps bombers returning. Elias tensed, but he kept his voice steady. "We're safe up here. Nothing can reach us."

Mira's brow furrowed in the vision. "But I hear something... like before."

He opened his eyes first, the Dreamwood fracturing. The bunker vibrated slightly, distant engines growling. Mira blinked awake, disappointment mixing with the previous hooked excitement. "It was better this time," she said. "But the noises... they always come."

As night fully settled, Elias stayed awake longer than usual, listening to the bunker breathe. The rumble outside had faded to a distant growl, but it never truly left. Mira lay curled against him, her breathing slow and even, one small hand still gripping his sleeve as if afraid the Dreamwood might slip away if she let go.

He thought about what she'd said, about how the noises always came. She was right. They always did. The Dreamwood wasn't a wall, not really. It was a bridge. A way through the fear, not around it.

Elias stared into the dark, tracing the outline of the cracks in the ceiling with his eyes. Tomorrow, he'd make it stronger. More paths, more places to hide. Maybe a river deep enough to drown out the sound of engines. Maybe roots thick enough to hold the ground together.

For the first time, the Dreamwood didn't feel like just an escape. It felt like something they were building together.

As the bunker settled into uneasy sleep, Elias held onto the thought, letting it anchor him against the long, uncertain night.

Chapter 4
Threads of Imagination

The bunker door creaked open with a low groan, releasing them into the pre-dawn haze that blanketed the ruins. Elias shivered as the cool air hit him, carrying the familiar mix of damp stone and distant smoke that never fully cleared. The world outside was vast and hostile, streets twisting like veins through the wreckage of what had once been bustling neighborhoods, and they felt nothing as he remembered. Their mother stepped out first, her posture tense but determined, a worn scarf wrapped around her neck to fend off the chill. She glanced back at Elias and Mira, her eyes sharp in the dim light. "We move quiet and quick today," she said, voice barely above a whisper. "Patrols are out early. Stick close."

Elias nodded, taking Mira's hand in his. He was used to these runs by now, but the weight of responsibility pressed harder each time. Their family had shrunk, and it fell to him to keep Mira steady, to be the one who didn't falter. Hunger gnawed at all of them, a constant companion after days of thinning rations. Last night's "meal" had been a shared cup of watery soup from boiled roots, leaving Elias's stomach fighting in protest. The empty sacks slung over their shoulders felt like promises, though, promises of food, if they were lucky, danger if they weren't.

As they stepped fully into the smoky gray light, Elias scanned the alley ahead, his free hand brushing against the rough wall for balance. The pre-dawn chill seeped through his jacket, a reminder of how the war had stripped away even the small comforts, like warm mornings in their old apartment overlooking the harbor. Back then, Nova City had pulsed with life at this hour; vendors setting up stalls in multicultural districts, the air filled with the sizzle of street food from every corner of the world, bridges humming with early commuters linking continents in a web of trade and talks. Now, those bridges lay twisted in the bay, destroyed to cut off escape routes, and the districts were ghosts, their vibrant markets reduced to rubble where soldiers picked through the remains. Elias pushed the thoughts aside, focusing on Mira's small fingers gripping his. She walked with careful steps, her eyes wide at the shadows, still trusting him to lead her through the maze of destruction which was once their home.

They slipped into the shadows of the alley, feet padding softly over cracked pavement littered with debris from fallen buildings. The air smelled of wet earth and charred wood, a reminder of the fires that flared up nightly from stray shells or desperate survivors trying to stay warm. Buildings loomed on either side, their walls riddled with holes from gunfire, windows shattered like broken teeth. Elias kept his eyes ahead, scanning for movement, while his mind wandered to the Dreamwood. It had become an anchor during the last run, a mental refuge he could pull Mira into when the real world closed in. Today, he decided, would be different. He'd teach her to build it too, make it something they owned together. The idea excited him, a way to share the burden, to turn his solitary escape into a tool they could both wield against the endless threats.

The alley narrowed, forcing them to sidestep piles of twisted metal and broken glass that glinted faintly in the haze. Elias squeezed Mira's hand tighter, feeling her pulse quicken at every distant sound, a rat scurrying in the debris, the faint drip of water from a ruptured pipe. Their mother moved like a shadow ahead, her steps silent and steady, years of navigating the city's pre-war crowds now honed into a survival instinct. She paused at a junction, listening for any dangers, then waved them forward. Elias's stomach growled audibly, loud enough that Mira glanced up at him with concern. "We'll eat soon," he murmured, though he knew it was a half-truth. The rations back in the bunker were dwindling, and without a good haul today, the hunger would dig deeper, sapping their strength for the next patrol dodge or siren wail.

As they turned a corner into a wider street, their mother held up a hand, freezing them in place. In the distance, the low mutter of voices carried... soldiers, perhaps, rummaging through a nearby ruin. She motioned them back into a narrow gap between two collapsed walls, the space tight and cluttered with fallen bricks. They crouched low, breaths shallow, waiting for the sounds to fade. The gap smelled of mildew and rust, the bricks pressing cold against Elias's back, but it was cover, better than the open street offered. Mira huddled close, her shoulder against his, her breathing quick and uneven. Elias leaned close to Mira, his voice barely audible. "This is a good time to start. Remember the clearing with the rock and flowers? Let's add to it. But you do some of the adding. Start with hidden streams maybe, little ones that run through the ground, not out in the open, hiding like we are."

Mira's eyes widened, a mix of nerves and interest. "Me? What if I mess it up? I don't know what to say." Her voice was quiet, her fingers twisting in his sleeve, the fear of the soldiers mingling nearby, mixed with the uncertainty of creation, left her uneasy.

"You won't mess it up," Elias assured her, keeping his tone calm even as his heart pounded from the nearby voices. "Just picture it and describe what you see. Like, the stream could be narrow, hidden under bushes or rocks. Water clear and cool. You pick the details, where it starts, what it sounds like." He kept his eyes on the street's end, where shadows shifted, but his mind reached for the Dreamwood, holding the clearing steady in his thoughts; the flat rock warm under an imagined sun, the flowers swaying gently.

She bit her lip, thinking hard. The soldiers' voices grew louder for a moment, boots crunching as they got close, then receded as they moved on. Mira whispered, "Okay. The stream starts from a crack in the earth, under a big tree. The water's shiny, like... like glass, and it flows quietly, hiding under green moss. It makes a soft trickling noise, like rain bouncing between the leaves of the trees."

Elias felt a spark of pride. "That's great. Now add something living in it." The image bloomed in his mind, the stream snaking through the clearing like a secret watery pathway, Mira's words giving it shape and sound.

"Little fish," she said, warming to the idea. "Silver ones that dart around. And water plants with long leaves that wave in the current." Her voice gained a tentative rhythm, the act of building pulling her focus from the danger outside.

Their mother signaled the all-clear, and they crept out, continuing down the street. The addition lingered in Elias's mind, weaving into the Dreamwood like a new path. It made the run feel less like a desperate scramble and more like a game, something they controlled. The street opened into what had once been a lively thoroughfare, lined with skeletons of shops where families had bartered spices and fabrics from across the globe. Elias remembered fragments from school, how Nova City's markets had been neutral zones, stalls from every culture blending without borders, a testament to the peninsula's role as a bridge between divided powers. Now, those stalls were splintered wood and empty shelves, patrolled by invaders who saw the city's openness as a weakness to exploit. The thought fueled his steps, a quiet resolve to protect this small act of creation with Mira.

They reached the edge of an old market square, now a field of toppled stalls and scattered crates. Their mother knelt behind an overturned cart, rifling through the debris. Elias and Mira joined her, digging carefully. "Look for anything sealed," she motioned, flipping over a toppled shelf. "Cans, bottles… nothing that's been opened." The ground was uneven, mixed with shards of pottery and rusted cans, the air heavy with the scent of decay from spoiled goods long exposed.

Elias pried open a half-buried box, finding a couple of dented tins. Vegetables, maybe, the labels were long peeled and faded. Mira uncovered a roll of twine, useful for repairs. But as they worked, footsteps approached again, heavier this time. Their mother pulled them down, and they squeezed under the cart, the wood pressing against their backs. Dust filled Elias's nose, forcing him to stifle a sneeze. "Keep building," he whispered to Mira. "What if the stream branches off? One part goes to a hidden pool."

She nodded, eyes squeezed shut against the fear. "The pool is small and round, with smooth stones around the edge. The water's still, like the big mirror we had in our living room, reflecting the trees. And… tadpoles, swimming in circles."

"Good," Elias whispered. "Add flowers along the banks. Ones that float or grow tall." The cart's underbelly was cramped, splinters digging into his palms, but Mira's words painted a serene contrast, the pool a calm center in the Dreamwood's growing landscape.

"Pink flowers on lily pads," she added with a smile. "They open in the sun, smelling sweet. And tall stems that rustle when you walk by."

The soldiers passed by and continued down the street, their conversation a low grumble he didn't understand, rifles clinking as they avoided debris. Elias's pulse slowed as they moved away. The Dreamwood was growing richer with Mira's touches, the hidden streams becoming a network that tied the clearing together. It helped him focus, pushing back the hunger pains and the aches in his legs from crouching. As they emerged, the sun's first rays broke through the haze, casting long shadows that danced like warnings across the square. Elias pocketed a loose nail from the debris, thinking it could reinforce their bunker's corner, a small act of defiance against the decay and deterioration.

They emerged and pressed on, sacks a bit heavier. The market led to a row of gutted shops, and their mother chose one with a caved-in roof, but what looked to be an intact backroom. Inside, the air was musty, filled with the scent of moldy paper. They searched shelves and under counters, finding a bottle of cloudy water and a small knife with a dull blade, better than nothing for cutting bandages or food. Mira beamed at her find, a frayed but intact blanket. Elias used the moment to expand. "Now make the pool deeper. What lives at the bottom?"

"Colorful pebbles," she said. "And snails with swirled shells. The water's warm near the edges, like a bath." Her enthusiasm bubbled, the shop's dim interior fading as she spoke, the Dreamwood pulling them in briefly amid the dust motes swirling in the light.

Their mother packed the items, but a sudden shout from outside froze them. It was a patrol, closer than before. Their hearts raced as they ducked behind a counter. The soldiers entered the shop next door, banging through debris, cursing in their harsh language. Elias pulled Mira close and felt her body trembling. "The stream now," he breathed. "Add a waterfall feeding the pool," his voice silent but heard.

"The waterfall's gentle," she whispered back. "It splashes over rocks covered in vines. Mist rises up, making rainbows in the light."

They waited there, huddled together, the building session their lifeline. The soldiers lingered, one kicking a crate that rolled from the next shop over toward their hiding spot. Elias held his breath, fearing the worst. But the soldiers finally left, grumbling something that sounded like disappointment. Relief washed over him, mingled with the growing strength of the Dreamwood. Mira's additions made it feel alive. The shop's backroom held a few more treasures: a rusted tin of nails, a length of cord, some bungee cords. But the patrol's intrusion had soured the air, a reminder nothing was truly safe, and that they needed to get back as soon as possible. Elias shouldered the sack, the weight a small victory, as they slipped out. The morning light was now fully breaking, illuminating the scars of the city in harsh detail.

Deeper into the district, the streets narrowed, flanked by taller ruins that blocked the rising sun. Their mother spotted a warehouse at the end of an alley, its doors hanging loose, promising bigger finds. "That's our target," she said. "Stay alert, this is not a safe area, but we need to check it out." The alley felt like a trap, walls closing in with jagged edges from recent blasts, the ground uneven with potholes filled with stagnant water that splashed beneath their feet. Elias's arm throbbed faintly from an earlier brush with debris, a dull ache that accompanied the constant pull of exhaustion. Mira walked closer to him now, her earlier excitement tempered by the thickening tension, her small sack bumping against her leg with each step.

They approached cautiously, but the sky darkened with a familiar whine: artillery incoming. The first shell whistled down, exploding a block away with a deafening boom that shook the ground. Dust and debris rained, and their mother shouted, "Inside, fast!" The blast's force pressed against them like an invisible hand, the air filling with the sharp tang of explosions and pulverized stone. Elias grabbed Mira's arm, pulling her along as they stumbled toward the warehouse doors, hearts slamming in their out-of-breath chests. The building emerged dark and ominous, its frame groaning under the vibration, but it was shelter, better than the open street where bombs were falling.

They bolted for the warehouse, but the second shell hit closer, the blast wave knocking them off balance. Shrapnel flew like deadly hail; sharp metal fragments flying sideways, embedding in walls, ricocheting off the pavement. Elias felt a hot sting on his arm, a shallow graze, but their mother took the brunt of it. A jagged piece sliced into her calf as she turned to shield Mira, and she went down with a sharp cry, leg buckling under her. The pain in her voice cut through the ringing in Elias's ears, raw and immediate as she clutched the wound, blood pooling dark on the ground. Mira froze for a split second, her face draining of color and eyes widening, before dropping to her knees beside her.

"Mom!" Mira's voice pierced the chaos, high and terrified. The shelling continued, booms rolling in waves, the air thick with smoke and the unpleasant bite of explosives. Elias's world narrowed to the sight of his mother on the ground, her face twisted in agony as she tried to push herself up. The warehouse doors were only steps away, but the next shell could land anywhere. Elias dropped to his knees beside her, the metallic scent of blood mixing with the dust, his hands hovering uncertainly over the gash. It was deep, the shrapnel embedded like a cruel thorn, tearing through muscle and cloth alike.

Their mother gritted her teeth, face pale, sweat beading on her brow. "Get it out," she gasped to Elias. "We can't stay exposed out here." Her words were clipped, fighting through the pain, but her eyes locked on his with a fierce urgency, the same look she'd had when teaching him to tie knots or spot safe paths in the ruins. He nodded, swallowing the bile rising in his throat, his fingers trembling as he gripped the shard. The metal was warm from the blast, slick with blood, and he hesitated for a heartbeat as the whine of another shell was building in the distance.

Mira knelt too, tears streaming down her cheeks, her small hands pressing on their mother's shoulder for support. "It's okay, Mom," she cried, voice breaking, though her eyes begged Elias to make it true. He pulled as hard as he could. The jagged metal finally came free, blood surging to the surface. Mira sobbed harder, and Elias tore strips from the scavenged blanket, pressing the first one hard against the gash. The cloth soaked through quickly, but he layered another, then another, wrapping the rest tight around her leg. "Keep pushing right here," he told Mira, guiding her hands. She did, her fingers trembling but steady, the pressure turning her knuckles white. Elias tied off the bandage, knotting it securely, the blood flow slowing to a trickle. The pain twisted their mother's features, her breath coming in short, ragged bursts, but she didn't scream. She was holding it in, for them, seeing how strong they were in the face of danger.

As he worked, their mother spoke, her voice strained but calm and deliberate, as if the words were a way to fight back the agony.

"This leg... it's just a scratch. We are going to be ok." Her words sank into Elias like lead, stirring a whirlwind of thoughts as he adjusted the bandage. Hope felt so fragile in that moment, like a spiderweb caught in a storm. The injury in front of him was a brutal symbol; one random piece of metal and their fragile family could shatter further. He looked at Mira, her face streaked with dirt and tears. He felt the weight of it all. A flash of Theo crossed his mind. His brother, always the fixer, bandaging scrapes from their pre-war games with quick hands and jokes to distract from the pain. Theo would have known exactly how to pull the shrapnel out without flinching, turning the moment into a story instead of terror. But Theo was gone, lost shortly after their father when debris from a missile strike rained down. Elias shoved the memory down hard with a shake of his head, focusing on the knot, refusing to let the ache surface now. He couldn't afford to break, not with Mira watching and their mother counting on him.

“We have to move,” their mother said, testing the leg with a wince. It held, barely, but pain etched her every movement. “Help me up. The bunker isn't too far if we cut through the back alleys.” They lifted her together, her arms over their shoulders, Mira on one side, Elias on the other. She was lighter than she should be, hunger whittling her down, but the weight still pulled at Elias's arms. Once she was up, leaning on Elias for support, Mira grabbed the sacks, slinging them across her back with determination. The shelling had eased to sporadic booms in the distance, but the street was a mess of fresh craters and haze. They limped forward, every step a test. Their mother's face was a mask of grit, but she leaned heavily, her injured leg dragging slightly.

The return stretched into agony. The first detour came quickly: a patrol's flashlight beam sweeping the main path, forcing them into a side street choked with collapsed scaffolding. Elias supported more of their mother's weight, his shoulder burning under the strain, while Mira scouted ahead, her small size letting her peer around corners without notice. The air grew thick with smoke from a nearby smoldering building, the heat radiating off the ruins like a warning. Elias's graze on his arm stung with sweat, a minor hurt compared to the gash on their mother's leg, but it reminded him of how close they'd come.

Another patrol forced them into a storm drain, the water cold and foul-smelling up to their ankles. Mira gagged at the stench, but Elias hushed her, the sound of boots overhead making every splash a risk. Their mother bit back a groan as the uneven ground jarred her wound, blood seeping fresh through the bandage. "Almost there," Elias reassured, though the bunker felt miles away. In the dim light filtering through grates, he caught Mira's eye and nodded subtly. "The pools... tell me more about the snails."

She blinked, catching on, her voice shaky. "They have patterns on their shells, like maps. Slow swimmers, but they know all the hidden ways under the water."

Elias built on it, the words a distraction from the filth and fear. "And the sandy bottom shifts when they move, uncovering shiny stones that light up the pool." The image steadied them, Mira's shoulders relaxing a fraction as she added. "The birds come to the edge, dipping beaks in for drinks, their songs mixing with the stream's trickle." The image carried them forward with renewed strength, pushing them in an uncertain retreat toward safety.

Hours later, they reached the bunker, descending the stairs into its dim, crowded depths. The familiar damp enveloped them, a mix of relief and exhaustion washing over Elias as other survivors rushed to help, offering water and space. He took charge in their corner, propping the leg and rewrapping the wound with cleaner cloth from the medic's kit. Mira fetched supplies, her small frame bustling with purpose. The bunker hummed with low voices and the clink of bowls, but Elias tuned it out, focusing on the task: cleaning the gash with boiled, clean water, applying a thin layer of herbal paste that smelled of bitter earth. Their mother's color returned slowly, the pain easing under the care, but the limp would linger, a new scar in their fragile routine.

With her resting, Elias turned to Mira. "Ready to go in deep? See what we made?" The bunker's evening hush had settled, lamps casting flickering glows on the walls, the air heavy with the scent of boiled rations and weary bodies. Mira nodded eagerly, though her eyes still held the shadow of the day's terror, and they sat cross-legged, closing their eyes together. The Dreamwood pulled them in gradually... the clearing first, then the streams twining into view. Sensations built: the feel of moss underfoot, the scent of fresh water. Then, visuals sharpened. Elias saw Mira standing by a pool, vivid and real. Her tangled hair, the dirt on her knees from the run, her eyes sparkling. She gasped in the vision. "Elias! I see you. You're by the stream, waving at me. It's like we're really here!"

He looked down at himself in the mental space, arms scratched, knees bloody from kneeling on broken pavement, then back at her. "I see you too! Come on, let's explore it." The clarity hit Elias like a rush, the Dreamwood no longer a solo construct but a shared realm where Mira's form moved with her real-life energy, her steps light on the imagined grass. It was as if the threads they'd woven during the run had tightened, pulling their presences together in a way that felt almost tangible, a bridge across the isolation war forced on them.

They moved together, visually linked. Mira ran to a waterfall, splashing her hands, and Elias watched the droplets fly from her fingers. He led to a new cave, and she followed, her form casting a shadow on the walls. They added more. She placed fireflies over the water, the few berry bushes along the banks. Seeing each other made it profound, the betrayal a faint memory. Elias watched Mira laugh as a firefly landed on her palm, her joy cutting through the day's horrors like sunlight piercing the bunker's gloom. In this space, her tears from the shelling dried, replaced by wonder, and Elias felt a swell of protectiveness. He'd created this for her, but now she shaped it equally, her additions breathing life into the streams and pools they had built under duress, necessary to still their racing hearts and minds.

Elias reflected there, the fragility of hope still tugging, but this shared sight strengthened their bond. It was their world, unbreakable. The cave's vines glowed softly, like the neon lights that lit up the streets before the bombings snuffed them out, illuminating Mira's face as she turned to him, her voice clear in the vision. "Look, Elias, turtles are coming up from the sandy pool. They have shells like the snails! See their shells?" He nodded, the details she'd added earlier now vivid: the turtles surfacing slowly, snails at the bottom of the pool, patterns on their backs glinting like hidden maps, guiding them to new corners of the forest. Elias added a ledge by the waterfall, wide enough for them to sit side by side, the mist cooling their skin.

Mira climbed up beside him, her imagined self peering out. "The blue birds are flying over the reeds. Their songs are getting louder, like they're welcoming us." The sounds filled the space, a chorus that drowned out the faint, real-world murmurs from the elderly voices in the bunker, lamenting lost districts, children whispering games to pass the time. Elias let the vision expand, drawing from Mira's cues: the birds swooping low, their long tails trailing like ribbons in the breeze, landing on the lily pads she'd described earlier. It was her touch that made it feel infinite, the pools not just hidden but alive with her animals and plants, a testament to her growing trust in the refuge.

But even here, Elias couldn't stop his thoughts from drifting to the day's misfortune; the shrapnel's sting on his arm, their mother's pale face as he'd pulled the metal free. Theo's memory surfaced again. He had always known how to mend, turning hurt into stories, but the war had taken that from them, leaving Elias to fumble in the dark. He suppressed it once more, focusing on Mira's bright eyes in the vision, refusing to let the past fracture this moment. The Dreamwood was their mending now, threads of imagination stitching over the war's deadly grip on reality.

Surfacing from their created world, Mira smiled as she opened her eyes. "We saw everything! I can't wait to go back, Eli." Her real voice carried the same excitement, cutting through the bunker's dimness like a candle lighting a dark room. Their mother murmured approval from her mat, her bandaged leg propped higher now, the herbal paste working its slow magic. "Sounds like a fine place," she said softly, her eyes half-lidded but warm. "Tell me more about those fireflies."

Mira launched in, describing their glow and dance, while Elias added the berry bushes' sweetness, the two of them trading details like secrets. The bunker faded around them and other families' conversations faded. Nova City had been built for such sharing, its districts a mosaic where cultures wove together without force, pacts forged over meals that fed body and hope. The superpowers had hated that, their divisions threatened by a place that proved connection could outlast grudges. Now they choked it all, starving the ports to break the spirit. But in this corner, Elias and Mira wove their own pact, the Dreamwood a quiet rebellion against stark reality.

Elias lay with Mira curled against him, their mother's breaths steadying nearby. But their rest shattered with the first low thump-thump overhead, a rhythmic pounding that built into the roar of what could only be helicopters swarming the skies, their rotors slicing the air like knives. Searchlights pierced the bunker's vents in harsh beams, sweeping the ruins below, while bursts of gunfire joined a barrage of shells slamming closer and closer with each pass. Mira jerked awake, clutching his arm, her face pale in the dim light, as their mother tensed with a sharp inhale, one hand flying to her bandaged leg, the other to gather what little supplies they had into a bag. The assault closed in, relentless and unyielding, forcing Elias to grip the Dreamwood tighter in his mind, knowing the next hours would demand every thread they'd woven just to hold the fragments together.

Chapter 5
The Shattering Storm

Thumping from the helicopters overhead turned into a steady drumbeat that rattled the bunker's vents, pulling Elias from the fragile quiet he'd carved out with Mira. He bolted upright on their threadbare mat, his arm still around Mira, sleeping between him and mother, the Dreamwood's lingering warmth fading like a half-remembered dream. Mira stirred, her eyes fluttering open in confusion, while their mother tensed beside them, her bandaged leg propped up on a rolled blanket on top of a milk crate. The herbal paste had dulled the pain from yesterday's shrapnel, but her face tightened now, the lines under her eyes deepening as the helicopter rotors grew louder, slicing through the night air.

"Elias," she whispered, her voice low and urgent, one hand already fumbling for the small pack of supplies they'd scavenged. "Wake your sister. This isn't a patrol, I don't know what it is, but we may have to leave fast."

The words hung heavy in the bunker's dim hush where other families shifted uneasily, their frantic whispers rippling through the crowded space like warnings. Elias's heart kicked up, a familiar dread that matched the growing roar outside. The helicopters were defenders, he told himself, scouting the skies over Nova City's fractured skyline. A lie he told himself to feel better, though he knew it wasn't the truth.

Mira rubbed her eyes, her small body curling closer to him as the first distant boom echoed down the subway, not from the helicopter, but something heavier, deeper. Artillery. The ground vibrated faintly, dust sifting from the ceiling like fine ash. "What's that?" she asked, her voice thick with sleep, fingers clutching his sleeve. Elias swallowed, forcing his tone steady. He couldn't let her see the fear coiling in his gut, the way it twisted memories of the last raid into something sharper.

"Just noise," he said, though the lie tasted bitter, like the one he told himself about the helicopters overhead. "Remember the waterfall we made? The one feeding the pool? Let's hold onto that." He glanced at their mother, who nodded faintly, her free hand pressing against her injured calf as if bracing for the pain to flare up as she started to move. The bunker filled with voices. The elders muttered about the city's power grid flickering out weeks ago, leaving them blind to incoming threats like this; parents shushing children as the booms grew closer, each one a punch to the earth.

The barrage hit full force without mercy. The first direct strike slammed into the street above their subway bunker, the explosion ripping through concrete. The walls shuddered as screams erupted around them. Chunks of ceiling cracked and fell, one grazing Elias's leg, causing a small gash and swelling immediately. Mira yelped, burying her face in his chest, while their mother grabbed his arm, pulling them all lower and closer to the wall. The air thickened with dust and the bite of ruptured gas lines, making every breath a fight.

Elias blinked, and while his eyes were closed for that split second, the Dreamwood fractured. A sharp crack split the central tree by the clearing while branches snapped like brittle bones. The streams Mira had woven ran dry in an instant, pools draining to cracked mud. The fireflies blinked out one by one. It was as if the blasts punched straight through, shattering the green sanctuary into jagged pieces that scattered like glass on the road outside. Elias's chest tightened, a wave of nausea rising as the mental world he'd built for them crumbled. This wasn't like the tank rumbles or siren wails; those had tugged at the edges. This tore at the core, leaving him exposed while the war's roar flooded in unchecked.

"Eli, it's breaking," Mira whispered, her voice cutting through as another shell whistled down, detonating closer. The force buckled the floor beneath them. People scrambled, guards shouting orders to seal the doors, but panic spread faster. Their mother winced, shifting her weight off the bad leg, sweat beading on her forehead. "We can't stay," she said, voice strained. "It's collapsing. Elias, grab your sister, we move when I say."

He nodded, gripping Mira tighter, his free hand finding their mother's. The next blast was the worst yet, a thunderous crack that split the bunker's far wall, debris cascading in a mess of stone and metal. Alarms blared faintly from the vents, drowned out by screams as water, from rain and busted pipes, began flowing in, turning the floor slick and cold. Elias closed his eyes for a split second, trying to summon the Dreamwood's remnants for a bit of courage, but it was chaos there, too. The cave's vines wilted and the waterfall stuttered to a drip. Guilt clawed at him. What good was his mind if it shattered like this, leaving Mira trembling, her trust in him cracking alongside it?

Their mother yanked them up as the ceiling shifted, a massive section collapsing in the main chamber, swallowing crates and people in a cloud of rubble and dust. Guards herded survivors toward a narrow escape route, flashlights cutting erratic paths through the dust-choked air. Elias scooped Mira onto his back, her legs wrapping around his waist, while he hooked an arm under their mother's good side. She limped heavily, pain etching her face, but she pushed forward, the three of them rushing with the frantic crowd. Rain poured through the breaches now, a relentless sheet that soaked them to the bone, turning the tunnel into a slippery gauntlet of jagged concrete and broken glass. Elias's mind raced, fear rising. What if the next shell buried them like the ceiling just did to the others? What if he couldn't rebuild fast enough, and Mira saw how truly broken everything was?

The side tunnel spat them onto the street amid the storm, the night sky a churning black lit by flares and explosions. Nova City's ruins loomed like broken teeth, buildings gutted by fire, the distant harbor a void of blockaded shadows. Shells rained down in waves, craters blooming yards away, hurling dirt and shrapnel that pinged off the pavement. Elias ran, Mira's weight an anchor on his back, their mother leading the way with a heavy limp. The Dreamwood flickered in his thoughts, a desperate grasp at the cave's entrance, but the blasts kept shattering it, each boom a fresh fracture. They had to find cover, something solid, before the world swallowed them whole.

Rain lashed the streets of Nova City like a punishment, turning the evacuation into a blind scramble through the dark, wet landscape. Elias's legs burned as he carried Mira on his back, her arms locked around his neck. Her breath came in hot puffs against his ear, irregular from fear and the downpour soaking her clothes. Explosions walked the skyline, artillery shells arcing in from enemy lines beyond the bay, their impacts shaking the ground in a relentless, continuous rhythm. Elias dodged a fresh crater, its edges slick with mud, the air thick with the stench of wet earth and explosions. His leg throbbed from the gash earlier, swollen under his torn pants, but he ignored it, he had to, focusing on the weight of Mira on his back and their mother half leaning on him with her recent wound.

"Left, go left! Towards the warehouses!" their mother shouted over the roar of explosions, her voice cracking as her injured leg dragged, blood seeping anew through the bandage from the jolts. The uncertainty from the bunker lingered in her tone; she'd sensed something off about those helicopters from the start, not just a patrol but a harbinger, focusing the hell on their already broken refuge. Elias veered, spotting a cluster of shadowy figures ahead. Other bunker escapees, coughing and stumbling through the rain. But the shells didn't discriminate; one detonated a block over, the shockwave knocking mother sideways as Elias fell, Mira's cry sharp in his ears as they bounced off the ground, landing in a deep puddle. Pain flared in his scraped palms and the gash in his leg, but he pushed up fast, hauling their mother to her feet.

The Dreamwood was in tatters now, the cave's entrance buried under imagined rubble in his mind, its walls caving as the bunker's had. That lie about the helicopters being safe had crumbled, too, just like everything else.

Mira, who'd been trying to remain in the Dreamwood amid the fires and explosions, dug her fingers into his shoulders. "Eli, I can't… It's all gone. The ferns, the pool… everything's smashed." Her words hit like another shell, guilt surging through him. He'd promised her safety in that green world, scenes of streams and fireflies woven together during scavenging runs. But the barrage had pulverized it, the blasts echoing inside his head until the sanctuary felt as ruined as the city around them. Nova City was now fully under siege. The invaders hammered it, not just for the oil rigs dotting the peninsula or the ports that fed global supply chains, but to erase the proof that unity could outlast grudges.

"Whisper it back," he said, dodging behind a toppled tram car as shrapnel whined past, pinging off metal. Rain streamed down his face, blurring the world into gray smears, but he focused on her voice, small and shaking beside his ear. "The cave... start with the rocks outside. Big ones, mossy, hiding the door." Mira hesitated, her body quivering from the wet and cold, but then she murmured, "...the rocks are round, wet from rain, but strong. They don't break." Elias latched onto it, his mind stitching the shards: the moss clinging stubborn, the entrance a narrow slit just wide enough for them. It wasn't perfect. The waterfall above it sputtered weakly, pools drained to mud, but it held, for the moment, a dim glow inside promising shelter.

Their mother stumbled, her leg giving out on a slick patch, and Elias caught her before she fell fully, the three of them collapsing against a shattered wall. Pain twisted her features, rain mixing with sweat and blood on her brow, but she gripped his arm. "Take Mira, get to a warehouse, get somewhere safe." The words sliced him deeper than any shrapnel. No. He wouldn't lose her, too. He wouldn't leave without her, not after Theo's quick laugh was silenced by falling debris, and their father's steady hands were ripped from them at the factory inferno. Elias shook his head, helping her up again. "No!

We're not leaving without you." The street ahead erupted in a fireball, heat blasting their faces, forcing them into a side alley choked with rubble. Other survivors streamed past, some dragging wounded, others vanishing into the downpour, but toward what? There were no bunkers left intact; the subway line was a tomb now, its tunnels flooded and collapsed.

Mira's whisper grew steadier as they pressed on, her words a lifeline in the storm, keeping Elias going. "Inside the cave... the walls are smooth stone, cool to the touch. And vines hang down, thick ones, blocking the wind." Elias nodded, even as thunder from the bombs, not the sky, rumbled overhead. He added to it, voice low against the chaos, words coming in between gasping breaths, "The ledge... by the pool, it's still there... dry and flat... We can sit, watch the waterfall drip." The image solidified a fraction as the cave's interior unfolded: flickering light from imagined crystals in the walls, the air fresh with earth and water scents, far from the rain's bitter slap. Mira's contributions pulled it tighter, her fear channeling into creation, the vines now twisting like protective arms, the pool refilling drop by drop.

Reality clawed back, hard. A shell struck the alley's end, the blast wave hurling them forward, Elias's vision spotting black as he shielded Mira. They tumbled to the ground once again, coughing up grit from their lungs. Their mother groaned, clutching her leg, fresh blood staining the wrappings, thinned from the rain. "Can't... stop," she gasped, but Elias saw the exhaustion in her eyes, the way the war had whittled her down. At only thirty-two, she was moving like an elder, every step in agony. Elias's mind reeled, isolation pressing in: alone in this downpour, family fracturing right in front of him. The Dreamwood was his only sanctuary, but that too was in shambles. That earlier lie about safety... it mocked him now, as the helicopters' distant thumping faded into the explosions all around.

He helped them up, spotting a fallen overpass ahead. A massive slab of concrete sheared off by an earlier strike, propped unevenly against a pillar wall, forming a shallow, hollow shelter, like a makeshift cave.

"There," he pointed, urgency sharpening his voice. The area was cramped, barely ten feet deep, water pooling at its mouth from the storm, but it was better than the open street. Elias shoved Mira inside first, then their mother, easing her down against the rough wall. He wedged in last, the space tight, their bodies pressed close. Rain sheeted down the concrete slab's edge, dripping in steady curtains that turned the entrance into a watery veil. The hollow shelter amplified every distant boom.

Mira huddled between them, shivering, her head on Elias's shoulder. "It's like... our cave," she whispered between tears, eyes wide in the gloom, catching the parallel from the Dreamwood even through the terror of the escape. Elias nodded, relief flickering in his mind. The real cover's walls loomed close, pressing them together.

But in his mind, the Dreamwood's cave expanded to rival the small space, its stones smooth and vast, the drips from the slab becoming the waterfall's gentle flow, cascading over the entrance in a soothing rhythm. "Exactly," he said softly, pulling her closer. Their mother leaned against the opposite wall, leg extended stiffly, her hand finding Mira's. "We'll wait here, just for now." Her voice held the strain of knowing it was temporary.

As the explosions rolled on, Elias and Mira attempted to rebuild their fractured world, their whispers weaving against the storm. "The waterfall's stronger now," Mira said, her tone gaining some wonder. "It pushes the bad sounds away, like a door." Elias built on it, describing the mist rising cool and clean, beading on the vines she'd placed. The pool at the cave's rear filled gradually, tadpoles darting in the shallows, snails tracing patterns on the rocks. It wasn't seamless; the fractures lingered, shards of shattered trees glinting in the mental corners, but their shared words seemed to mend it. The cave grew solid, a refuge where the rain outside felt distant, and almost comforting. Elias's thoughts turned inward, the effort stirring both sadness and conviction: with father and Theo gone, this was his duty now, holding the fragments together for her, even as doubt clawed in. How long could he keep piecing it together before the war broke them beyond repair?

Their mother watched silently, her presence a steady anchor, but Elias saw the pain in her silence, the way the siege had stolen her strength, bit by bit.

The attack seemed endless. The shelling continued, crashing in waves, the rain turning the streets into rivers of mud. Other survivors' shouts faded into the night, some finding other hiding spots, others silenced in the fire. In the hollow cave, time blurred. Minutes or hours... Elias couldn't tell. He kept whispering, adding details to fortify the cave: glowing fungi on the walls for light, a hidden nook with soft moss beds. Mira contributed too, her voice softer now, the stress relaxing. "The turtles from the pool... they came inside our cave." It steadied him, her ideas threading through his, making the cramped space bearable. But the isolation lingered. Nova City's fall wasn't just stone and steel; it was this: families huddled in the dark, imagination the only light against the endless night.

In their cramped confines, the Dreamwood's cave continued to take shape, its imagined vastness easing the press of real concrete against Elias's back. He shifted slightly, careful not to jostle their mother. Mira nestled closer, her head heavy on his shoulder, eyes half-closed as she murmured additions to their sanctuary. "The nook... make it bigger, with berries inside. Sweet ones, like the bushes by the stream." Elias nodded. "Yeah, clusters hanging low, red and plump. We pick them, sit on the moss, let the waterfall sing outside while we eat them."

The words wove tighter, the cave's details sharpened. The glow of the fungi cast warm light across the pools on the walls, and the turtles danced across the floor with their bright shells etched like maps of hidden paths. Elias felt the fractures mending, the shattered tree from the barrage now a sturdy root pushing through the cave floor, its branches curling upward to support the ceiling. It wasn't without flaws, though. Jagged edges remained, reminders of the blasts that had torn through, but Mira's touches filled the gaps, her innocence breathing life into the stone itself. She smiled faintly, a welcomed sight, her small hand tracing patterns in the air as if touching the vines. "The mist from the waterfall... it smells like clean water, not this wet dirt."

Elias eased a fraction, but the doubt lingered, a quiet storm in his thoughts clawing to the front. Holding this world together took everything he had. The war's chaos burrowed deeper, stirring the memories he shoved down, bringing them to light. Theo would have laughed through it, turning the cave into a fort with silly rules and endless stories. But Theo was gone, leaving him to fumble alone. And their mother, her injury a fresh wound on top of the old ones, how much more could she take before the terrors outside claimed her too? Elias glanced at her, catching her eyes in the faint light filtering through the rain veil. She managed a weak nod, her hand squeezing Mira's knee. "Keep going, Elias. It's working." Her voice held strong, but the pain undercut it.

The rebuilding of the Dreamwood pulled them through the shelter's cramped hours, whispers turning terror into tentative peace. Mira added birds to the cave's entrance; their calls and songs drowned out the sporadic booms rolling in from the horizon. In this shared space, the real rain's chill faded, the drips transforming into the waterfall's gentle rush, camouflaging the cave entrance like a natural door. Mira's excitement built, her body relaxing against him. "Look, Eli, the turtles are climbing the roots now. They know the way." He smiled, adding fireflies to flicker along the vines, their lights guiding the turtles. For a moment, the war felt far off, Nova City's ruins just a shadow beyond their mental walls.

Their mother shifted, wincing as she adjusted her leg. "The rain's easing a bit, and it's quieted down outside. We should get ready to move." Elias nodded, peering through the watery veil. The street beyond was a wasteland of craters and smoldering debris, rain pooling in the scars, distant fires flickering under the gray sky. An eerie quiet took over. Mira, sensing them moving around, opened her eyes. "Can we stay in the cave a little longer? It's nicer than here." Elias pulled her closer, the real shelter's chill seeping back. "We'll come back. The waterfall will keep the cave hidden for us."

As they started to exit the hollow concrete safe haven, dawn hinting at the horizon's edge, a new noise filtered in... not bombs, but engines creeping towards them. Elias tensed, hand on Mira's shoulder. The sound recalled the helicopters from earlier, stirring that old lie he had told himself... ally or enemy?

The vehicles advanced closer, tires churning over rubble, voices calling out in the rain; harsh at first, then clearer, in the familiar accents of the city's defenders. Headlights pierced the downpour, sweeping the street, searching for any survivors. It was a convoy of trucks, evacuating people to refugee camps. Elias's pulse quickened. Salvation or another trap? The engines idled closer, guards shouting, "Anyone out here?" No enemy tongues, no rifles raised in aggression. Mira lifted her head. "Eli... is it safe?"

Their mother pushed up on her good leg, face set. "Sounds like it's safe, let's go with them." Elias hesitated, mind flashing to ambushes whispered in the bunker before the chaos. He pushed the thought down, helping her to her feet. Mira grabbed his hand, her grip tight despite the tremble, and they slipped out toward the trucks.

The dash was a blur of slipping in the mud and shouting. Elias supported their mother, her limp heavy and constant, Mira tugging at his other side as they wove through the debris. Shells still exploded in the distance, but the convoy seemed safe: six trucks, canvas-sided, packed full with other wide-eyed refugees. A guard spotted them and waved urgently. "This way! Hurry!" Elias pushed forward, heart pounding against his chest. Mud sucked at their feet, rain stinging in newly opened wounds. His leg ached with each step, but the fear crumbled as soon as real hands pulled them aboard, not just imagined vines in their cave.

They reached the lead truck. Guards hauled their mother aboard first, followed by Mira. Elias climbed in, the canvas flapping shut behind him. The interior was chaos. Bodies were pressed close as elders chanted prayers. Children were crying, some missing the parents they had been with earlier. The engine roared to life, tires spinning through the muck, the convoy lurching forward into the gray dawn.

Mira leaned against him, exhausted but smiling faintly. "We made it, Eli. The cave helped. It protected us." Elias nodded, arm around her, their mother across the aisle, eyes meeting his with quiet relief. As Nova City's jagged skyline receded in the distance, Elias felt the Dreamwood settle, scarred, but steady. The war's storm was not over, just shifting to new ground.

Chapter 6
Memorializing Loss

The truck lurched through the mud-slick outskirts, its engine growling against the weight of too many bodies packed inside. Elias sat wedged between Mira and some other survivors, their mother directly across from them. Mira's head rested on his shoulder, her breathing steady now but shallow, as if the Dreamwood's cave still halfway cradled her. Their mother leaned awkwardly. Her leg extended stiffly, the bandage dark with fresh blood from the scramble. The convoy rumbled on, six vehicles in loose formation. Elias felt no real safety in the truck, though. Shells still blew in the distance, reminders that the war's grip on Nova City wasn't loosening.

Whispers filled the cramped space. Refugees trading broken thoughts over the engine's drone. A woman across the way clutched a bundled child, muttering about routes cut off by patrols. An elder nearby coughed into his sleeve, voice low and raspy: "Heard the lines are holding the ports, but for how long?" Elias tuned it out mostly. His leg throbbed from the gash, but the words stirred a quiet depression. Home felt like only a memory already; their apartment by the harbor. It was probably just rubble now. Would he ever stand there again, watching ships sail in without fear? The thought pressed heavy, but he shoved it down, shook it away with a strong head flick, focusing on Mira's warmth against him. She needed him steady, not lost in what-ifs.

"Eli," Mira mumbled, adjusting as the truck hit a rut. "The cave... It's still there, right? With the turtles?" Elias nodded, squeezing her hand. "Yeah. The waterfall's keeping it safe, remember?" But even as he said it, doubt flickered. The rebuilding in the hollow cave shelter by the overpass had mended some cracks, but the jolts of the ride tugged at the edges. Their mother caught his gaze, staring at her bleeding leg. "There's gotta be doctors at the camp who will fix this right up," she said, gesturing to her leg. "Don't worry. You should try and get some rest." Elias managed a nod, but rest felt impossible. The convoy's guards rode up front, scanning the flanks for threats. Ambushes were common on these runs, at least that's what Elias pieced together from the whispers of others. Enemy scouts were picking off stragglers to choke the escape routes, and ambushes meant to stop the convoy in a crossfire of bullets and hopelessness.

As the truck climbed a low rise, Elias let his mind drift to Theo. The memory came fast and sharp as the shrapnel that lodged in their mother's calf. Theo, two years older, always the one with quick fixes and quicker laughs. Elias pictured him in the old apartment, bandaging a playground scrape on Mira's knee, turning the pain into a tale of pirate battles on hidden islands. "See? Now you're a warrior queen," Theo had said, eyes sparkling like the fireflies they'd later added to the Dreamwood. But that was before the bombs and missiles started. Debris rained from a sky torn open, and Theo was caught in the collapse while fetching a bucket of water. Elias had been in the bunker with Mira and their mother, hearing about it only after it happened. Theo's absence was a hole, one Elias had patched with stories and suppression, but here in the truck's sway, it gaped wider.

He closed his eyes, pulling Mira into the vision without a word. "Do you see those groves beyond the cave?" In the Dreamwood, they stepped from the waterfall's mist into a new clearing, trees rising tall and solemn, their trunks etched with faint patterns. Elias guided it slowly, his voice low against the rumble of the engines. "These are for Theo. Remember how he told stories about forests that never ended? This one's his. Wide branches with leaves whispering his jokes." Mira's breath hitched, but she nodded, committing fully now. "Yeah... and strong roots, holding everything up. Like he did for us." The grove took shape, sunlight filtering through the canopy in soft shafts. It was a quiet spot where the war's noise faded to nothing.

Just then, the trucks braked hard, tires skipping to a stop. Shouts erupted from the guards, "Contact front! Flank left!" Gunfire cracked outside, sharp and close. Bullets pinged off the armored sides of the trucks. The convoy halted in a ragged line, engines idling as passengers ducked low below the canvas flaps. Cries and panic filled the air. Elias pulled Mira tight. Their mother's hand clamped on his arm, her face drained white from the pain of the sudden stop. "Stay down!" she hissed, but her voice shook. Elias's heart slammed just like the brakes did on the trucks. Another fracture, the Dreamwood's grove splintering at the edges. Theo's tree tilted like it might topple. Mira whimpered, "Eli, it's breaking again, I'm scared," but she held on, whispering back, "The roots... make them deeper, and stronger." Elias latched onto it, fortifying the vision mid-panic; roots twisting underground, anchoring the grove against the jolts. It held, barely, the imagined leaves rustling calm over the gunfire's snap.

The ambush lasted only minutes, but it seemed like hours. Enemy scouts on foot, rifles flashing from a ruined building a hundred yards off. The guards returned fire in bursts. The truck rocked as a grenade detonated nearby. Elias shielded Mira, his legs wound pounding with the movement. He kept whispering, with his eyes open, the grove a thin barrier against the chaos. "Theo's tree has fruit now," sweet, like the berries he sneaked us when we were in trouble." Mira added, her voice gaining strength, "And birds nesting in it, singing songs." Her full commitment broke through, no hesitation, turning the memory into a memorial that pushed back the fear. Their mother pressed closer, her eyes fixed on Elias as if to say, "Keep going." The gunfire tapered off. The guards shouted all-clear as the convoy revved forward again, leaving the attacking scouts scattered in the mud.

Elias surfaced from the vision, sweat beading despite the chill. The grove lingered in his mind, solid now, a place to return to when the losses pressed too hard. But the ambush had tested it, the unfamiliar road pulling at the edges like the camp would soon do. Theo's absence felt raw, a weight that made Elias wonder if any path led back to the life they'd lost. The truck pressed on. The outskirts unfolded into gray stretches of tents and barbed wire, but as they got closer, the concept of home seemed farther away than ever.

The convoy ground to a halt at the camp's edge as midday sun broke through the smoky clouds, casting light on the sprawl of tents stretching across a barren field. Elias blinked against the glare, helping Mira down from the truck as guards waved them toward the gates; makeshift barriers of wire and crates, manned by weary sentries. The air buzzed with activity. Refugees shuffled in lines for rations, voices overlapping in a mix of accents. There was a distant thud of construction hammers building more shelters. Overcrowded didn't capture it. Elias supported their mother as they stepped forward, her limp worse now. Each shift in weight drew a stifled wince. Mira clung to his free hand, eyes wide at the chaos and the unfamiliar press of strangers. It smelled of unwashed clothes and boiled rations.

"Go see the medics first," a guard directed, pointing them to a central tent marked with a faded red cross. Elias nodded, relief mixing with wariness as they joined the queue. The line moved slow with the wounded from the convoy filling the spots ahead: a man with a bandaged arm, children coughing from dust. Mira tugged his sleeve. "Eli... It's loud here. I don't like it." He glanced at their mother, who nodded to a quiet spot along the wall in the sunshine near the tent. "Come on, we'll quiet the noise over here," Elias said as he guided Mira to the spot their mother pointed out. They sat close, knees touching, and slipped into the Dreamwood where the quiet grove was waiting.

Elias deepened it there, his voice soft against the camp's ruckus. "Look. More trees now, one for each thing we miss. This grove is for all of us. Its roots link them to the big central tree." Mira leaned closer, her commitment clear as she shaped it without prompting. "One for Theo's stories... branches full of nests with birds telling them over and over." The vision bloomed: trunks smooth and knotted, leaves forming canopies that blocked out the sun's glare, a central clearing with stones arranged like seats around a fire pit with warm flames, not destructive ones. Elias felt connected to Theo stronger now, memories surfacing like roots breaking ground. "He'd like this," Elias whispered, adding a stream winding through the grove, its water carrying faint echoes of laughter.

The camp clawed back, a shout from their mother in the line pulling them out. It was their turn, and the medics ushered them into the tent with its rows of cots under buzzing lights, the air sharp with antiseptic. A doctor, sleeves rolled up, knelt by their mother first, unwrapping the saturated bandage to reveal the shrapnel gash, raw and inflamed. "Shrapnel wound?" she asked, voice efficient but kind. Their mother nodded, biting her lip as the woman cleaned it with steady hands, applying stitches and fresh gauze. Elias watched, leg throbbing in sympathy, until the doctor turned to him. "Your turn. Let's see that leg." He rolled up his pant leg, the gash swollen and dirt-grimed from the run. She worked quick, irrigating the wound and bandaging it tight. It hurt, but not as much as some things recently. "You can walk on it, but take it easy. Don't want it getting infected out there."

As the doctor finished, their mother caught Elias's eye, gratitude softening her pain. "You got us through all that, Eli. You're such a good big brother." He shrugged it off, but inside, Theo's shadow stirred. His brother would have been the one joking with the medic, easing the sting. Mira hovered close, her hand brushing his bandaged leg. "Does it hurt less now?" Elias nodded, though the ache lingered, deeper than skin. The medics directed them to a supply tent for basics. They received a thin blanket each and a tin cup filled with meager rations of bread and dried meat, which was way better than the slimy beans they'd been eating. Elias carried the bundle, Mira grabbed the food and skipped a step ahead despite the exhaustion. The camp's uneasiness settled fast. Tents butted against each other, voices spilling from flaps, arguments over space, children wailing, parents lost in convoys. Guards patrolled the perimeter, rifles slung scanning for infiltrators.

They were assigned a tent at the field's edge. A small canvas sagging on poles, space for three if they slept close. Elias helped their mother inside, propping her leg on their pack. Mira dropped the rations and peered out the flap. "It's like a big bunker, like the last place. Everyone's too close, though." Elias knelt beside her on the hard-packed dirt. "We'll make it ours. Like the grove." But doubt clawed as the afternoon wore on. The tent walls were thin, letting in every shout and cough from neighbors. He tried pulling Mira into the Dreamwood again, but his focus slipped; a nearby argument over water rations shattered the grove's quiet. Theo's tree flickered like a bad signal and Mira frowned, rubbing her temples. "I can't see it clearly. Too much noise."

Elias pushed harder, reassuring Mira to drown out the background noise. "Theo's tree, add a swing from the branches, like the one he built in the yard." Mira latched on among the noises around them. "Yeah, and vines with flowers for the ropes! Strong so it doesn't break." The grove reformed, the swing creaking gently in a breeze that swept through the campground, a spot to sit and remember without the pain cutting so deep. The camp tested their vision relentlessly. Overcrowding meant no privacy for whispers, rumors filtering in like free-flowing water. Elias heard an older man outside grumble to a group, "Heard patrols hit two convoys yesterday, picking them off to keep us pinned. The supplies won't last much longer." The words fueled his wonder about home. Would the apartment still be standing, or was it just another crater? He didn't know. The siege felt endless, trapping them in this sea of tents.

Their mother rested with eyes half shut, the stitches holding but pain keeping her awake. Elias shared the bread with Mira, the crust dry and crumbly in his mouth. As evening fell, Elias lay back, mind turning to Theo again. The grove called to him, a place to bury the day's fractures. Home felt like a fading light, and Elias wondered if the Dreamwood could carry them all the way back, or if the war would snuff it out first.

Night cloaked the camp in a haze of lantern glow, the air cooling to a damp chill that seeped through the tent's seams. Elias lay on the thin blanket, Mira curled beside him, their mother dozing unevenly across the small space. The day's jolts, the ambush, the medics' hands, the endless shuffle of feet outside; it all left him exhausted and blank, with Theo's memory the only constant. He couldn't shake it. In the quiet, Elias slipped into the Dreamwood alone, the grove unfolding like a half-forgotten path. Theo's tree stood, branches heavy with the swing Mira had strengthened, but

Elias deepened it now, adding groves that spread outward; clusters of trees for the family.

He pictured one for their father, a sturdy oak with roots delving deep and tying into the other trees, bringing them energy, much like the generators he'd fixed and how they supplied power to everything else. Another for Mira, a slender birch with leaves that shimmered like her questions during rebuilds. But Theo's dominated, its bark rough under imagined fingers, holding the weight of what they'd lost. Elias sat in the swing in the vision, pushing off gently, remembering Theo's voice reciting tales of endless woods. Guilt twisted in him. Why hadn't he been there that day, fetching the water instead? The war had stolen pieces one by one, leaving him to patch it together. But the groves felt like a start, a way to hold them close without letting them fade. Mira wiggled beside him, sensing the Dreamwood. "Eli? Are we there?" He whispered yes, drawing her in. "The groves... they're for us. Add to Theo's, maybe a path through them, leading somewhere safe."

Mira's voice came soft but sure, no wavering now. "A path with stones, smooth ones, like the ones you showed me first. And flowers along it, ones that glow at night. And a cute fox, hopping along the side, in and out of the trees." The vision expanded, the path winding between trees, petals unfurling in the mental dusk, lighting the way. Her full buy-in now made it sincerer; the groves no longer just Elias's refuge but theirs to share, a memorial alive with her touch. They walked it together, the swing swaying behind in a breeze, birds jumping from branch to branch with songs that carried Theo's laugh. For a stretch, the tent's confines faded, the camp's noise a distant buzz. Elias felt the weight lift a fraction, the doubt about home easing into something bearable.

Morning revealed the camp's full face. Sunlight slanted through gaps to reveal the dirt floor streaked with last night's damp air which collected on the flaps and dripped down. Their mother woke first, testing her leg with a grimace, the stitches holding but the wound tender. "Better," she said, sitting up slow. Elias, up next, helped her with the rations, and Mira was peering out the tent flap, drawn to the movement beyond. "People everywhere," she said, a mix of curiosity and unease. "Too much."

The day wore on in lines with more waiting. Rations first: a watery stew doled out in dented bowls and water runs under watchful eyes. Elias stuck close to Mira, her character shining in small ways throughout the day. During a long wait, she whispered grove details unprompted. "The birds in Theo's tree, they fly ahead, show us the path." She made the best of it.

Rumors swirled thicker now, caught in fragments. A group by the supply tent muttered about patrols tightening the noose, cutting off fallback routes; another about holdouts in the city core, fighting for every block. Elias overheard it all, fueling a quiet dread. Home wasn't just the apartment; it was the life they had before this. The walks by the water, Theo's stories under the stars. Would the war let them return, or was this tent their new forever? He tried to shake it off.

Their mother noticed his quiet, touching his arm as evening fell. "I've been listening to this place you've been building. It sounds nice, Elias. That grove seems to help her a lot." Mira curled up, already murmuring grove details as she fell asleep. Elias tried to get comfortable next to her, but he felt something in his bones.

Outside, a low rumble built in the distance. Not engines this time, but something heavier. Voices all around rose in alarm. Elias froze to listen. He peered through the flap as shadows moved in the growing dark, the camp stirring like a beehive when an invader got too close.

Chapter 7
The Thump's Freezing Grip

A low rumble outside the tent built steadily, pulling Elias from the quiet he'd settled into. Night had fallen thick over the camp, with lanterns casting faint pools of light between the rows of canvas, but the sound cut through the noise and distant coughs like a warning. He sat still on the blanket, Mira curled beside him, her earlier whispers about the grove fading as the noise became recognizable. Their mother shifted slightly, eyes narrowing as she listened too. The rumble wasn't engines on the ground. There were no tires crunching gravel or guards barking orders. It was from above. A rhythmic thump-thumping that vibrated the air, growing closer with each beat.

Elias's breath caught, his body freezing as the noise sharpened. He knew this noise now; helicopters slicing through the dark. The camp stirred around them, voices rising in confusion from neighboring tents, flaps rustling as people peered out. "What is that?" a woman muttered nearby, her words carrying through the thin walls. Elias knew what it was. The sound brought back memories, sharp as broken glass: rotors overhead in Nova City, destroying their safety, not bringing help but unleashing fire from the sky. Missiles streaked down without warning, buildings crumbled. His chest tightened, and his limbs became heavy. He couldn't move, couldn't even call to Mira. The sound of the helicopters nearing filled his head, drowning out the grove's steady roots he'd built earlier that evening.

Their mother pushed up on her good leg, wincing as she reached the flap of the small tent. "Helicopters," she said, voice low but urgent. "Stay put." She slipped outside and moved into the darkness, the canvas falling back with a soft slap. Elias stared at the doorway, his pulse matching the rotors' cadence, sweat beading cold on his skin despite the night's chill. The camp's lanterns grew brighter as more people emerged from their tents. The thump-thumping swelled, multiple helicopters. A formation, coming to wipe them out.

Mira, startled in her sleep, sat up suddenly, rubbing her eyes as the noise rattled the tent poles. "Eli? It's loud again." She tugged at his shirt, but Elias remained frozen in place, his mind lost in the past. The distinct sound of rotors brought it all back: smoke rising thick, screams cutting through the air. His breath came shallow, the world narrowing to the thumping blades. The fear pinned him like the debris that had buried his brother. Mira shook his arm gently, her face creased with worry in the dim light filtering through the canvas. "Eli, you're shaking. Like when the tanks came. Is it bad?"

He wanted to answer, but the sound held him fast, fracturing his thoughts into jagged pieces. The helicopters were close now. Voices outside swelled as the first helicopter banked low over the central field, ropes dropping from each side. Crewmen rappelled down, securing crates that thudded to the ground. More followed, three in total, rotors whipping the night air without mercy, spraying dirt against the edges of the canvas tents. The helicopters arrived over the barren fields, using the darkness for cover to avoid drawing enemy fire.

Their mother returned through the flap, face set with caution. "It was a supply drop. Stay here, I'm going to go see what I can grab." She knelt beside Elias, hand on his shoulder, but he barely registered it. Mira watched him, her small fingers digging into his sleeve. She glanced toward the flap, where lantern light flickered from the field, then back to him. "Eli... Remember the cave? The one we made strong?"

Elias nodded faintly, but he couldn't break free, his body still unresponsive. The helicopters hovered, crates piling in the dark field. Cheers broke out sporadically as word spread. They brought food and water. But for Elias, the sound was a trigger, pulling him back to the chaos of that night, the way rotors had masked the strikes until fire bloomed everywhere. His mind splintered under it.

Mira didn't wait for him to lead. She scooted closer, her voice steady despite the tremble in her hands. "Close your eyes with me.

We're going to the waterfall first. The mist is cool, pushing the loud away." Her words were gentle, trying to guide her brother into the one place that had helped her many times. Elias blinked, the thump-thumping fading a fraction as he followed her lead. For the first time, she pulled him in, the Dreamwood unfolding under her prompt. The waterfall rushed and vines thickened across the cave entrance, blocking the rotors' beat. "The rocks are solid," she continued, voice soft but sure. "Holding us safe inside."

Elias latched on, the cave's interior blooming around them, smooth stone walls, the pool at the rear rippling gently. The fear eased, his breath deepening as Mira added, "The turtles are there too, swimming slow, not scared of the noise." He nodded in the vision, the freeze thawing as the imagined water cooled the heat in his chest. Outside, the helicopters finished their work, the last crate thudding down before the formation pulled away, rotors receding into the night. The camp buzzed with subdued excitement, people gathering cautiously around the field inspecting the haul in the dark.

Elias surfaced slowly, the tent's confines sharper now. Mira grabbed his hand. "Better?" she asked, a small smile breaking through her worry. He squeezed her fingers. "Yes, thanks Mira," he sighed, relieved a bit. "I was scared too, but the cave made it quiet. I wanted you there." His thoughts faded in the dark. How could he protect her if noises drove him to freeze like that?

Their mother returned. "They'll distribute some supplies in the morning. Go back to sleep." Elias laid down, the rotors' memory lingering like a bruise. Mira had stepped in, her initiative a quiet shift, but it highlighted his fractures, the way anxiety clawed deeper without warning. The Dreamwood held, thanks to her, but he pondered how long he could lean on it before the war crushed it.

The camp settled into a dull quiet after the drop. Elias eventually dozed off to sleep, Mira at his side. Dreams tangled with reality. Rotors blended into the grove's rustling leaves. Theo's tree tilted under an unseen wind. Steady, for now, holding fast thanks to Mira's quick thinking.

By dawn, voices stirred outside. Guards organized in the field under lantern light. Elias woke to Mira's nudge, the air cooler now, carrying the sound of crates being ripped open. Their mother tested her leg as she stood, painful, but working. "Let's go see what they've brought. Stay close."

Joined by other early risers, they shuffled toward the central field. The crates stood in neat rows, lids pried open to reveal stacks of tins, water pouches, bandages; much-needed rations after weeks of scraps. Guards directed the flow with firm voices: "Families with children first. One line, keep it moving." Elias kept Mira's hand in his, the crowd pressing but orderly in the chill. He caught doubt hanging in the elder's mutters ahead of them, "Won't go far with all of us here, it doesn't look like enough."

The line moved slowly as dawn broke fully. The sun crested the horizon, bringing heat which thinned the cool morning air. Elias's leg throbbed with each step, but the anticipation pushed him forward. Mira bounced slightly, her earlier worry forgotten. "I hope it's not slimy beans." Elias smiled, but the sound of helicopters replayed faintly in his mind, a reminder of the fear she'd pulled him from. The drop was a lifeline, but in the war's grasp, nothing came without cost. Dawn's light sharpened the camp's edges as the line snaked toward the crates, the air thick with the scent of smoke and murmured hopes. People pressed forward, voices overlapping. Their relief was edged with urgency.

Guards barked directions, rifles slung across their chests, forming barriers to keep the flow single-file. "Two cans per family, one water bottle. No pushing." The first groups emerged with bundles, faces lighting up at the weight in their arms. Elias caught glimpses of the haul, dented tins of fruits and vegetables, strips of dried meat. It looked substantial in the piles, but the line stretched long behind them. Thousands were packed into the camp, bellies waiting after weeks of thinning gruel. Mira tugged his sleeve. "Look, Eli. Jerky like Mom got yesterday. I liked that." Her eyes sparkled at anything but beans.

The war weaponized hunger, starving any resistance to force surrender. Here, it showed in the crowd's hollow eyes. Elias's stomach growled; the brief fullness from last night's bread had already faded, but he focused on Mira, keeping her between him and their mother. It wouldn't be long until he had more food in his belly.

Their turn came as the sun climbed another hour into the sky. The guard at the crate, sweating and impatient, shoved two tins into Elias's hands. Beans, and a half-full water bottle. "Jerky is gone. Move along." Elias tucked them away, glancing at the shrinking piles. Behind him, groans rose as the portions dwindled. A woman ahead argued for more: "We have kids, that's not enough!" The guard's response was empathetic but sharp; there just wasn't going to be enough for everyone. Mira frowned at their haul. "Only beans?" She put her head down, the hope and excitement she held an hour ago about jerky now gone.

Their mother squeezed her shoulder. "It's something, better than nothing. Let's get back." But as they turned from the field, the discord ignited. At the pile's edge, two men lunged for a dropped tin, fists swinging in a blur of dust. Shouts spread, a woman shoving another over a water pouch, other children scattering as adults grappled in the dirt. Guards made their way in, batons cracking against arms as they tried to break up the violence, but the scuffle rippled outward. Families clashed over scraps, desperation turning neighbors into threats. Elias pulled Mira close, hurrying them through the chaos. Her rigid body was tense against his side. "Why are they fighting? The helicopters brought food for all of us. Even if it is just beans."

Elias had no good answer. The scene twisted in him. The drop was too slight, the famine's grip tightening daily. Nova City's blockaded ports, once symbols of shared trade, now fueled their starvation. He guided them past a group yelling in the haze, a man's bloody nose staining the dirt. Their mother limped faster. "Get inside." The canvas flap fell shut on the rising commotion outside.

Inside, the air hung stale, the thin canvas doing nothing to mute the shouts filtering through. Their mother sank onto the blanket, leg extended and propped up, while Elias set the tins down. Mira paced the small space, kicking at the dirt floor. "It's not fair. I don't like the beans." Elias knelt beside her, "The grove. Let's put the beans there but make them taste better." The vision took hold, the fire pit waiting, tins opening to reveal warm stew instead of cold sludge.

Mira built on it, smiling. "And water that never ends, like a stream filling the bottles." In their shared space, they ate the beans, but they didn't taste the cold disappointment thrust upon them from the war. Their mother, contemplating, pushed herself to her feet. "Stay here. I'm... going to check the lines, see if anything's left."

Elias sat uneasily as his mother left, Mira watching him. "You were scared last night, with the helicopters. But I helped, right? Like you help me?" He nodded and managed a smile, assuring her question, the reversal still sinking in. Her initiative pulled him from the freeze, a fracture in what was supposed to be his role as protector. The camp's unrest pressed on, though, yells turning to thuds as fists continued to fly. Guards' shouts barely contained it. The drop had cracked the fragile order of the camp, turning relief into rivalry.

A short while later, their mother returned, slipping through the flap with a bundled cloth under her arm. She sat down and unwrapped it carefully. Mira's eyes widened, and her bottom jaw fell as she saw the contents: a loaf of bread, soft and whole, three thick strips of jerky, and two full water bottles. "Mom, how? There wasn't enough and people were fighting."

"From the overflow crates," she said, voice hushed. "No one's counting every person in this mess." Elias stared at her, her act bold and clearly against the rules, but his hunger overrode the caution. She tore the bread, passing pieces to both of them, saving a little for herself. Jerky followed, salty and tough. Mira chewed slowly, a grin breaking through between bites. "It's like the meat in the stew in the grove, just a little tougher. Way better than beans!"

Their mother sipped from a water bottle, eyes steady on the tent flap. "Eat it quick, we'll need the energy." Elias saw the risk his mother took, and watching Mira's face light up, could understand why she did it. She broke the rules to comfort them. He took note.

Afternoon heat baked the camp, the sun turning the thin canvas tents into ovens. Elias sat with Mira, just outside of the tent in the small shade it provided, the smuggled meal's satisfaction lingering in their stomachs. Their mother rested nearby, leg elevated, the extra water bottles hidden under a blanket she kept close. The fights from the drop had simmered to scattered arguments, but the tension was coiled tight. Elias picked at the last breadcrumbs while Mira leaned against his back. Now, with full bellies and nothing to do, the Dreamwood called to him.

"Let's go back to the grove," Mira murmured as if sensing his thoughts. She closed her eyes first, guiding without prompting. Elias followed again, the tent dissolving into the grove's quiet grass, swaying in the breeze. Theo's tree stood tall, swing creaking softly, the path Mira had lined with glowing flowers winding through. "There's a basked of bread by the fire. It's filled with jerky and water and fresh steaming hot bread." Her voice wove the details: flames low and steady, the loaf appearing whole again, strips of meat dangling within reach, water bottles refilled from the nearby stream. Elias added to it, the scene solidifying. "The fire warms without burning, and the berries from before grow thicker." They sat by the fire pit, passing food that sustained without end. Birds from Theo's branches hopped down to share the crumbs. Mira's commitment shone, her additions turning the grove into a haven of abundance, a stand against the famine's scarcity. The helicopter noise from the rotors' fear receded further as well with the cave's vines now extending to wrap the grove, shielding it from outside noise.

But even in the safety of their shared space, Elias's mind churned with doubts. The freeze last night had exposed cracks; trauma from the raids and losses burrowing in, fracturing his resolve like the camp's fragile peace was disturbed with minimal rations. The war's mental toll pressed harder in the isolation of the overcrowded tents.

Surfacing from the vision, the tent's reality rushed back. Mira opened her eyes, smiling. "It felt real. The jerky was chewy, like ours." Their mother adjusted her bandage, the wound cleaner now but tender. Elias tore the last of the jerky into three pieces and gave the larger ones to his mother and sister. It's what Theo would have done.

Outside, the camp's discord lingered in mutters and shuffles. Elias pondered the famine's reach, starting to understand it. The blockades don't just starve bodies; the lack of food erodes the minds, turning people against each other. And he was right. The superpowers were betting on desperation to shatter unity. He felt it in his fracturing thoughts, the Dreamwood a vital hold but stretched thin by endless threats. To protect Mira meant mending himself first, but the war chipped away relentlessly.

He closed his eyes last that night, listening to his mother's slight snores and Mira's steady breathing. The day's fractures eased into a heavy but welcome exhaustion. Sleep came in fits. Images of the grove paths wound through his thoughts, a temporary shield against the camp's uncertainties. For a few hours, the world outside didn't exist, and the three slept soundly in their small space.

It wasn't destined to last, though. Morning shattered the fragile rest with a deafening drone overhead. Planes, slicing low through the sky, their engines roaring as they passed. Elias jolted awake, Mira clinging to him in confusion. Their mother sat up with a sharp intake of breath, the noise ripping her from her slumber. White leaflets fluttered down like snow, blanketing the tents and fields. Enemy words were printed bold telling civilians to leave the camp before it was bombed. The camp erupted in fear and scrambling feet, the message igniting fresh panic. Elias's mind flickered: they found them, everywhere they went. He wondered how long the refuge hidden in their minds could withstand the invaders' tightening noose, or if they would invade that, too.

Chapter 8
The Labyrinth of Fears

Leaflets blanketed the camp like a sudden storm, white scraps catching on tent flaps and piling in the dirt. Elias's heart beat fast, the planes' roar still fading overhead as they sped away, their droning engines having ripped through the morning's quiet and calm. Mira clung to him, rigid with confusion. The noise had barely settled as the invaders' message burned into Elias's mind. "Leave this area. Resistance is futile. Leave now or face destruction." The leaflets gave a grave warning: leave or die.

Shouts erupted outside, voices overlapping in a wave of alarm that swept through the tents. Guards barked orders from the perimeter, their tones edged with urgency. Families scrambled from their shelters, bundles clutched in arms, children wailing amid the chaos. Elias pushed to his feet, leg throbbing under the tight bandage, and grabbed their pack from the corner. Mira rubbed her eyes, voice shaky, "Eli, what do they mean? Are we leaving?" Their mother stood with a wince, "We have to go now, grab your things. Elias, put the water and tins in the bag."

Elias stuffed the smuggled water bottles and remaining jerky into the pack, his hands moving on instinct despite the uneasy feeling growing inside him. The camp dissolved into a frenzy around them. Tents collapsed in hasty folds, people shoving past each other toward the gates. Guards waved them through with rifles raised at the sky, as if expecting more planes. The air filled with dust, kicked up by hundreds of pairs of feet stampeding along.

Their mother limped ahead, leading them through the press of bodies toward the supply tents, where crates from the night drop still stood half-distributed. "We take what's left, grab anything you can." Elias kept Mira close as they wove past a gaggle of arguing elders, one clutching a leaflet and gesturing wildly at the horizon. "They'll bomb it all, mark my words. The city's next." Elias shoved the thought down, focusing on the path ahead, but the words lodged in his chest, stirring a fresh wave of unease. The leaflets weren't just paper; they were threats, promises of fire that turned the camp's fragile safety into a trap.

At the crates, chaos reigned. Guards doled out whatever remained: scattered tins of beans and vegetables, a few water bottles, bandages, and a few handfuls of jerky. Elias shouldered forward, grabbing a few dented cans without labels and a strip of cloth for extra wrapping, while their mother snatched a half-empty medical kit, three bottles of water, and a handful of jerky. Mira tugged at his sleeve, eyes wide at a child nearby, sobbing over a torn leaflet. "Eli, why is he crying? Are they coming now?" He pulled her back, the pack heavier on his good shoulder, and scanned the sky. They were clear for the moment, but the planes' droning lingered in his ears like a warning pulse. "We're fine. We are leaving this place, so we'll be ok." Mira squeezed his arm as they moved to the gate.

The gates loomed ahead, a makeshift barrier of wire and crates now flung wide open, streams of refugees pouring through. Elias supported their mother's arm, her limp slowing them as they joined the flow. The leaflets crackled underfoot, words of surrender blurring into the dirt: warnings of bombed homes, calls to abandon the fight. Elias's mind raced, anxiety coiling tighter with each step. The camp had been their uneasy safety, but now it felt like a target painted on their backs. What if the planes returned? What if the tanks followed, grinding through the fields to seal the escape? What about the helicopters and their destruction? He glanced at Mira, her face set with determination despite the fear in her eyes, and forced his voice to steady. "We'll find cover out there, like before with the cave."

Beyond the gates, the barren fields stretched toward Nova City's jagged edges, the skyline a broken line of toppled towers and smoke trails. The refugees scattered in loose groups, some heading for the roads, others veering toward the rubble of the outskirts. Their mother steered them off the main path, toward a cluster of half-standing structures: a small residential section that had once housed dignitaries, now reduced to shambles of cracked walls and collapsed homes. The scent of charred wood filled the air as they approached, the ground uneven with debris from old strikes. She pointed to a low wall, partially intact, offering scant shelter. "There. We'll rest a minute." Her leg was throbbing; she just needed to sit for a moment to dull the pain.

They ducked behind it, breaths coming hard. Mira crouched low, peering over the edge at the dispersing crowd in the distance. "Everyone's running. Why are they running?" Elias scanned the leaflets caught in the nearby rubble. Their messages foreshadowed a grim future: *futility, destruction, isolation.* The words pressed in, amplifying the sickened feeling taking over his body, turning his thoughts into a tangle of what-ifs. From inside the camp, it looked safe. But from this distance, a couple hundred yards away, it looked vulnerable, tents flapping like flags of surrender. He pulled Mira closer, his anxiety deepening, making every shadow seem like a threat closing in.

Their mother unwrapped the medical kit, checking her bandage amid the quiet. "We can't stay here long. We'll use the old alleys and paths to get through, stay off the main roads." Elias nodded, but his mind churned, the leaflets' warnings burrowing like splinters. The war didn't just destroy buildings; it propagated doubt, making every step feel like a gamble. Mira fidgeted with a leaflet scrap, her voice cutting through his spiral. "Eli, it's scary. There's so much stuff on the ground," she said, referring to the toppled building and destroyed cars everywhere. He met her eyes, seeing his own unease reflected, and reached for the one tool they had left. "Let's make our own way through, paths without all this stuff in the way."

She squeezed her eyes shut as Elias spoke softly, the rubble fading as the Dreamwood took hold. The grove unfolded, Theo's tree steady, but ahead, the path twisted in unfamiliar turns. There was a new maze of hedges and vines, and walls rising to block the way. His anxiety sharpened as the leaflets seemed to seep in, forming barriers in their paths. "It's a labyrinth," he said, scanning the area. Mira could sense the fear as Elias described the place beyond the grove, not fully letting go of the real-world terrors. "I'll find a gap through, like hiding from the guards," she said, her hand firmly grasping his, pulling him forward. "We'll just push through it."

The maze stretched, turns leading to shadowed corners where leaflets littered the ground. Warnings of fire and isolation twisted the vines into knots. It was becoming harder to breathe, Elias's anxiety delving deeper, a sense of being trapped, not just in the Dreamwood, but in the endless running and hiding. Mira pointed ahead, her voice cutting through the haze. "There, a break in the hedge. We'll go that way." The path opened slightly with her help, inspired by the wall's shelter, a narrow alley in the lush green. Elias latched on, the vision holding against his pulses of doubt. But the real world clawed back, a distant growl building from the fields. The grind of treads on broken concrete... it could only be tanks, and they were approaching the camp.

The growl grew from a low vibration to a full-throated roar, shaking the ground beneath their hiding spot. Elias's eyes snapped open, the Dreamwood's maze fracturing at the edges as reality crashed back. Mira blinked too, confusion crossing her face, while their mother tensed against the low wall. "Tanks again," she whispered. The sound rolled closer, heavy treads pulverizing the broken earth, engines snarling like beasts. Elias pulled Mira down lower behind the rubble, heart pounding as the first shell whistled overhead, slamming into the camp's perimeter with a deafening crack.

The impact ignited a wildfire. Flames leapt from the central field where crates and tents ignited in a chain of blasts. From their vantage on the outskirts, Elias watched in horror as the residential ruins gave way to a view of the camp erupting; tents shredding under explosions, people scattering like ants from a kicked nest. A plane flew in low overhead, its drone merging with the tanks' roar. The air filled with burning canvas and fuel, black plumes rising thick against the morning sky. Shouts carried on the wind, sharp cries cut short by the next shell's thunder, the ground bucking as if the earth itself recoiled.

"Stay down!" their mother hissed, yanking them toward a deeper pile of debris. It was a collapsed section of wall off a building and shattered roof tiles that offered a shallow hole, much like the overpass did. Elias scrambled after her, dragging Mira behind, the pack dragging heavy on his shoulder. Debris rained from the sky, chunks of stone and twisted metal pinging off the ruins around them. Elias seemed to ingest all of it: the relentless grind of treads vibrating through his bones and the sharp scent of scorched earth and gunpowder stinging his nose. He pressed Mira into the hollow area, shielding her with his body as another shell struck nearer.

Mira whimpered, burying her face against him and trembling with each boom. "Eli, it's too loud. Is the camp gone?" Elias held her tighter, his own anxiety spiking, thoughts racing in jagged bursts. The tanks were tightening the noose, shells walking the field to scatter survivors. The plane circling low in the sky sowed more panic. From the debris, he glimpsed the destruction: tents engulfed in a wall of flames, crates exploding, smoke pouring into the sky, figures fleeing toward the city's edge only to vanish in the haze. The war's randomness clawed at him, turning preparation into peril, every shadow a potential crater. His leg burned from the scramble with fresh blood seeping through the bandage. But he ignored it, focusing on Mira's trembling hand grabbing at his side. "The camp is fine, we're just going another way," he lied, hoping to ease her tensions a bit.

Their mother crouched beside them, face smeared with dirt, eyes scanning the horizon. "They will pass if we're quiet, we'll wait it out here," she said, plopping down next to them. The assault intensified. Shells cratered the outskirts now, one landing close enough to shower their hiding spot with shrapnel and debris. Their shallow hole shuddered, air thickening with grit that coated their throats, forcing coughs that Elias stifled with his sleeve. The chaos pressed in from all sides: the tanks' engines a constant snarl while shells whistled like vengeful spirits. How many more strikes before the ruins swallowed them? Elias's mind raced as the camp's flames lit the sky orange.

Mira's voice broke through, muffled against his shirt. "Eli... it's the maze. It turns everywhere... no way out." Her words cut the haze, pulling at the Dreamwood even here in the debris, though it seemed she was losing hold. Elias latched on, the idea sparking despite the racket. "Yeah. We'll use it. Find paths in the chaos, just like we have been." He closed his eyes briefly, the rubble fading as the labyrinth reformed. The hedges twisted sharper now, like the debris piles, forming dead ends that mirrored the road ahead. Mira pointed to a gap in the chaos. "Through there, we can fit I think."

The vision held fragile; the tanks' rumble nearby bleeding into the mental ground, but it gave them a foothold. Elias pushed through the gap first and whispered back, "The path, it's narrow, but we can make it." Another shell hit nearby, the blast hurling a wave of dust that choked the air, forcing them to huddle tighter. Their mother pressed close, her hand on Mira's back. "Quiet, they're moving past."

Time stretched. The assault pounded without mercy. Shells walked the camp's remains, flames roaring higher as the plane banked for another pass. Elias shielded Mira from a flying shard of rubble, the chunk of probably concrete hitting him square in the back. The sensory overload battered him. Heat radiating from the fires. The metallic tang of blood mixing with smoke. The ground's relentless tremor vibrating up his legs as Mira clung to him. He remembered freezing when the helicopters came, and how he felt about not being able to protect her. He tuned it all out, whispering about the maze. "There's a new turn at the rocks ahead." The new path forked through the debris-inspired walls, a way to navigate the labyrinth they've created.

The tanks pressed past, shells shifting focus to the field's far side, the immediate threat easing. Their mother peered out, face grim and dirty. "They're pulling back. We move now, toward the city." Elias helped her up, Mira scrambling after. The air was hazy with smoke from the burning camp, leaflets smoldering all around. From this vantage, the destruction unfolded: tents reduced to ash and craters scarring the earth. More survivors fled in ragged lines. Elias's anxiety lingered, a deep churn that made the ruins ahead feel like just another trap. But he didn't let Mira look towards the camp. Instead, he grabbed her arm and reminded her of the new turn ahead, a path for them to forge as they moved to the city, like how they'd found the gap in the Dreamwood.

They pressed on, weaving through crumbled walls of old dignitary homes, broken glass crunching underfoot. The plane's noise faded, but the tanks' distant grind still echoed off what walls were left standing. Mira scouted small gaps in the rubble, her earlier maze idea turning practical in their current situation. "Like the paths, we find the breaks."

The residential ruins swallowed them as they moved deeper, shattered facades of once-grand homes offered fractured cover amid the outskirts' sprawl. Elias's back hurt, bruised from the concrete shard that hit him, but he pushed forward, Mira's hand on his shirt as she stayed close. Their mother limped beside them, her face etched with strain. The camp's flames a were a fading glow behind them. Elias's anxiety coiled tighter, a nagging feeling that turned every distant rumble into approaching tanks. His mind was weary from analyzing every sound.

They ducked into one of the homes, mostly collapsed. Mira sat on the broken tiled floor, breathing heavy after maneuvering through all the rubble. "Stay here, I'm going to go check inside for anything usable," their mother said as she slipped through a hole in the wall, deeper into the wreck of a home. Elias looked around, ruins giving way to more ruins, destruction leading way to more destruction. Like a mousetrap with no way out. "It never ends," he accidentally muttered out loud. Mira looked up, her face smudged with dirt and soot, eyes wide. "Then we go back to the maze and make paths from what's here, we can get past it I think," she said with conviction as she stared into his eyes.

Elias nodded. Her suggestion pulled at him. "Yeah, the hiding spot. The way we slipped through the hedge, let's use it." They closed their eyes together, and the broken house faded into their grove, paths twisting into the labyrinth once more. Hedges rose higher, like the home's walls, different turns forking out into shadowed alleys, mimicking the ruin's narrow gaps. "It's a maze everywhere, Mira. What do you see?" "There! A break in the hedge. If we push the stones aside, we can get through it." She shaped it, the wall shifting under her prompt, revealing a narrow passage past all the debris they navigated to get there. "See. We make it wider, like the alleys." Elias followed the path, and light started to pierce through cracks in the hedges, seemingly lighting the way. Mira continued to add details, a vine bridge over a pit and a rope swing over a stream. The maze stretched, challenges piling on. But Mira seemed to find a way around every obstacle. Meanwhile, Elias delved further into his fears. One turn led to a chamber of swirling smoke, mirroring the camp's inferno. He froze in the vision, but Mira continued and pulled ahead. "The air is clean. It smells like fresh rain and pine trees. Breathe Eli, it's nice." Elias took a deep breath, the swirling smoke fading away. "There's a breeze," he said, "pushing the smoke away." The path emerged clearer, with new tree branches forming from the chaos.

"Look, flames! Good ones!" Mira smiled through her shut eyes, and Elias felt it. She'd found their fire pit through the mess. The glow of the flames led to their familiar grove, paths converging into a hub of stability. Elias added the final touch, a high-lookout in Theo's tree where they could see over the entire hedged maze to plot their routes. His anxiety eased fractionally, the probe into the Dreamwood yielding direction, not defeat. The clearing of the labyrinth held them for a moment, a pocket of calm where the vines receded, loosening into gentle arches over the new pathways. Elias paced at the edges of the clearing, looking at the new paths. Mira added bright pink flowers along the route that got them out. "This won't close up," she said, voice firm and in control. "We keep it open, no matter what." Elias watched her, the sight stirring a quiet resolve. The anxiety hadn't vanished, but it had form now, navigable with turns and sunlight peeking through, no longer blind walls with no escape.

Slowly opening his eyes, Elias surfaced to shallow cover, the stone wall pressing close but no longer suffocating. Mira blinked too, her real hand finding his knee amid the debris. "The paths... they're real now. Like the ones we'll take through the city," she said with eagerness. Their mother returned with a fire-singed sheet folded into a pouch. "Lucky us, I found some canned pears and carrots, and electrolyte pouches for the waters. And for you Mira," She reached out with a small crocheted doll with button eyes. Mira's eyes lit up as she grabbed the doll, squeezing it tight against her cheek. "I love it!" she shouted out. A fresh spark ignited in her. Elias was equally as happy seeing her rejoice in the newfound toy. At the least, it would help her in tense situations where he may struggle.

The camp's smoldering remains dotted the horizon, thin trails of smoke curling upward, the flames reduced to embers under the midday sun. Scattered figures moved in the distance, refugees picking through the wreckage or fleeing toward the city. The immediate threat had passed. The sound of tanks and planes were absent. Elias's mind replayed the maze's lessons, the new paths a fragile toolkit against the war's randomness. Anxiety lingered, but Mira's flowers stuck with him, small patches blooming through the charred earth. "We follow the flowers," he said to himself as he peered out of the broken home, staring at the rubble and broken buildings in front of them. "We'll find the breaks in the ruins like the gaps in the hedges."

Their mother gathered the pack, slinging it on her back. "We need to go. The city will hide us better than these open fields." Mira stood, brushing dust from her knees, her earlier tremble gone. "And if we get stuck, we go back, make more paths." Elias rose with her, the shallow shelter feeling less like a cage now.

As they stepped out, the ruins unfolded ahead. Crumbled homes gave way to narrower streets choked with fallen beams and shattered stone. Elias and Mira led out front, Mira scouting gaps with a newfound sureness. Elias replayed the day in his mind. The attack had cost him, stripping away illusions of control, but it forged something stronger: paths from peril, a way to press on when all felt lost.

Chapter 9
Rivers of Memory

The sun beat down mercilessly as they pushed through the outer ruins towards the edge of the city, the three-hour trek turning every step into a battle against uneven ground. Elias's bandaged leg ached with each footfall, the wound pulling tight under the strain, but he kept his pace steady for Mira's sake. She walked between them, the crocheted doll from the previous day's scavenging tucked under her arm. Their mother led the way, her limp more pronounced now. The air hung heavy with the faint scent of smoke and burnt canvas from the camp they'd left behind, a distant smudge on the horizon that seemed to follow them like a bad memory.

As they neared, Nova City's outskirts unfolded in a desolate sprawl; buildings reduced to skeletal frames leaning against one another, their walls scarred by blasts that had come and gone months ago. Craters scattered the streets, filled with stagnant water that reflected the fading light in murky pools, and twisted rebar jutted from the concrete like broken bones. Elias scanned the path ahead, his eyes catching on every flicker of movement; a loose scrap of fabric fluttering in the breeze, a rat scurrying into a gap. The quiet out here unnerved him more than the chaos of the camp. No engines growled in the distance, no shouts cut through the air. Just the vast emptiness that made the world feel too big, too exposed. He thought of the tanks from before, their treads grinding paths through similar ruins, grabbing at Mira's hand to make sure she was still there.

Mira looked up at him, her face smudged with dust, tangled hair sticking to her forehead. "Eli, when can we stop? My legs hurt." Her voice carried a mix of complaint and hope, the kind that tugged at his heart every time. Elias forced a reassuring tone. "Soon. Mom said there's a place up ahead, somewhere we can spend the night." Their mother glanced back over her shoulder, her scarf slipping loose, revealing the lines etched deeper around her eyes. "There should be an old theater up ahead. It was made of brick, so hopefully it'll be in decent condition." She didn't complain about her leg, but Elias saw the way she paused to catch her breath, leaning on a fallen signpost for a moment before pressing on, favoring the wound.

The road curved slightly, revealing glimpses of what the city had been: a faded billboard, half-buried in rubble, advertising a festival from years back with families gathered under strings of lights. Elias remembered hearing stories about those days, before the superpowers turned their grudges into bombs. The districts buzzed with visitors from across the bridges, and trade flowed free through the ports. Now, those bridges lay twisted in the bay, and the ports sat silent under the blockade, starving the city from the inside out. He shook off the thought, focusing on Mira's steady steps beside him. The pack on his back held their scavenged finds: pears and carrots from the ruined home, a couple of water bottles that sloshed half-empty as they stepped. But thirst bothered them all, turning the dry air into something thick and insistent.

As the theater came into view, Elias felt a small lift in his chest. It stood like a relic from another time, the marquee drooping low over the entrance, its letters chipped and illegible; something about stars and stories. The front facade held firm, cracked but unyielding, with two short towers flanking the doors that might have once lit up the night. The roof had given way in sections, letting in shafts of late afternoon sun, but the main body of the building remained solid, promising shelter. Faded posters plastered the outer walls with bold colors muted by time, showing adventurers on rivers, families picnicking by sparkling water, and movie heroes standing tall against painted sunsets. One caught Elias's eye: a wide blue stream winding through green hills with boats bobbing gently.

Their mother reached the doors first, pushing against the rusted hinges with a low creak that echoed inside. "This'll do," she said, stepping through. Elias followed, guiding Mira over the threshold, the air inside shifting to something cooler, laced with the musty scent of old velvet and spilled popcorn long gone stale. Dust swirled in the beams of light piercing the ceiling gaps, and rows upon rows of seats stretched out toward a massive screen at the far end. It was torn in places, fabric hanging like ragged curtains, but still imposing, as if waiting for the next showing. The concession stand sat off to the side, its counter splintered, glass display cases reduced to jagged piles of broken glass that crunched underfoot. A few posters inside clung to the walls too, one depicting a serene riverbank with children skipping stones.

Mira's eyes grew wide as she took it all in, twisting to see every corner. "Eli, it's huge! Bigger than the grove!" She darted to a row of seats that were still upright, perching on one and bouncing slightly, the springs creaking beneath her. Elias set the pack down nearby, easing onto the seat beside her, his leg grateful for the pause. Their mother claimed another, stretching her bad leg out with an audible exhale, propping it on a toppled armrest. "This used to be a great place," she told both of them, her gaze drifting to the screen. "People from every district and from across the world came here. I should have taken you guys here before..."

Elias pulled out the near-empty water bottle and took a careful sip. The water was warm, barely touching the dryness in his throat, but it was something. He passed it to Mira, who drank deeply, a trickle escaping down her chin that she wiped away with her sleeve. "Almost gone," she said, handing it to their mother. She took a long drink, her throat working visibly, then capped it with a sigh. "We'll find somewhere to get it filled. The pears and carrots, you two should eat those now." Elias rummaged in the pack, dividing the food between him and Mira: soft pears that yielded under his fingers, carrots still crisp enough to snap. Mira bit into a pear, juice dribbling, and her face lit up. "They're sweet! Like the berries in the grove!"

But thirst lingered, sharper in the still air. The ruins outside offered no relief; just polluted puddles they'd passed, brown and uninviting. Elias's gaze wandered back to the poster of the river, the painted water seeming to move in the shifting light. Mira followed his look, tilting her head. "That looks better than our bottle of water." She shifted on her seat, kicking her feet against the leg of the one in front. Elias felt it then, the Dreamwood stirring like a reflex in the newfound calm. The theater's quiet made it easier somehow, the seats like soft banks of sand. "Want to add it? The painted water?" Mira smiled and nodded eagerly, not closing her eyes this time, her stare fixed on the poster as if pulling the image straight from it. "Yeah. Let's make a river. Starting right here, by the seats."

Their mother watched, a small smile tugging at her lips despite the fatigue in her eyes. Elias settled deeper into the seat, letting Mira lead, her words spilling out steady and bright. "The river comes from a spring under the big central tree in the grove, hidden, but strong. It flows out wide, rushing over rocks, water so clear you see the bottom." Elias pictured it, the current building in his mind, cool and alive. But with his eyes open, the vision layered over the theater. The rows of seats became gentle banks lined with ferns, the concession stand a rocky outcrop where the spring bubbled up. "The water's deep enough to swim," he added, his voice joining hers. "The current is gentle, just float along."

Mira leaned forward, pretending to trail her fingers along the armrest as if dipping into the flow. "Fish are darting by, silver ones flashing in the sunlight. And the banks have those yellow flowers from the clearing, waving in the breeze." The image sharpened. The river carved through the Dreamwood, sunlight glancing off the surface, washing away the dust of their walk. Elias felt the imagined coolness seep into him, easing the rawness in his throat, making the real bottle of water feel less empty. Mira continued, her excitement building: small whirlpools along the edges, slow pools where the current swirled, perfect for resting in. "We can float there, on our backs, looking up at the trees."

For a stretch, the theater transformed in their shared sight. The torn screen turned into a distant waterfall feeding the river, the dust particles swirling like water spray from splashes over rocks. Elias's anxiety from the trek faded, the quiet ruins outside vanishing against the rush in his head. He remembered snatches of the harbor before everything broke: their mother by the water's edge, Theo tossing pebbles to make them skip, the splashes drawing laughs from Mira as a toddler. The memory carried a pain, but the river smoothed it, turning it into something that flowed freely rather than sticking around. Their mother shifted in her seat, her voice soft and tired.

"Your place sounds peaceful. It sort of reminds me of somewhere I went as a girl. We should find somewhere like that when we get out of here."

Mira expanded, describing boats carved from fallen branches, paddles dipping smoothly in the gentle flow. The thirst didn't vanish, but it dulled, the vision quenching what the bottle couldn't. As the light outside turned golden, slanting through the holes in the roof, they let the river settle, a steady presence now, flowing around the edges of the Dreamwood. Mira leaned against him, content with their new addition, the doll held tight with both hands. Elias glanced at their mother, her eyes half-lidded, and felt a quiet hold on the moment. The pause, the stories, the water they'd made their own, the lack of bombs falling.

The golden light faded as afternoon stretched into evening, the theater's interior cooling with the drop in temperature. Elias and Mira lingered in the river's flow for a while longer, their voices trailing off as the vision held steady, a comforting light against the growing shadows. Mira continued eating the carrots, "These are the best. No slimy stuff."

Their mother sat up a bit, watching them with a tired smile. She took a pear slice but set it aside after one bite, her eyes on the dented tin of beans from the camp supplies. It sat unopened in the pack, its label long peeled away, the metal warm from the day's heat. "You two finish those," she said, nodding at the fruits and vegetables.

"I know the beans aren't your favorite. I'll eat those." Mira pulled a disgusted face at the mention, her nose wrinkling. "They're gross, like eating dirt from a can. You can have some of my pears!" Their mother chuckled softly, the sound light despite the strain in her voice. "You eat the pears, you need them more than I do right now. I'll stick with the slimy gross beans," she laughed, making a face back at Mira that made her giggle.

Elias hesitated, carrot halfway to his mouth. "You should have carrots then, Mom." But she shook her head, prying the tin open with the lid, popping it open with a faint hiss. The smell wafted up immediately. It smelled off, sour, like food forgotten too long on a warm counter in the sun. Elias's stomach turned, but their mother spooned a portion without flinching, eating methodically. "It's not that bad. Just needs to be eaten." She took a few bites, chewing slow. She didn't make any faces as Mira watched, her own carrot forgotten. "Does it taste okay?" Their mother nodded. "They taste like everything else these days."

Elias forced down his share, the carrot crisp but the sweetness overshadowed by worry. The war had twisted meals into risks. Rations sat in blockade shipments, spoiling before they reached hands like theirs. Their mother finished half the tin, setting it aside with a quiet burp, and leaned back against the seat. "There. Now rest. We'll head out when it's dark, try to find a place to stay for a while."

Elias nodded, catching a full glimpse of her. She looked paler in the fading light, her hand resting on her bandaged leg.

After a couple of hours, Mira finished her pears and drank the juice from the can, curling up beside Elias in their chairs, her head on his arm. "The river had better food. Fish we could cook at the fire pit." Elias agreed, though his eyes remained on their mother. She closed hers, breathing deep, but after a while, a sheen of sweat broke on her forehead. Elias sat up straighter. "Mom? Are you okay?" She opened her eyes, blinking slow. "I'm fine. Just the walk catching up." But when she shifted to adjust her leg, a wince crossed her face, sharp and quick. Mira noticed too. "Your leg? Is it hurting more?"

Their mother waved it off, but Elias leaned in and touched the bandage gently. It felt warm, too warm, and a dark spot bloomed at the edge, seeping through the cloth. "It opened again," he said, concerned. She pressed a hand to it, her color draining. "Probably nothing. Those beans though..." Mira's eyes widened. "The beans were bad? Like when I got sick from that water?" Their mother tried to sit up fully, but dizziness hit, her head lolling back. "Maybe. It could be nothing though."

Elias's mind raced, the theater's quiet turning oppressive. An infection had flared, the tainted food stirring in her belly, the reopened gash from weeks ago bleeding yet again. He remembered the medics' words at the camp, "keep it clean, watch for redness," but out here, with no proper care, the task seemed impossible. It was definitely infected, and on top of that, she probably had food poisoning from the gross beans. "We need medicine," he told her. "The kind you gave us when we were sick." Mira nodded fast, scrambling for the pack. "There's stores nearby. We can find some!" Their mother gripped Elias's arm. Her hand was hot and clammy. "Absolutely not! You two stay put. We'll figure it out in the morning." Another wave of nausea hit, and she laid back across a few chairs. Elias helped her lie flat across the seats, propping her head up with a folded jacket from the pack. Mira dribbled the last of the water into a cup, mixing in a bit of the electrolyte powder. Their mother sipped slowly as her breaths came shorter. Her eyes fluttered shut as the fever hit, and within minutes she was asleep. Guilt washed over Elias. She'd taken the beans to spare them the taste and the sickness landed on her instead. Mira knelt close, her small hand on her mother's. She looked at Elias, "We can go. We'll be fast like the river."

Elias agreed. They needed to. He gathered the flashlight and knife, and Mira tucked her doll away. The night outside waited, full of illusions and quiet dangers. He took a breath, the river already stirring in his mind. The Dreamwood, maybe it would help guide them.

The dark settled thick over the ruins as Elias and Mira slipped out of the theater, the doors creaking shut behind them. The moon rose pale, casting the streets in silvery patches. Elias kept Mira's hand in his tight, his pack light with just the flashlight and knife. The outer ruins lay still and quiet; no distant rumbles, no lights flickering. The quiet pressed in, broken only by the occasional shift of debris settling. Elias's eyes darted up and down the alleys, a long stretch of shadow from a toppled lamppost making his pulse jump. "Stop," he whispered, tugging Mira behind a low wall. She crouched with him, breathing quicker. "What is it?" The shadow held still, then stretched as clouds passed the moon; it was nothing. Just light playing on the ground, not soldiers.

Mira exhaled, squeezing his hand. "It was a trick, from the moon?" Elias nodded, standing back up slowly. "Yeah. Stay close, the stores are just across the road there." A row of buildings loomed ahead, walls blasted open from old strikes leaving jagged entrances like wounds of the city. A bakery ruins first, its counter visible through a gap in the wall, then what might have been a pharmacy, shelves toppled over inside. Elias led, Mira matching his pace. The quiet held; no patrols, no tanks, no helicopters, no signs of danger.

They reached the bakery wall. Elias peered through the hole before helping Mira climb over the loose bricks. The interior smelled of stale grains and char, and shelves were scattered with broken bowls and flour sacks gone hard. Mira scanned the floor, her doll peeking from her pocket. "Look, that flat spot by the oven." She stepped onto the edge of a low counter, balancing with her arms out. "Like the riverbank. We can jump across." Elias paused, the urgency pulling at him to keep looking for medicine, but her spark cut through. "Okay, quick." Mira nodded, eyes bright even in the dim. "And rocks to hop on." She jumped lightly to the next flat surface, a small desk upturned near the back. She landed with a soft thud and a grin. "Your turn! Skip across like a stone!"

Elias hesitated at first, then stepped up on the low counter edge, jumping across after her. The desk wobbled under his weight as he landed. The motion loosened something in him. A short laugh escaped as he landed. "The water splashes up, cold on our legs." Mira bounced again, giggling, her voice filling the air. "Fish nipping at our toes! Faster current here." For a minute, the bakery came alive in their words. The riverbanks and water overlayed the ruins, turning their search for medicine into something much lighter. Elias felt the guilt he carried over their mother ease, the play chasing worry away like sunlight on shadows. Mira added details out loud. "The spring feeds it strong, pushing us to the next bend," her steps quick and sure.

A faint groan was heard overhead; debris shifting on the weakened roof. It sobered Elias up fast, back into forage mode. He grabbed her arm, "Careful. That could fall." Mira nodded, face serious. They rummaged quickly, finding only a few rusty cans, no medicine. "Next one," Elias said, helping her through the wall gap into the clothing shop beside it. The air here carried a musty wool scent, racks bent like bare branches, mannequins toppled in heaps. Moonlight slanted through a high broken window, throwing shapes that made Elias tense. A pile of fabric for a second looked like a crouched figure, a soldier looking for them. "Wait," he hissed, pulling Mira down. She froze with him, but the light moved, revealing just folds in the cloth. "Moon trick," she whispered.

Relief hit, and inside the shop's deeper shadows, Mira's energy bubbled back. "The river bends around these racks, like trees in the water." She skipped ahead lightly, weaving between the fallen displays. "Paddle time! Push through the branches." Elias followed, his voice joining as he rowed with an imaginary stick, the motion drawing a real chuckle from him. "The current's strong here. It carries the boat fast." Mira spun in a skip, arms wide, her laughter short but bright, echoing off the walls. The play pulled him in. The foraging felt lighter, and the river turned the twisted racks into a fun maze. "Whirlpool ahead. It's slow so we can catch our breath," he added, and Mira hopped onto a low shelf, pretending to float. "The fish are swimming beside me!"

The joy held for those beats, the two of them side by side, words painting the scene over the dust. Elias's worry softened. The jumps reminded him of simpler days, like Theo racing them through parks. But a distant clank, a loose pipe rattling in the breeze, brought them back to reality. "Serious now," Elias said, scanning the back of the collapsed store. Mira dropped from the shelf, returning to forage mode. They searched drawers and pockets in the mannequins, finding buttons and thread, nothing more. "On to the next one," he said, and they slipped through another gap, the night deepening around them.

Two buildings down was a half-collapsed pharmacy. An open wall let in the moonlight, counters exposed like a stage. Elias went first, the flashlight beam cutting through the dark. A shadow stretched long from a fallen sign, his heart stopping for only a moment. It was just the light bending on glass shards. "Moon trick, again," he muttered, getting more used to the dark. Mira continued her Dreamwood adventure. "River turns sharp here. There's a pool by the counter." They talked it out, voices low but energetic, the current guiding their hands under shelves. In the side room, away from the entrance, the play started again. Mira darted to a sturdy box, jumping up on it like a rock. "Hop across! To the deep part," Elias said as he joined, landing beside her. "The water pulls hard here, swim strong." Her skip followed, laughter bubbling as she paddled in place. The moment was light and free from the war's horrors they'd been facing. For the first time in a long time, they were being children as children were meant to be, not as children were during the war.

A creak from unstable flooring cut it short as the floor sagged beneath Mira. Elias steadied her, pulling her off the area by her arm. "Watch it, the floor could give out there." Face set, Mira continued to search, but the real find waited for a breeze from the Dreamwood. As she searched, Mira called out. "There's a breeze here, pushing you around the corner." As Elias played along and swirled around the corner into a mostly intact stockroom, the moonlight shone perfectly on a shelf with a glass door. He opened it, and there they were, a handful of bottles of medications, lying sideways at the edge of the shelf, hidden behind a higher shelf that had fallen on top of them. "I think I found some medicine," he said to Mira. "It led us to them, the breeze did!" Mira said softly, her eyes sparkling in the revelation. Not knowing what was what, Elias pocketed all the bottles. "The river needs to take us back now." Mira, excited, jumped up and down in place, landing in the river, then "swimming" to the front of the store and out through the broken wall that let them in.

The theater doors creaked open, louder in the night, stars sharp overhead through the roof gaps as Elias and Mira scurried inside. The air felt thicker now, laced with the faint sweat of fever, and their mother was still stretched across the seats in a sweaty sleep. Mira reached her first, kneeling by her side. "Mom, wake up. We found it, the medicine from the river!" Their mother's eyes cracked open, focusing slow in the starlight, her face slick with sweat. As her eyes trained on Elias, he pulled bottle after bottle of medicine out of his pocket and placed them on her chest. "I told you to stay put. Where did you get this?" Elias ignored the stern question. "I don't know what they are. I grabbed them all." He shone his flashlight on the faded labels so she could see. Their mother, too weak to push the issue, looked through the bottles he had brought back. Penicillin, third bottle she pulled up. "This is it," she said as she coughed, opening the bottle and taking two of the pills, hard to swallow without any water left. Mira's smile was ear-to-ear. To her, the Dreamwood found the medicine; it was real.

Elias grabbed her arm. Mira hovered close, doll in her lap, chattering to fill the quiet. "We jumped rocks in the bakery, like the ones by the spring. And the current took us right to the pool where fish were swimming guard, but the breeze pushed us to the medicine!" Their mother managed a weak smile, the effort pulling at her. "Sounds... like you had an adventure." Elias, fearing a tongue-lashing, was relieved at the words and the faint smile. The color in her cheeks stayed high, but her breathing eased a fraction as the medicine started working against the infection.

He turned to the bandage next, peeling it back gently. The wound was red and angry. The edges were swollen, and the poison from the beans probably didn't help. Mira fetched a clean cloth from the pack. Elias cleaned the wound the best he could and wrapped it fresh. Their mother winced but held still, her hand on Mira's head. "You did good. Both of you, you're so big." The guilt hit Elias again; she'd eaten that tin to keep the slimy taste from them, taking the bad on herself, and now the fever burned because of it. But Mira's words about the river helped, the way the vision had guided their steps, turning shadows into sculptures and ruins into paths.

As the dose settled, their mother leaned back, eyes closing fully. "Go to sleep, you'll feel better in the morning," Elias said, pulling the blanket over her, much like she'd told him a hundred times growing up. The theater's quiet enveloped them, the posters' faded scenes watching over like silent guardians. Elias sat on the floor nearby, back against a seat, his mind turning to the day's adventure. The foraging had been full of tricks, the soldiers that weren't there, the creaks that sounded like danger, moon tricks. But the river had made it bearable, overlaying the dark with lighter jumps. The laughter pushed back the fear. He'd felt it lighten him, Mira's skips drawing laughs he didn't know he had anymore. Their playing was a direct rebellion against the war, and it was just what they needed.

Mira yawned beside their mother. "The whirlpools were the best." Elias yawned in agreement, his thoughts drifting to the memories the swim had stirred fresh in his mind: at the harbor's edge, their father teaching them how to flick a stone just right to make it skip across the surface. Theo cheered for each skip as the water rippled out in perfect circles. He thought of their bonds under the war's constant grind, eroded, but holding.

He adjusted the blanket, checking her forehead: cooler already, the fever breaking into a light sweat. Mira dozed off fast, the adventure tiring her out. Elias stayed awake a while longer as the night sounds filtered in. The siege waited out there. But tonight, the Dreamwood did more than soothe. It had led them to what they needed, its river currents practical as a map. He embraced it fully then, the sanctuary, not just an escape, but a tool, woven from their words, strong enough to navigate the never-ending dark.

Chapter 10
Shadows Creeping In

Sunlight slanted through the theater's roof gaps, painting the dusty seats in warm stripes as morning stirred the ruins outside. Elias blinked awake first. Mira slept curled nearby, her crocheted doll tucked under her chin. Across the row of seats, their mother shifted, eyes fluttering open as she tested her leg with a careful flex and stretch. The shrapnel wound, cleaned and rebandaged the night before, felt less angry, and the swelling and redness had faded. She sat up slowly, fever gone.

"Elias," she said quietly, voice hoarse but stronger than the day prior. He scooted closer, helping her prop the leg on the folded jacket. "How do you feel?" he whispered so as not to wake Mira. She managed a small smile, the lines around her eyes softening. "Better. The medicine's working its magic." She reached for the pack, pulling out the penicillin bottle. There was enough for a few more doses. With steady hands, she shook out two pills, swallowing them dry with a grimace. "I've got to get us some water," she mumbled.

Mira woke as their mother moved about, rubbing her eyes and sitting up with a yawn. "Mom? You're not hot anymore?" Their mother nodded, pulling her close for a quick hug. "Cool as the river you two dreamed up. Thanks to your adventure, and that breeze finding the medicine." Mira beamed with joy. "We didn't know where it was, the current pushed us that way." Elias watched the exchange, a sort of relief washing over him. The night had been long. His mind replayed the foraging shadows and moon tricks, with guilt over the beans still eating at him, even though it was no one's fault. But seeing her color return, hearing her laugh softly at Mira's enthusiasm, eased it. For a moment, the theater felt like a true refuge; faded posters on the walls whispered stories of unity, the large screen a silent guardian against the ruins beyond.

Their mother stretched again, testing her weight on the good leg. "We can't stay here forever, but we can take it easy here today. I've got to get us some water... those bottles are bone-dry." Elias nodded, glancing at the pack. Thirst had been a constant shadow since the camp. "There's pipes out there leaking from the old lines. I saw one near that wall gap yesterday." She considered it, eyes flicking to the door. "Close enough. I'll go refill what I can. You two stay put, no wandering. I'll be right back."

Mira frowned, hugging her doll. "But what if we go with you? The river could show us the way." Their mother shook her head gently, ruffling her hair. "I'll be back before you know it with all the water you can drink." She gathered the empty bottles in the pack. Elias walked her to the door, the rusted hinges creaking as she pushed it open. Outside, the ruins lay under the climbing sun; no rumbles, no shouts. A thin layer of morning dew stuck to a fallen street sign, mocking their thirst. She turned back, eyes meeting his with a fierce glint. "I'm proud of you both. Keep this door closed." Mira waved with the doll's hand, and their mother slipped out, the door thudding shut behind her. Elias wedged a loose seat against it to lock it shut.

The theater fell quiet again, light shifting as clouds passed overhead. Mira bounced on her seat. "She'll find the spring! Like in the grove." Elias managed a nod, but unease settled in, a familiar feeling from the tank rumbles and leaflet warnings and helicopters. The quiet felt too absolute. He sat beside her, pulling out the last carrot remnant for them to share. "We'll add a pool by the door when she gets back, deep enough for bottles to float in and get refilled whenever we want." "With fish guarding it! Silver ones, darting fast," Mira exclaimed, munching on the last carrot. The Dreamwood stirred like a reflex now. But without their mother anchoring the space, the theater's shadows seemed longer and the posters' faded smiles appeared to hold secrets unknown to them.

Time stretched. The sun climbed higher in the sky, warming the exposed theater seats. Mira chattered about river bends and whirlpools, her doll "swimming" along in the armrest. Elias listened, half-distracted, his mind wandering to the door. How long had it been? Mira noticed his worry. "She's okay. The paths are open now, remember? No mazes." He forced a smile, but his worry remained. The lull pressed in, the quiet amplifying doubts he'd shoved down: Theo's last fetch for water was the last time he'd seen him. "Let's check the river," he said finally. Mira nodded eagerly, closing her eyes, her hand finding his. "We'll start from the spring with the turtles, and it'll carry us to the river."

The theater's hush deepened as Elias and Mira settled into the seats, the door's wedge holding firm against the world outside. Sunlight pooled on the floor, dust motes dancing like tiny fish in an unseen current. Mira leaned against him. "The spring bubbles up right here, under the seats. Feel it? Cool water pushing through the cracks." Elias let his eyes drift half-shut, the vision layering over the velvet rows; armrests softening into mossy banks, the faint drip from the roof becoming the spring's first trickle. It was easier with her leading, her words painting without the weight of his worries. "Yeah," he sighed in a bit of relief, "it flows out wide, carrying leaves fallen from the trees in the grove." The river took shape, gentle at first, winding around the concession stand like a fallen log in the stream.

Mira's enthusiasm built the scene, her free hand gesturing as if trailing fingers in the water. "Fish come first, blue ones with gold fins, swimming in circles. And the banks have tall grass, waving like they're saying hello." Elias nodded, the current soothing and washing away the ache in his leg. For a moment, the theater felt alive with the

Dreamwood. The seats were smooth rocks, the screen a distant waterfall shimmering in the light. Mira added boats from twisted vines, small and steady. "We paddle slow, looking for the pool by the door. That's where Mom will fill the bottles." The image steadied him, the river a promise of return, its flow countering the noise in his head created by the droning silence.

Elias's gaze flicked toward the wedged door, the silence outside too complete. No footsteps, no call of her voice, just the ruins' vast emptiness, like the isolation he'd felt after losing Theo and Father. Mira chattered on, though, describing eddies where turtles basked, but Elias's mind wandered, the spring's bubble turning distant. "What if the pipe's dry?" he said softly, more to himself. Mira tilted her head. "Then the river makes more. See? It springs stronger." She squeezed his hand, trying to settle him, but a chill settled in, the vision flickering like a cloud passing the sun.

The quiet pressed heavier now, the theater's posters watching with their frozen smiles. Adventurers on rivers, families under lights, all untouched by the war that had cracked the walls they sat on. Elias was uneasy and shifted around, his thoughts drifting to suppressed fragments: the factory raid's smoke, Theo's laugh cut short, the raid on the bunker. He'd shoved them down for Mira, for their mother, building the Dreamwood as a shield. But alone with her gone, the weight of it all surfaced. Mira's voice faltered as she noticed. "Eli? The water is warming, do you feel it?" He blinked, focused on the water;

ripples stirred at the river's bend, not from fish, but something deeper, coiling like smoke under the surface.

At first, it was subtle: a shadow rippling across the current, unseen by Mira, its edges blurring into troop silhouettes and faceless figures from the bunker barrage. His breath caught as the chill spread. "Mira... do you see the ripples?" She squinted, head tilted. "The ripples? Yes, the turtles are swimming around." But it wasn't from the turtles; to him, the shadows thickened. Why did he let her go alone? His pulse quickened, the river's flow slowing, banks closing in like the theater's walls. Mira frowned, her hand tightening. "It's vines, dark ones tangling the boat. I'll push them away, watch!" She gestured, words reshaping the visible edges; vines dissolved into harmless foam and the current rushed free again. But the core shadows lingered for Elias, unseen by Mira, creeping along the depths beneath the boat.

The vision held, but Elias's anxiety deepened. These weren't like the maze's hedges from the ruins; they were his alone, surfacing in the quiet without her anchoring presence. His guilt twisted sharper. Had shoving down the memories invited them here, poisoning their sanctuary? Mira pulled at his hand. "Eli, it's better now. The fish are back. Look at the silver flashes!" She couldn't see the remnants trailing behind, whispers growing on the wind that only he could hear like a snake's hiss: *You let her go alone.* He forced a nod. "I see them... keep going." The isolation inside persisted, though.

Mira fought the vines she perceived, but his ghosts evaded her, a solitary burden in their shared world.

Mira's additions brightened the river, adding yellow flowers along the banks and a gentle bend leading to the door-pool, but Elias's focus wavered as his mind couldn't stop thinking about their mother. Mira paused, sensing his drift. "What's wrong? The water's clear." He hesitated at first, but the truth found his lips. "Shadows… in the deep parts. Like the raids, but you don't see them. That means they're here for me." Her eyes widened and a feeling of shock took over. After a brief moment, determined, she yanked at Elias's arm, "Then we'll get rid of them together, like the maze. Tell me what they look like, I'll make the current stronger to carry them away."

Elias swallowed heavy, the theater's dust catching in his throat as he met Mira's gaze. Her eyes held that spark, the same one that had pulled him from the helicopter freeze nights ago. "They're… like the troops from the bunker," he whispered, voice low against the quiet, ashamed. "There's dark figures in the water, creeping from the edges. Whispers in the wind." Mira's brow furrowed. She didn't completely understand, but she didn't pull away. Instead, she leaned closer, her hand still in his. "I see vines like that, dark ones, tangling the boat. But the river's stronger. Watch, it'll flood them!" Her words reshaped the visible fringes: the current surged in the vision, foam bubbling where shadows met the surface for her, washing the shadows into harmless mist. The boat bobbed free, flowers blooming brighter along the banks as the shadows dissipated. Relief flickered in Elias, but the core lingered, unseen.

The Dreamwood held, fragile as the wedged door, but steady. Elias's thoughts continued to spiral, delving into the fractures he'd already patched over. Why are the shadows here, in their sanctuary? Mira's help banished the edges she perceived, her innocence reshaping the light, but his core burdens evaded her touch, isolating him even in their shared float. "They're mine..." he sighed, voice cracking. "Only here for me."

Mira's eyes opened briefly in the real world, her face serious but kind. "Eli, we can fix it," she said, leading with unprompted details. "Vines from the grove wrap the shadows tight, like roots holding Theo's tree." Elias built on it, the river surging to carry away the smoke, birds nesting in the vines to sing over the whispers. Partial victory bloomed. The water cleared fully for Mira, the boat gliding toward the door-pool, bottles imagined filling with crystal clear water. Elias felt the tension loosen, his worries quieting as he joined and voiced more. "The raid's fire... it burns out in the stream." Mira helped, reshaping the flames into harmless embers floating away. The shadows receded to the edges, no longer invading the current, though they lingered in his periphery, a reminder of the fractures.

Time blurred in the vision, the theater's light shifting as the sun climbed directly overhead. Elias's mind churned on, Mira's innocence illuminating what she could. It eased the isolation, turning solitary ghosts into something shared, even if she couldn't see them. "It's better," he admitted, the pool shimmering ahead. Mira grinned. "The door's opening, Mom's coming with the water!"

But the quiet cracked like a glass plate falling to the floor. Distant shouts filtered through the walls: harsh voices in a foreign tongue. Elias's eyes snapped open, the Dreamwood vanishing in an instant. Mira blinked too, confusion washing over her face. "What was that?" He pulled her close, heart instantly slamming against his chest. The shouts grew and footsteps approached the theater. Patrols, moving fast through the ruins. The door rattled against the wedge.

With a strong kick, the theater doors busted open. "Hide, now!" Elias hissed, grabbing Mira's hand and bolting toward the screen at the far end. Her doll tumbled from her lap, but she didn't stop to retrieve it, her small feet pattering behind him as they ducked behind the torn fabric. The material hung heavy, muffling their breaths. Outside, shouts sharpened. Flashlights pierced the gloom through the gaps. Elias pressed Mira against the wall, his body shielding hers, the screen's folds their only veil. "Quiet, no noise," he whispered, holding a finger over his lips.

More soldiers from the patrol pushed through the door and walked around the theater. They were looking for anyone who had left the refugee camp. Elias's heart hammered, hard enough he thought it might give away their hiding spot. Tanks, leaflet warnings, helicopters, planes... now soldiers on foot. Mira whimpered softly, her hand digging into his arm, but he gently clamped a palm over her mouth, eyes locked on a sliver of light through the fabric. Shadows danced on the screen from the other side; silhouettes with rifles raised, boots crunching glass near the concession stand.

In his mind, the Dreamwood fractured further, the river's pool darkening with those unseen remnants. Troop shapes merged with the patrols inside the theater. Had the shadows warned him, or lured him into this trap? The soldiers fanned out, one kicking over a row of seats with a clatter that made Mira flinch. After what seemed like an eternity, some of the soldiers filtered back out of the door, but one lingered. His flashlight beam swept the screen's base, inches from their feet. Elias held his breath, the fabric's tear brushing his cheek. The beam of light fell on the small crocheted doll between the seats. He picked it up, stared at it intently for a few moments, then threw it back on the ground and moved out with his comrades, the door slamming shut behind him.

Outside, chaos rippled. The patrol's main force swept the streets, random gunfire snapping in bursts. Their mother, who was desperately making her way back, was stuck a few buildings down, the patrol all around her. She spotted them first, though, and was able to avoid detection as she moved silently back towards the theater, all the water bottles now filled with mostly clear water. Her eyes were locked on the theater, dreadfully trying to see if the patrol was there. Believing she saw a clear path, she started to move towards the theater, just as a soldier rounded a corner and locked eyes with her. As the soldier froze for a second, she hurled a piece of concrete with jagged rebar sticking out in his direction and doubled back, now rushing away from the theater. The soldier yelled as the concrete hit his leg, and gunfire erupted down the alley. She zig-zagged her way as fast as she ever could, the adrenaline numbing the pain in her leg. As the guards chased her down, she moved deeper into the alleys and further from the theater. The raid's speed scattered everything. She had to keep moving or risk being caught. She hadn't seen the soldiers near the theater, believing the kids were safe. She'd make it back to them, eventually, if she could remain uncaptured.

Footsteps receded, leaving the theater in ringing silence. Elias exhaled, peeling back the fabric to peer out. The streets teemed with movement; patrols flushing refugees, gunfire echoing from the alleys. "Mom!" Mira's voice cracked, small and desperate, but Elias clamped a hand over it again. "She's okay, she's moving like the current, she'll find the way back here." But he wasn't sure as the shadows whispered in his mind. What if they found her? The raid had split them in an instant; the theater no longer safe, patrols swarming the outskirts, just as the leaflets had promised. Elias pulled Mira toward a side exit, a jagged hole in the wall leading to a collapsed side alley. "We have to leave." "What if mom comes back and we're not here?" Mira whimpered with tears running down her cheeks. Elias didn't have an answer, but his mind shifted to a show he used to watch. "We'll leave a clue for her, just in case." He grabbed a handful of broken armrests and made an arrow where they had slept, pointing to the side exit. "Okay, now we have to go before they come back." Mira grasped his hand and they slipped through the hole into the chaos now illuminated by sunset.

The streets twisted into a labyrinth of their own, crumbled walls and piles of debris offering fractured cover as they moved. Shouts in the distance were a mixture of other refugees and soldiers, gunfire popping like warnings. Elias led, Mira's hand locked in his. They dodged craters and toppled signs, weaving around rubble and abandoned cars. "Stay low, keep your eyes open looking for the patrols," he urged as a patrol rounded a corner ahead, flashlights sweeping from side to side. He yanked Mira into a narrow gap between buildings, hearts pounding against the broken cement. The soldiers continued, calling out in the half-dark as the sun dipped below the horizon. Elias's mind drifted instantly to their mother. She's alone out there, fever barely broken, and it's his fault for not insisting they go with her. Guilt twisted sharper in his head... what would Theo think of him letting her go out on her own?

They pressed on, weaving through the fractured skeleton of what used to be Nova City, moonlight casting long illusions with its endless shadows. Piles of rubble turned into crouching soldiers, wind-whipped fabric as their cloaks. Mira panted beside him. "Where is mom? You said the current would bring her back." Elias swallowed the lump in his throat, scanning the alleys. "It will. She's getting through the labyrinth, just like we did. We just have to keep going."

That's when they heard it. A scream. Louder than the gunfire, it cut the night in half. Sharp, high-pitched. A woman's scream, echoing through the streets from the direction Mom had fled. And then silence, followed shortly by a distant shot. Elias froze. Mira grasped him hard. His blood ran cold at the scream, the echo bouncing off the ruins like a ghost in the alleys, sending a large shiver down his spine. Was that her? The shadows laughed at him, unseen, leaving them alone in the dark.

Mira whimpered, pressing closer in the narrow gap, her small body trembling against the cold stone. "Eli... that sounded like Mom, didn't it?" "No... that could be anyone. She's hiding like us. Like how we hid in the cave." But his words rang hollow in his own head, the shot's crack lingering in his ears. The shadows from the Dreamwood coiled around his mind, fearing the worst. She'd gone for water, just like Theo had, and now they're both gone.

Moonlight slanted through the gaps in the walls, casting jagged patterns that danced like threats everywhere he looked. Distant shouts multiplied. The soldiers swept the ruins block by block. Elias scanned the alley ahead, debris piles offering limited cover. "The paths... from the maze. Find the breaks." Her voice steadied him, a rope to hold onto through the panic, but the shadows nipped at his thoughts: She's gone, like Theo... and it's all your fault.

They slipped out, hugging the wall's edge as Elias led, Mira's hand in his as she crouched behind. A beam swept nearby, a flashlight from a patrol probing a side street. They dove behind a shattered fountain, water long gone. They waited until the light disappeared. He wanted to move in the direction of the scream, but the patrols swarmed there. Shadows of soldiers merged with his unseen ones, blurring real peril and memory.

Mira tugged his sleeve. "Eli? You're shaking." He blinked, realizing his free hand clenched white-knuckled on the pack. The freeze, the same as from the helicopters; he could feel it creeping back in. But he was able to break it now, thanks to her. "I'm... okay. Just... moon tricks." She squeezed his hand. "Not tricks. The river's here, flowing around them." The words layered in his mind faintly: debris as river rocks, alleys as bends. It steadied him enough to move, weaving toward the scream, dodging open stretches where moonlight exposed them.

Time stretched in the dark, alone, the raid fading to sporadic bursts of gunfire in the distance. The separation wasn't just distance; it was the war peeling them apart, piece by piece. Elias's guilt twisted with fear. What if the shadows were right? He pulled Mira into a basement, revealed by a collapsed sidewall of a market building. It wasn't very deep, but it offered a broken cover overhead and shielded them from the cooling breeze and any possible flashlights. "Tell me about the pool again, the one waiting for mom." He wanted to, but in that moment, he couldn't find the words. Mira looked up at him, yearning for comfort, and the best he could manage was, "We'll sleep here till the morning."

Elias peered up through the ragged entrance, moonlight now illuminating the wasteland that used to be his home. "It's quieter now, I think they've left." Mira, still trembling, laid her head on his lap. "The river will lead us to her, like it did to the medicine." Elias stared at the wall blankly, not acknowledging her this time, the scream replaying in his head, over and over. The gunfire that followed, cracking as he blinked. They were alone now. And he didn't know what to do.

Chapter 11
The Tightening Grip

She bolted down the alley, boots pounding cracked pavement, the pack slamming against her back with every stride. Water bottles splashed inside, the only sound louder than her heavy, long-winded breaths as she ran from the soldiers. Patrol shouts rang out behind her; harsh, clipped words she couldn't make out but knew meant trouble. Elias and Mira waited in the theater, door wedged shut, counting on her to return. That thought drove her legs forward, the shrapnel scar in her calf burning like fire with each impact.

The pain hit hard on the next step, a stabbing feeling that nearly dropped her to her knees. She gritted her teeth, forcing through it. Not now. No time for that. The kids needed her; she couldn't slow down. She veered sharp left, slamming into a narrow gap between two leaning walls, the space so tight her shoulders scraped brick. The shouts faded a fraction, but she didn't stop, crouching low as she pushed deeper. The leg throbbed once more, hot and insistent, but she clamped down on it, her mind locking on their faces: Elias's steady gaze, Mira's quick smile. Pain could come later.

Ahead, the gap opened to a wider street, lined with gutted shops, their fronts blown open like empty mouths with jagged teeth. She scanned fast, seeing no patrols in sight. She broke into a run again, weaving past what used to be a family van, split completely in half. The theater was two blocks over, close enough she could picture the rusted doors. Elias would have it barred solid, Mira clutching that doll telling one of her made-up tales to pass the time. The patrol wouldn't go in there. They'd just move past it.

A flare burst overhead, orange light flooding the shadows in the street. Boots thudded nearby. Soldiers, two of them, rifles out, sweeping the area with flashlights. She hid beneath a section of what used to be a shop's overhang, now a roof over a crater in the ground. One barked a command. She pressed flat, the leg screaming as she shifted her weight. Not now. The kids. She counted breaths, slow and silent, until the flashlight beams passed and the soldiers continued on.

She waited ten seconds, twenty, then rose, slipping across the street to a doorway. The shop interior was empty, shelves tipped over, glass crunching underfoot. She moved through quick, eyes on the back wall. A hole blasted clean through to the next alley, perfect. She climbed through the hole, twisting her body to get through, her leg buckling for a split second. No time for the pain. She landed hard on the other side, rolling into a crouch, and kept moving forward.

The alley twisted right, forcing her to duck under a fallen beam, the wood splintered and sharp. Her hand brushed it, slicing into her skin drawing a thin line of blood, but she ignored it. The patrols were spreading out, shouts converging from multiple directions now. They had the perimeter locked tight, pushing everyone inward like cattle to a pen. She cut left at a fork, avoiding the main road where a vehicle idled, engine rumbling and waiting. Lights from its cab cut the haze, soldiers leaning out, rifles scanning the streets.

Her leg pulsed steady now, a background fire she could shove aside. Elias's voice was in her head; calm and practical. He'd keep Mira safe. She had to get back to them. The vehicle revved, pulling away slowly, but she was already moving, darting across an open stretch to the next building.

Inside, the air hung thick with old rot. She paused only to catch her breath, scanning for the exit. A side room led to another gap, this one smaller, forcing her to squeeze through on her belly. The leg dragged, pain flaring sharp as gravel bit into her knee. She pulled herself free on the other side, standing quick, pulling the pack through behind her.

The next street bustled with movement, but it wasn't the soldiers. Other refugees, a dozen or so, huddled in doorways and behind piles of bricks. They moved as a loose group, adults shielding kids, bundles clutched tight. She fell in at the edge, keeping pace without joining fully. Safety in numbers, but she couldn't afford to get tangled up. One of the women glanced her way, face tired and dirty. "Patrols are at the east end and pushing in," she muttered, low enough for only her to hear. She nodded, eyes forward. East meant the blocked road. They'd have to go west, circle around. Elias would head that way if things went wrong. Smart boy.

Shouts erupted ahead, soldiers spilling in from a cross street. The group scattered, some diving into buildings, others bolting for alleys. She went right, slamming through a half-open doorway into what used to be a shop. The leg gave a hard jolt like lightning as she landed, but she bit it down. She crouched behind the counter, peering out. Two soldiers herded three refugees. An older man, a woman, and a boy, no older than Mira. The woman fought, twisting in their grip, but a rifle butt to her side dropped her. They dragged them toward a vehicle idling at the curb.

The boy cried out, high and desperate, as they shoved him in. The woman twisted back, eyes locking on the remaining group for a split second, pleading for help, wordless. Then the doors slammed shut, and the vehicle sped forward, tires spinning in the dirt.

She pressed a hand to her mouth, the image sticking in her mind. Not her kids. But it could be. The soldiers moved on, lights sweeping side to side. The remaining refugees regrouped slowly with pale faces. The woman who'd warned her earlier was now by her side.

"They're taking them back across the gulf for processing." Her voice shook. She nodded, throat tight and dry from the dust. Processing. Vehicles full of families, gone. "I've heard we have allies on the way to help... they need to hurry," the woman said, staring at the sky in hope. Rumors were that there were a handful of nations that had once reached peace in Nova City instead of war, and they were now banding together to push back against the overreaching superpowers.

The group reformed, smaller now, continuing west. She stayed with them, the pain in her leg a steady drum she tuned out. Elias and Mira couldn't end up in one of those vehicles. They'd hide and wait for her. The street narrowed, buildings closer, offering better cover. She scanned every shadow, every doorway.

The group hit a dead end, a wall of rubble blocking the way. The group turned south, but she veered north, trusting her gut, knowing she had to get to the theater before the soldiers had a chance to. The leg protested the quick shift, but she kept going. The refugees' footsteps faded behind her. Alone again, but closer to the theater.

A piercing scream ripped through the air. High pitched, a woman's voice, from the direction the other refugees turned. She froze, spinning back. The sound triggered her to want to help. The scream was desperate and cut short by a scuffle. More shouts, boots pounding. Her pulse jumped again, picturing Elias and Mira being dragged into a vehicle with the soldiers.

She doubled back fast, staying low, the leg holding under the strain. The scream came again, closer, joined by a child's cry. She reached the corner, peering around. The refugee woman from the group, the one who'd spoken to her, grappled with a soldier in the street. Her kid clung to her leg, screaming as another patrol closed in. The woman swung a loose board, catching one in the shoulder, but a rifle butt dropped her hard. They hauled her away, the child kicking and crying, toward the waiting vehicle. The vehicle pulled away with dust clouding the road as its tires spun. The cries faded with it.

She sank against the wall, hands shaking. The woman had a kid, just like Mira. Just like Elias. Patrols took what they found without mercy. Elias and Mira were close. She had to keep moving. Thirst burned her throat. She took a small sip of water from the pack but saved the rest for the kids. The theater couldn't be far.

The alleys blurred into a maze of turns and dead ends, each one looking the same, glowing orange as the sun dipped below the horizon. She wiped sweat from her eyes, the pack digging into her shoulder. The leg burned steady now, the initial fire dulled to a constant throb she could ignore. She rounded a corner, spotting the marquee in the distance, sagging against the sky. Relief hit her as her steps quickened. Almost there. The streets around it looked clear, no patrols in sight. She broke into a jog. The doors loomed, rusted but intact. She reached them, pounding with her fist. "Elias? Mira? I'm back!" But as she pounded, the door pushed open, not barred like she'd instructed Elias when she left. The interior lay dim, seats empty where they'd been all night. Her stomach dropped. "Kids?" She stepped inside, the door thudding shut behind her. Dust swirled in the fading light, undisturbed. She moved to the seats, overturning cushions and checking under the rows. Nothing. The pack slipped from her shoulder, bottles bouncing out and rolling across the floor as it thumped down.

Panic surged. "Elias! Mira!" Her voice bounced off the walls, too loud in the quiet. She spun around, scanning the space. No sign of them. Her hands shook as she called again, louder. "Elias! Where are you?"

That's when she saw it. The doll. Lying in the dust near the screen, button eyes staring up from the grit. Mira's doll. Abandoned. She snatched it up, clutching it tight, the fabric rough in her palms as her tears hit the ground. They wouldn't leave it. Something happened. The patrols. The gunfire she'd heard on the way. Her breath came shorter, hyperventilating, the leg buckling as she fell to her knees. Pain shot up her calf, sharp now, the numbness she forced as she rushed back to the theater gone.

She pushed to her feet, limping to the seats, still searching as she moved. Empty. "The concession stand, they're hiding there." She checked behind the counter, glass crunching under her boot. Nothing. Her mind raced. The raid, they made it to the theater. She knew it.

She tore through the rows, calling their names, voice cracking. The theater felt huge, empty, her kids' names echoing off the walls as she called out, mocking her. They were gone. Patrols took them. No. Elias was smart. He'd get them out. He just would.

That's when something caught her eye. The floor near their sleeping spot, armrest fragments, arranged in a rough arrow pointing toward the screen's edge. Her breath caught. Elias. She knelt, fingers tracing the wood. It led to a pile of rubble behind some fallen seats. A side exit, hidden, one she hadn't known was there.

Hope sparked, small but fierce, as a huge sigh made it out of her dust-riddled lungs. They made it out, they had to have. Alive. She retrieved the water bottles and the pack, stuffing the doll in, and pushed through the rubble. Her leg glanced off the broken wall as she made it to the other side, but she didn't feel the pain she knew was there. The alley beyond stretched narrow, leading away from the main street. They had a head start. She'd catch up. They couldn't be too far away.

The alley twisted, forcing her to sidestep beams and broken signs. A picture replayed in her head, the doll laying lifeless on the floor of the theater. A reminder. She had to find them. Elias would keep them low and hidden. Mira would stay quiet and cling to her brother. She wiped dirt and sweat from her forehead and tears from her cheeks, scanning for tracks. Nothing, just rubble and destruction everywhere.

A shout carried from the main road, patrols still active. She pressed against the wall, waiting it out. Her leg throbbed, demanding rest, but she ignored it. The kids were out there. Alone. Scared. She slipped forward when the shouts faded, the alley opening to a cross street.

Empty. She crossed fast, ducking into the next gap. The ruins stretched on, buildings blown open, alleys filled with junk. She called out, louder than she should have with the patrols nearby. "Elias? Mira?" Silence. Doubt crept in. Wrong way? She pushed on. They were close. Had to be.

The cross street led to a row of apartments, walls leaning like they'd give up any second. She moved between them, eyes on the ground for signs: footprints, broken sticks. Anything. Nothing. No time to stop, she kept pushing. She scanned a doorway, the frame splintered. "Kids?" The word came out raspy, swallowed by the quiet. No answer. The row ended at a small opening with a patch of dirt. Footprints were etched into the dirt. All large and scurried, except for two smaller sets, impressions not as deep. Her pulse quickened. It had to be them. She continued in the direction the footprints seemed to go.

A rustle ahead stopped her in her tracks. She dropped low behind a crumbled wall, the stone rough under her hands. She heard footsteps, two sets of footsteps, lighter than the soldiers had been. Her heart jumped. "Mira? Elias?" she called out, hopeful.

Two figures emerged from the path: other refugees, an older man and woman. They froze at the sight of her, eyes wide. She stood slow, hands out. "Have you seen any kids? Boy, eleven, girl, seven?"

The man shook his head, voice low. "I saw some kids about an hour ago... they ran towards the markets. It's crawling with soldiers over there, though." A sigh escaped with a whisper, "Thank you." The markets. West. The market was a tangle of stalls and small buildings, good for hiding but bad for patrols. She adjusted the pack on her back and began moving. Elias would avoid the open parts, stick to the edges. He's a smart boy. Mira might be scared, but she'd hold his hand tight.

The path opened to the market's edge, stalls collapsed into heaps of wood and cloth, buildings half alive. She wove through, eyes down for signs. Small prints in the dust, fresh, not yet disturbed. Hope pushed her faster, her leg complaining but completely ignored. The small prints led to the north side of the market area, past the central fountain, toward the blocked road. Her stomach twisted. Patrols were there. Elias wouldn't go straight. He'd circle around.

A cry pierced the air. High-pitched, from the road. She froze, turning fast, forgetting to breathe. Mira?

She ran toward it, the leg buckling once more, pain shooting up as she continued to pound on it. Not now. The cry came again, closer now with a scuffle following. She reached the stall's end, peering around. Another woman with a child, trying to escape a soldier. Her child kicked at his legs, screaming. Another group of soldiers closed in, grabbing the boy. They hauled them both toward a vehicle at the curb. She pressed against the stall, hands clenched. Anger for the woman and her child swelled, but relief soothed her as it was once again not them.

North was blocked with vehicles and soldiers. They'd gone around. They had to have. She circled the market's edge, scanning for breaks. A gap in the fence led to back lots. Night fell fast, stars pricking the sky. She called soft at each shadow, each new building, every stall with a possible hiding spot. "Elias? Mira?" Silence. They were out here, somewhere, hopefully.

The night deepened. She paused at a low wall, sinking down. She grabbed the doll out of the pack and stared at it with tears in her eyes. They wouldn't be moving now. She could walk right past them. But they were here, she could feel it. She pushed beneath an old dumpster, just high enough to squeeze under and stay out of sight. She'd wait till first light here. The pain had crept back in her leg, but so did hope. She'd find them when the soldiers left and the sun peeked in the morning.

Chapter 12
Knots of Doubt

The basement air hung thick and stale, a dim pocket beneath the collapsed market building where Elias and Mira had huddled the night before. Elias woke first, his body stiff from the cold stone floor, the jagged edge of a broken crate digging into his side. Moonlight had given way to a gray predawn haze filtering through the ragged entrance above. His leg throbbed dully under the bandage, a reminder of the raid's chaos, but it was the ache in his chest that pulled him fully awake. The scream, replaying in his mind on a loop he couldn't escape.

He sat up slowly, rubbing his eyes, the events crashing back vividly: the theater door bursting open, soldiers moving in, hiding behind the screen, Mira's hand trembling in his as they fled. And then the scream... sharp, a woman's voice. Not hers, he told himself again, but the doubt he pushed down, shadows of patrols and whispers from the Dreamwood twisting it into something worse. He glanced at Mira, still curled on the scrap of blanket they'd scavenged trying to keep warm. The spot next to her, empty.

Elias shifted closer, trying his best to share his body heat. The basement was shallow, barely ten feet deep, its walls cracked, concrete veined with rust from exposed rebar. What remained of the market's foundation arched overhead like a precarious lid, chunks of ceiling dangling down. They'd entered through a hole where the sidewalk had caved, a short drop to the basement floor, landing amid piles of splintered wood and shattered crates that smelled of old spices and rot. No patrols had followed. The raid's shouts had faded into the night, but the isolation pressed in, heavy on his heart.

Mira stirred, her eyes fluttering open, bleary at first. She sat up with a small yawn, rubbing her arms against the chill, then froze as the reality hit. "Eli?" Her voice was small, edged with the remnants of sleep, but her gaze darted around the dim space, landing on the empty spot where their mother should have been. "Where's Mom? Did she find us?" Elias's throat tightened. He'd hoped she'd be here by now, slipping through the entrance with the water she'd set out to find with her steady voice to anchor them. But the basement was empty, except for the two of them.

"Not yet," he said, forcing calm into his tone, though his heart stuttered. "She'll follow the signs. Remember the arrow?" She'll see it." Mira's face crumpled, her lower lip trembling as she hugged her knees. "But it's morning now. The river was supposed to bring her back, like the medicine. I thought... I thought the Dreamwood would work." Doubt clouded her eyes, the spark from their foraging adventure dimming. She looked at the blank wall opposite, as if expecting the waterfall to appear, cascading over imagined rocks to wash away the fear. But nothing came, just the faint drip of moisture from a crack above.

Elias gave her a hug, wrapping his arms around her back. "It will. The paths are still there. Mom's strong, she'll find us." But even as he spoke, the unease built. The scream replayed in his head. What if it had been her? What if the shadows from the river were right, and letting her go alone for water like Theo did had doomed them all? Mira turned away gently, staring at the floor. "You always say that, but she's not here. The cave, the river... It's just stories, Eli. They don't make things real. Mom's gone." Her voice cracked, tears welling as she wiped at her eyes with the back of her hand. The doubt hit Elias like a punch in the stomach, her words mirroring the fractures he'd felt in the theater; the shadows only he could see.

No. He couldn't let it crumble now. The Dreamwood had gotten them this far: the breeze leading to medicine, the maze's paths through ruins. It wasn't just stories; it was their shield, the one thing the war couldn't touch. "Mira, listen," he said, scooting closer, his voice urgent but soft. "It's not gone. We built it together, remember? The waterfall from the storm, the one that kept us safe in the cave? We just have to go back in, rebuild it stronger." Mira shook her head no, curling tighter.

A low rumble rolled in from outside. Not tanks, or artillery, but the first heavy patter of rain on the ruins above. It started soft, droplets tapping the debris like fingers on stone, then built steadily, the sound swelling into a steady drumbeat that vibrated the basement walls. Elias peered up at the entrance, where gray sheets of water began to slide down the collapsed sidewalk, turning the hole they'd entered through into a waterfall of its own. The air carried the earthy scent of wet concrete and distant smoke from the camp's embers. Mira flinched as a stronger gust rattled the overhead beams, sending a trickle of dust sifting down. "See? The storm's here, and Mom isn't. The Dreamwood is lies."

Elias's mind raced; he wouldn't let the doubt win. "That's it," he said, grabbing her shoulders gently, turning her to face him. "The storm is going to help, it's making the waterfall again. Remember the one over the cave entrance? Come on, close your eyes with me." Mira resisted at first, her body tense, tears streaking her cheeks. "Why? It doesn't work. She's not here."

"Because it has to," Elias pressed, his voice cracking with his own buried fear. If they stopped believing, what was left? The rain pounded harder now, the entrance a curtain of water cascading into the basement, pooling at the low point near the back wall and seeping through cracks in the floor. The space felt smaller, the air cooler and heavier. Mira wiped her nose, glancing at the growing puddle. "Fine... but if it doesn't work..." She squeezed her eyes shut, and Elias did the same, pulling her hand into his. He started soft, "See the stream? It's coming in through the hole, just like the waterfall over the cave. But it's ours now; strong, not scary. The water's clear, rushing over smooth stones."

Mira hesitated, her grip loose at first, but Elias pushed, describing the cave's entrance forming around the pooling water, vines draping like curtains to block the storm's roar. "The waterfall mist is cool on our faces, and inside, the pool's waiting, and the turtles are there." Slowly, Mira's hand tightened, her voice joining haltingly. "The stones... they're round, like the ones in the grove. And the water sings, pushing bad things away." The vision took hold; the basement's chill transformed, the pooling rain becoming the cave's welcoming flow, the drip-drip a soothing melody that drowned out the thunder outside. Elias felt the doubt ease in her grip, the Dreamwood pulling her back slowly, despite the storm's fury and their mother's absence.

The rain didn't relent. It hammered the ruins above, turning streets into rivers, the torrent filling their shallow hideout. Water lapped at their feet now, cold and insistent, seeping through the cracks and swirling around the low point in the broken floor. Mira's eyes snapped open, fear flashing. "Eli, it's real rain! The basement is flooding!" Elias opened his too, the vision fracturing as water rose around them, the stream escaping through floor fissures but pooling more in before it could all evacuate. Lightning cracked the sky in jagged bursts. Thunder rolled, shaking the beams overhead, dust and pebbles bouncing down. "We have to move higher," he said, pulling her to a raised ledge of broken concrete at the back, away from the pooling water. "The stories can't stop it. Mom's not coming and we're stuck here," she said, sitting down with a blank look and watery eyes.

Elias held her as the water climbed, his mind racing against the roar outside. The waterfall held in fragments; the stream as a beacon, not a threat, but the doubt was still there. Where was she? The scream, the shots… He shoved it down again, whispering more details to rebuild, for Mira's sake. "The cave's walls rise higher, the waterfall stronger." Mira nodded shakily, but the storm's pounding drowned his words, the basement a churning pool that tested their fragile faith.

Under the dumpster, the night stretched, the rusted metal pressing cold against their mother's back as she huddled in the narrow space. She woke with a gasp, the first heavy drops of rain hitting the lid above like stones, jolting her from the fitful half-sleep she'd fallen into. Dawn hadn't fully broken yet, but the sky growled with the promise of a storm, thunder rumbling distant as if the war itself were gathering for another strike. Her leg throbbed steadily, the shrapnel wound a dull fire that had flared back to life after the raid's adrenaline faded, but she ignored it the best she could, pushing up on her elbows. The doll clutched in her hand felt heavier now, its button eyes staring blankly in the gloom.

She'd fallen asleep heavy, being just a day removed from the fever and drained from the chase through the streets. But Elias and

Mira were still out there, alone. The woman's scream from the market still echoed in her ears, a warning of what could happen if she didn't move. No more waiting. The kids needed her. She shoved the doll into the pack with the water bottles, crawling out from under the dumpster on hands and knees as gravel and glass bit into her skin. Rain slicked the ground, turning dirt to mud that sucked at her boots as she stood.

The storm hit full force, rain coming down in sheets that blurred the world. Thunder cracked overhead, the sky flashing the ruins in a stark white. She tightened the pack on her back, the bottles sloshing as she started toward the market's edge where the footprints had led. "Elias? Mira?" Her voice cut weak against the roar, swallowed by wind that whipped her rain-soaked scarf across her face. The doll's absence in her hand now felt like a hole; she'd held it through the night, imagining Mira's laugh when she handed it back. Now, it was just her, the rain, and the gnawing fear that they were hurt, scared, waiting for a mother who couldn't find them.

She pressed on, the leg protesting every step, mud splashing up her calves and staining the wet gauze over her stitched-up leg. The alleys flooded fast, water rushing in shallow streams that tugged at her feet, carrying debris and leaflets from the drop down the road like little boats. Lightning illuminated a signpost, half-buried in rubble. She continued the direction of the tracks she'd seen the night before, now gone. The storm washed everything clean, earlier clues erased by the torrent. Panic clawed at her throat, but she didn't acknowledge it, focusing on Elias's face and his quiet strength. He'd keep Mira safe, hidden like they'd practiced in the bunkers. But how long could they last in this downpour?

Gusts drove the rain sideways, stinging her face as she ducked into a doorway, the overhang offering scant shelter. Water pooled at her feet, rushing around her boots. She leaned against the frame, catching her breath, the pack heavier now that it was wet. She fished the doll out of the pack, gripping it tight. "Mira, baby, I'm coming," she whispered to the doll. The kids; they were her bridge, her reason to push through the pain, the only reason.

The storm intensified, rain hammering the overhang, turning the street into a river. She stepped out, the water now ankle-deep, rushing toward lower ground. Any tracks were long gone, washed into the gutters. She veered left at a fork, toward what she remembered as the market's north side, the doll tight in her fist. "Elias!" She called out loud now, assuming the danger from the patrols would be minimal due to the imposing storm. Thunder drowned out her call, but she kept shouting. Lightning cracked again, revealing a collapsed stall ahead, its wooden frame splintered. She splashed through, checking behind it. Nothing but shadows and rain. Doubt crept in harder: wrong way? The patrols had pushed everyone south last night; maybe they'd doubled back. Her leg buckled on a slick patch, pain shooting up like lightning of its own, but she caught herself on a beam, biting back a cry.

Pushing forward, the stream deepened, water pulling fast, carrying sodden leaflets that bobbed like warnings: Leave or face destruction. She ignored them, splashing into a narrow alley where buildings leaned close, their walls forming a chute for the torrent. As she hopped over a downed light pole, the doll slipped from her wet grip, tumbling from her fingers into the rushing flow. "No!" She lunged forward, hand plunging into the cold current, but it was gone, whisked away on the foam, button eyes vanishing around a bend. Panic surged, and tears mixed with rain on her cheeks. Mira's doll, the one thing she'd clung to recently, lost, swept into the storm like everything else she had lost.

She chased it anyway, the stream guiding her north, deeper into the ruins. The water roared, funneling through a low point in the alley, pooling debris in swirling eddies. Lightning flashed and she saw the doll ahead, bobbing against a grate half-clogged with branches. She waded in, hand outstretched to grab the doll as a small wave knocked it loose, pushing it further away in the road river. She pressed on, chasing the doll, thunder masking her sobs. The kids had to be here somewhere, she felt it. And she wanted to bring Mira back her doll. The water turned toward a building, seemingly emptying into it. She rushed to grab the doll before it was sucked into the collapsed sidewalk of the building, but she was too late. The doll went over the edge like a barrel over a waterfall.

She paused at the edge, peering down. The drop was short, into a shallow basement it seemed. The water pooled at the bottom, and there was the doll, just sitting there at the edge of the pool. Relief, it wasn't rushing away anymore, she just had to grab it out. She lowered herself down, landing with a splash in the knee-deep pool that was draining out far slower than it was filling.

Water swirled around where Elias and Mira sat on the broken concrete ledge, the storm's fury turning their hideout into a shallow pool that lapped at the walls with insistent hunger. He'd pulled Mira to the raised ledge hours ago, the two of them huddled on the broken slab as the water poured through the entrance hole above. Mira shivered beside him, pressed against his side, the chill seeping through their thin, mist-soaked clothes.

"Eli, it's too wet," she whispered, voice trembling as another gust drove rain sideways through the hole, spraying their ledge. The basement's low point filled faster now, water starting to rise up to the slab. Elias wrapped an arm around her, his own teeth chattering, but he kept his tone steady. "The waterfall's holding. It's protecting the cave, not flooding it. The turtles are swimming and kicking their feet." But doubt flickered in Mira's eyes, the earlier fracture from waking without their mother still raw. The Dreamwood had pulled her back briefly, the stream transforming from threat to protection, but the storm's reality battered it. Where was Mom? Elias had pushed Mira into the vision to keep her calm, but now, as water climbed, even he wondered if it was all crumbling down.

Mira hugged her knees tighter, rocking slightly. "But she's still not here. The river was supposed to bring her." Elias swallowed, scanning the entrance where water cascaded like a veil, the hole they'd crawled through now a roaring funnel for the water filling the space. "She's coming. We just have to wait." But the basement felt smaller, the air heavy and damp. Theo's face flashed in his mind. Not again. He squeezed Mira closer, whispering more details in an attempt to rebuild their sanctuary. "The cave's deeper now, the waterfall stronger, carving a path straight to us." Mira nodded shakily, but her eyes stayed on the pooling water, doubt lingering like the chill running down her spine.

The storm deepened, wind howling through the ruins above. The water in the basement rose higher, creeping above the broken concrete ledge they were sitting on. Elias stood pulling Mira up with him, the slab their only dry-ish perch. "We can't stay down here much longer, we might have to go out there." Mira clung to him, tears cutting tracks through the grime on her cheeks. "Eli, I'm scared. The stories can't stop this." Her words hit hard, echoing his own buried fears, but he wouldn't let it break now. She'd carried him through the helicopter's freezing, so he wouldn't give up on it. He had to protect her.

He knelt with her, hands on her shoulders, eyes locked. "Close your eyes. All that water just feeds the waterfall over the cave entrance. Inside, it's warm and dry." Mira resisted, body tense. "Why believe? It didn't work last night." Elias's voice cracked. The scream flashed behind his eyelids as he blinked. "Because it's all we have right now." Slowly, she squeezed her eyes shut, and after a moment of silence, the scene in her mind started to take over.

Mira's voice rose up, "The stones under the water… smooth, guiding the flow. And the cave's bigger, with mossy ledges to sit on." The vision took fragile hold, the basement's chill easing as the roar of the water rushing through became the waterfall's song, the pooling a protective moat around the cave.

Just as Mira appeared to be grabbing back at the Dreamwood, reality dragged them back out. Footsteps splashed close. Running, heavy steps. Elias's eyes snapped open, heart immediately pounding. "Quiet," he whispered, grabbing a jagged piece of wood from the debris. He stood in front of Mira at the back end of the basement, fearing the worst. "It's more patrols. Stay behind me." The steps grew nearer, splashing through the stream toward their flooding refuge. As the water rushed in, something small tumbled in with it, splashing and coming to rest next to the pool.

Mira gasped, "My doll!" She lunged for it, but Elias grabbed her arm, yanking her back as the waterfall's veil parted, a dark figure peering in the open space. She got behind Elias, who was now shaking, holding his wooden spear shard, ready to defend his sister. The figure dropped down the hole, landing in the pool of water with a splash. Their eyes lifted to the figure, slick with rain, pack dripping.

"Mom?! The waterfall!" The words burst from her mouth as she ran forward, faith reigniting in a sob of relief. "Mira! Elias!" Their mother jumped forward, grabbing them both.

Elias dropped the wood, the tension shattering as he sprang toward her. Mira clung tight, doll pressed between them, tears mixing with rain turning to joyful sobs. "It worked! The stream... you came on the waterfall! Just like Eli said!" Their mother held them closer, voice breaking with relief and laughter. "I followed your arrow, Eli, and the doll washed away, right to you!" The family huddled together, the chill of the water forgotten in the warmth of their embrace, the pounding rain outside now a triumphant rhythm celebrating their reunion.

As thunder rolled in the distance, the storm's fury yielded with the first hints of easing wind and rain. Mira's face was lit up with unbridled joy, her earlier doubt completely washed away like the debris in the river on the road outside. "The Dreamwood's real, Eli! Stronger than the rain!" Elias grinned, relieved, pulling them all tighter, the guilt and shadows fading. Their mother ruffled Mira's wet hair, her own smile wide. "I'm never leaving you two anywhere again, ever." Laughter ensued freely now, echoing off the cramped walls, a spark of hope brighter than any of the lightning, carrying them toward whatever lay in front of them.

Chapter 13
Healing Branches

The storm's last gusts rattled the ruins as Elias pushed aside the debris blocking their basement exit. Sunlight peeked through the gray clouds like a hesitant invitation to the outdoors. Water still trickled in, but the downpour had eased into an inconsistent drizzle. Mira climbed out first with her reunited doll tucked securely under her arm. She squinted against the brightness, the fresh air wet with the scent of earth and faint smoke from recently extinguished fires. Her face lit up as the clouds parted just enough to show patches of blue sky. "Eli, look! The rain stopped!" Their mother followed, wincing as she swung her good leg over the lip. The pain in her leg had dulled to a steady ache, the penicillin from the nights before working its slow fix. She stood on the street, breathing deep, pack slung over one shoulder.

Elias emerged last, the chill of the flood clinging to his clothes but lifting as the sun's warmth hit him. No patrols had returned yet, and now the streets stirred with movement; figures emerging from doorways and rubble piles, refugees shaking off the night's terrors like wet dogs after a bath. A woman nearby wrung out her jacket, calling to a child huddled by a wall while two men pried open a crate half-buried in mud, pulling out dented tins that clinked in the quiet. The market area, once alive with stalls hawking goods from every corner of the world, lay in scattered pieces now. Wooden frames were splintered like broken bones, and torn and frayed awnings flapped in the breeze.

Their mother scanned the group, her hand finding Mira's. "We can't stay exposed out here." The other refugees talked about heading to the mall across the way. "We'll go with them to check out the mall. It's on the upper floors, so we won't be exposed to the ground patrols." Elias nodded, spotting the structure in the distance: a hulking building with wide glass fronts now shattered. Its sign was half-fallen but still readable: *Nova Global Exchange.* He'd heard stories of it from school videos before the raids shut everything down. A place where traders from distant lands set up shops side by side. Now it stood as a skeleton, escalators frozen mid-climb. But the third floor's height promised a view and walls that might hold. "They're already headed that way," he said, pointing to a loose cluster moving through the mud; five or six adults, a couple of kids trailing behind. Mira squeezed her doll tighter against her chest. "Can we go with them?"

They fell in at the edge of the group, not speaking at first, just matching their pace through the slick streets. The drizzle picked up briefly, but stopped almost as soon as it started, leaving puddles that reflected the breaking sky. A man at the front carried a makeshift pole with a cloth tied to it, waving like a flag to mark their path. A woman beside him passed around strips of dried fruit from her pack. Mira took one, nibbling as she walked, her free hand in their mother's. It was the first food they'd had in over a day. "It's sweet," she said softly, offering a bit to Elias. He chewed it slowly, the flavor cutting through the morning's chill. Plum, or something of the sort. A small reminder that not everything had turned to ash. The refugees didn't question them, their faces lined with the same weariness, but nods passed between them. It was like a silent agreement to share the road.

As they neared the mall, the scale of the building grew. A wide entrance with gaping holes and floors connected by stairs that spiraled up like frozen waves. The group funneled in through the main doors, feet screeching on the tiled lobby floor, slick with rain tracked in from outside. Shattered display cases lined the walls, and overhead, a massive chandelier hung crooked with crystals dulled by dust. Elias stuck close to Mira, his eyes on the shadows in the corners. The space felt less threatening up close. There were faded signs in swirling scripts that marked old shops: one with images of steaming bowls and chopsticks, another with shelves that once held colorful fabrics from far-off weavers. The air carried a faint mix of scents, baked into the walls: sweet pastries long gone, sharp spices that lingered like ghosts of the crowds that used to fill the halls.

The refugees split the work without words; two men cleared a path up the stairs, shoving aside fallen beams, while others checked the upper levels for stability. Their mother paused at the first landing, testing her leg on the next step. It was bearable now and didn't hurt nearly as much as it had the days before. "It's holding," she said, more to herself, and kept going, Mira chattering about the doll finding a 'high spot to watch from'. The third floor opened wide. A balcony overlooking the atrium below, with wide windows that let in the morning light. The group claimed a corner near a row of intact offices, their doors hanging loose but offering walls. A woman with a medical bag set up in one, gesturing for their mother to sit after noticing the limp on the way in.

"Sit here," the woman said, her voice carrying an accent from one of the old districts, pulling up a stool from the dust. Their mother eased onto it, rolling up her pant leg to show the bandage, stained with blood, but not bleeding fresh. Mira hovered close, watching as the woman unwrapped it carefully. The wound looked better; redness faded to pink, no pus seeping, and stitches holding firm. "You've been lucky," the woman said, dabbing it clean with a damp cloth from her bag. "This paste will draw out what's left of any infection." She spread a thick layer of the green mixture, smelling of crushed leaves and earth, wrapping it fresh with clean strips. Their mother winced once, but relaxed as the coolness settled in. "Feels better already," she said, flexing her foot. The woman nodded, tying off the bandage. "Keep it dry, we'll change it again tomorrow."

As the treatment wrapped, voices rose from the group in the next room. Elias sat with Mira on the floor, sharing the last of the dried fruit, but his ears caught the words. A man with a scarred hand leaned against a desk, speaking to two others. "Word has it those peace nations from the old summits, they're moving. Ships cutting through the gulf, loaded with gear to punch through the blockade." One of the listeners crossed his arms, glancing at the windows. "Ships? Against the carriers? If they slip past the patrols, sure, but the blockade has eyes everywhere." The scarred man shrugged. "Better than nothing. Remember the talks they held here? They brokered deals that held for years. Now they're grouping up, sending what they can to help."

Mira tilted her head. "What's a blockade?" Elias leaned in, keeping his voice low. "The ships that used to bring food and stuff... the bad guys stopped them, so they can't get to the harbor anymore. That's why we're stuck eating all the beans." She frowned, hugging the doll while making a disgusted face. "But the ships are coming back?" Elias nodded and shrugged, though the talk in the next room turned skeptical. A woman joined in with a sharp voice. "Hope's fine, but we've waited months. If those fleets don't show, we're just sitting ducks in these ruins." The scarred man pushed back. "They're coming. Some of the guards' scouts saw lights on the water last week." Elias listened, the words stirring something in him. A faint lift, like the sun breaking the clouds outside. Just a sliver of hope this would all end soon. The mall's wide spaces, once filled with traders from every land, now held these whispers of return, the building itself a sign of what could be rebuilt.

Their mother finished and pulled her pant leg back down, standing to test her step, the leg bearing her weight without the sharp pull from before. "That's better," she said, smiling at Mira. The group now claimed the balcony in full, windows wiped clear of grime to let in the light. The atrium below was a vast drop of scattered seats and twisted metal.

Elias joined their mother at a window, the city stretching out as far as they could see. Smoke trails from the camp, distant roads empty but for a few figures moving slowly, no patrols in sight. Mira tugged at his sleeve. "Let's go back in." He glanced at their mother, who nodded, settling on a cleared bench to take a breather. "Don't go far."

Mira led the way to a quieter spot off the balcony, a small lounge area with walls that still held patches of old murals and faded images of world maps dotted with flags. The space felt tucked away, the door hanging loose but enough to muffle the talks around them from the main room. She plopped down on a pile of seat cushions scavenged from a nearby office. The fabric was musty but softer than anything they'd sat on recently. "The trees start from the floor, growing up to the ceiling." Elias sat beside her. The air in the lounge carried a faint trace of the mall's past: polished wood under the dust, a hint of vanilla from long-gone candles in the corners. Mira's eyes sparkled, her renewed conviction fueling her words. "The branches hug like Mom, soft and strong, wrapping around the trunk to hold it up."

Elias felt the Dreamwood rise easily, the renewed pull from the night before making it flow without forcing it. No hesitation, no shadows creeping in. The faith they'd reclaimed in the basement flood carried them straight in. He closed his eyes halfway, the lounge blurring as the trees took shape. Trunks rose thick from the floor, bark smooth like the mall's old handrails, and their leaves unfurled green and wide. "The roots go deep, all the way to the ground level," he added, the vision steady as they continued. Their mother, sitting nearby, leaned back and closed her eyes, trying to imagine the place they had built. "Leaves that catch the light, turning pain into something that fades away," Mira added, hugging her like the imagined branches. They curved gently, like arms pulling you in close, trunk steady under their hold. The trees grew taller, filling the space. A soft glow spread from the leaves, warming the air like sunlight shining through the windows.

No fractures this time, just the build coming natural. Mira described the branches spreading out, each one tipped with small buds that opened slow, releasing a scent like fresh rain after the storm. Elias added a handful of small, colorful birds bouncing around, singing as they danced through the air. The vision bloomed full, the trees a circle around them, branches linking like the mall's old walkways, the glow touching the faded murals on the walls. Mira squeezed the doll again, and the branches responded, curling protectively around them. "They hold us, not letting go, not letting anything bad in."

As the vision settled and they opened their eyes, the lounge felt warmer, the light from the windows carrying a warmth that hadn't been there before. Mira grinned, "The trees will keep growing. The leaves can help mom's leg." Their mother reached over, ruffling her hair. "They already are. Feels like I could run up those stairs now," she added, trying to play along. Elias smiled, the ease of the Dreamwood leaving him lighter, their faith in the space stronger after the basement's test.

Back in the main area, the refugees had settled more. Small fires were started in metal bins to dry clothes and warm hands. The talk from earlier picked up, voices carrying clearer now as the group gathered around one of the firing bins. Elias sat with Mira near the edge as their mother joined a circle of adults to share a bit of the dried fruit. The scarred man from before spoke up again, gesturing with his hands. "The ships are closer than we thought. Those old fleets from the summit days, they're loaded heavy. Guns, supplies, enough to ram right through."

A younger woman nearby stirred her pot over the fire, adding a handful of scavenged grains. "Ships against carriers? We've seen what they do to anything that moves on the water." The scarred man leaned in, voice dropping but firm. "Not just any ships. Word is they're running quiet, hugging the coast, slipping past the patrols with decoys. If they punch through the gulf, it's fresh routes open. Food, ammo, maybe even some damn ground support." Elias listened closely. Mira's head rested on his shoulder as the doll's button eyes glowed with the firelight. Another voice joined, an elder with a wrapped arm. "All the good this city held back then... It's what's going to stop this war."

The talk flowed around them, not aimed their way but filling the air like the smoke from the fires. Mira whispered to Elias, "Ships like the big ones we watched in the harbor with Dad?" He nodded, picturing the vessels from old stories, sails full before the war grounded them all. Their mother's slight grin caught Elias's eye from across the circle. Their words built a picture. Hope.

As the sun climbed higher, the group turned to practical tasks: sorting finds from the lower floors, patching leaks in the sidewalls with tarps. Mira wandered to a window, doll in hand, pressing her nose to the glass. "The trees are out there too, growing in the cracks." Elias joined her, the view opening to the city's edge. Wet roads gleamed in the light, and figures moved in small groups toward the center of the city. Still no patrols in sight, the raid's sweep pushed back by the storm. Their mother limped over, her leg moving a bit better now. She pointed to a distant glint on the horizon, metal catching the sun, "What's that?"

Elias pressed close to the window, Mira's shoulder bumping his as they squinted into the distance. The glint sharpened into a shape. A convoy snaking along the outer road, bigger than anything they'd seen since the camp evacuation. Tanks led the way, their treads kicking up mud from the night's rain, followed by boxy armored carriers and a string of trucks loaded high. Soldiers marched alongside, maybe three hundred. The scale dwarfed the patrols; too organized, too steady for a raid sweep. Mira stood on her toes. "Those trucks look new." Elias nodded, and for a faint moment, the thump-thumping sound of the helicopter from the camp played in his mind. The vehicles moved with purpose, flags snapping on poles. Unfamiliar patterns. "Different," he said, the word hanging as the convoy turned toward the city core.

"Could be supply runners, or..." their mother trailed off, eyes tracking the lead tank as it rumbled past a checkpoint, no shots fired, no halt. The refugees in the main room stirred, voices rising in a mix of questions and guesses. The scarred man pushed to a window, cupping his hands between his eyes and the glass to see better. "That's no patrol push. Look at the spacing, the flags. This might be the ground wave." The younger woman from the fire peered over his shoulder. "Flags like the old summit ones? If it's the peace nations' crews…" The elder with the wrapped arm shook his head slow. "Hope it is them. If not, that's a lot of firepower headed into the city."

The talk spread while the group clustered at the windows, the convoy's rumble growing as it neared the mall's outer roads. No gunfire marked their path and soldiers waved to scattered figures on the roadsides instead of pointing rifles at them. Mira tugged at Elias's shirt. "They're going to the city? Do we need to leave again? … I like it in here." He glanced at her, the doll still tight in her grip. "I don't know."

Their mother squeezed his shoulder. A look of hope shone in her eyes as she stared at the convoy passing below, close enough to see details through the busted windows. Soldiers in mixed uniforms, some calling out in accents that didn't match that of the patrols'. Trucks with crates stamped in languages from the mall's old shops. One banner caught the wind. A simple design of linked circles. Elias remembered something from his school lessons, symbols of the summits that built the city, also linked circles. The lead tank slowed at a ruined intersection, an officer stepping out to talk with what looked like a city guard. Her gestures were calm, not demanding. Mira pointed, "They're helping!" The group behind them buzzed louder, the scarred man turning with a grin. "That's gotta be them! Ships must have made it through!"

Elias stepped back from the window. Their mother limped to a bench, easing down. "Whatever it is, it's moving things. We keep our heads down for now, but eyes open." The refugees dispersed back to their tasks, their talk turning to plans; scouting runs, ration shares, water retrieval.

The afternoon light slanted longer through the windows, drying the last damp spots on the floor. Mira played quietly with her doll near the murals, staging small scenes of vine boats on rivers, while Elias helped sort the group's finds. There were cans pried from lower levels and drinks in plastic containers. Their mother rested, joining the circle for a shared meal of warmed grains and fruit strips. The whispers about the convoy continued in bits as the scarred man sketched rough maps on a scrap of paper. The group worked and spoke with a renewed vigor which hadn't been there that morning when they arrived.

Elias continued to listen as he ate, the food sitting warmer in his stomach than it had in days. The mall's vastness was gentle, its high ceilings and wide spaces a change from the basement's close walls. The Dreamwood made itself present in small bits, a steady undercurrent.

The day stretched on, the light shifting gold. The convoy's rumble was a distant hum now as they pushed further into the city, carrying the first real sense of a shift in the air. But would it last? Everyone seemed hopeful, and for the first time, so was Elias.

Chapter 14
The Storm Within

The mall's third floor had proved steady over the next couple days since the storm cleared, the wide balcony space holding the small group of refugees together like a loose net. Sunlight cut through the busted windows each morning, warming the tiles. Elias helped the scarred man carry crates up from the lower levels, stacking them against the walls to keep out the drafts that still snuck in. The scouts, just the most able of the refugees, who headed out at dawn, came back with full packs. They collected buckets of rainwater they'd boiled over the fire bins, tins of vegetables dug from the rubble, and a few blankets that hadn't torn too bad. The group divided it without much fuss, passing tin cups around the flames in the evening. Mira stayed near the window ledges, her doll sitting beside her as she watched the streets below, pointing out people moving in the distance.

Their mother got around better now, the leg's ache easing under the wraps and herbal paste, letting her help with the sorting without much dismay. She sat with the woman from the clinic one afternoon, folding cloths from the group they had washed by hand into stacks. They swapped short words about what the scouts brought in. "They stuck to the side paths, the patrols haven't come close since the rain," the woman said. Their mother nodded, piling a blanket on top. "Gives us a chance to catch our breath." The group felt solid in those days, not tight like old friends, but reliable. Elias joined in where he could, hauling water up the stairs, his own leg faring much better under clean bandages. The mall's back areas, with their lines of shops, gave them room to spread out. There were racks of clothes hanging in some spots, protected by the roof which held up better there.

Mira took to the open stretches along the balcony. Her doll was always close as she set up little games with other kids who showed up from new groups. The space felt less closed up high. Elias watched her one morning, her laugh echoing off the wall as she pushed the doll along a ledge as if it were stepping carefully. The sound pulled him out of his thoughts for a minute. The raid felt pushed back now. The basement's flooded walls just a rough night that the Dreamwood had covered over. Their mother caught him looking across the space. "It's working," she said, pointing to her leg, but it fit the rest; the group, the mall, the stretch of days without alarms.

By the second afternoon, the scouts had pulled in more than just basics: a couple of tools from a hardware spot down below, enough to nail boards over leaky windows. The scarred man drove in the nails, the hammer's thuds filling the air with a steady rhythm while the group gathered loose rocks to hold tarps down over spots in the floor where water still seeped. Elias held a board in place for him. "The patrols hit east of here yesterday, but nothing here. The convoy's got them watching other spots," he spoke between thuds. Elias nodded like he understood. Just then, Mira ran up with a large smile, doll in hand, pulling at his shirt. "Mom said we can go look for clothes. Clean ones that are not all ripped!"

Their mother stood nearby, bending her knee to test it, the leg taking the motion without the bite from before. "The back shops have some racks that are full in places. Let's see if we can get something without all this mud and stains on 'em." The mall's walls stood firm, the doors to the stairs blocked with crates. "Stay where I can see you. Don't go past the escalator opening at the end of the hall." Mira hopped in excitement. "I want pants that aren't wet and don't smell like beans!"

They headed down the walkway together, the floor tiles slick in a few places from morning mist, but solid enough to walk steady. The back section spread out, shops on both sides with doors half-open. It was cooler back there because the sunlight didn't reach that far back. Their mother stopped at the first door, a space with racks of shirts and jackets, hangers still loaded in spots. She took a plain gray shirt off one of them, holding it up to see the fit. "This'll work." Mira looked around the racks, but didn't see anything in kids' sizes. "Can we try the next shop? There's nothing that will fit me here." Their mother checked the doorway, the balcony in view just down the hall. There really wasn't a danger in the mall, but she hesitated for a moment, remembering the last time she left them on their own. "Sure, but stay close. Yell if you need me. And stay with your brother."

Elias and Mira ran to the shop next door, the room tighter with shelves of pants and basic tops. Some were folded neat, like they'd sat there since the first hits came, unaffected by time. He grabbed a pair that looked his size, feeling it between his fingers. "These beat what I've been wearing." Mira went to a rack with kid stuff, pulling a sweater with a cat design and pressing it to her front. "Blue one. Matches the river fish." She turned in a circle, the sweater twirling like a sundress, and then started to dig for more. Elias nodded with a smile, draping the pants over his arm. The shop's quiet setting eased around them.

Mira's gaze went past the next shop's door, down the hall. "Eli, a playground!" She pointed to a colorful spot before the escalator opening. It was a small play area inside the halls with a green slide shaped like an alligator, mouth wide open. The floor sections had wheels that turned when you stepped on them. Elias, who was focused on looking through a rack of shirts, didn't hear her. Mira let the sweater fall to the ground as she skipped forward out of the shop. "Play time! I want to go down the slide!" She ran off.

Elias continued to look for clothes without holes. He lifted a simple single-color shirt, checking the sleeve length against his arms. He put the shirt with the pants he planned on taking back. Thinking of Mira's blue sweater she found, he looked up to help her find some more clothes. But the door stood open, the rack she'd been at empty, and her sweater on the floor. "Mira?" His voice stayed level at first, but the shop grew larger quick, the racks hiding the hall. He stepped to the door, glancing out in the direction they had come from, where their mother was to see if she'd run back towards her, but didn't see her.

His heart beat faster, a hard thumping in his chest like the rotors on the helicopters. "Mira!" He called a bit stronger, his voice moving down the hall. The shops beside stood open, but no sign of her. He went to the next door, looking inside; racks full, no Mira. The escalator opening sat at the end, dark to the backdrop. She wouldn't go there, not without telling him. But the hall ran long, doors half-open to more racks and dark spots. He walked quicker, checking the next shop; no Mira. "Mira, come on!" His chest tightened and fists balled. The pants and shirt he'd been carrying fell to the ground.

The mall's quiet grew thick. He turned back, checking the previous shop once more, then the next. No Mira. His breathing sped, the air hard to pull into his lungs. The raid at the theater flooded his thoughts. The doors breaking open, soldiers searching for them, Mira's hand slipping out of his as they ran from the theater. Could they be here in the mall now, still looking for them? The basement joined his thoughts now, water rising fast, her voice cut by the rush of the flow through the entrance. "Mira!" His voice broke, barely audible. Can no one hear him? Sweat broke out on his forehead, and his leg started hurting under the bandage as he turned, looking in shops again; still nothing.

The fear grew. His thoughts mixed fast; the artillery, the helicopter, the raids, Theo. He made his way back to the shop they'd started in and picked up the sweater she'd dropped, holding it against his hard beating chest like it could call her back from wherever she was. He moved to a backroom in the shop. The Dreamwood came on strong then, unasked for, without prompting. The floor shifted in his mind, the mall tiles to the basement's wet and broken floor; Mira's doll being sucked under the rushing water. Mira's face was lost in the dark, being pulled away into the shadows. The raid's noise played on repeat in his head. He leaned forward, air coming in hard pulls, the open space now too tight and closing in all around him.

Elias pressed his back against the shop's wall, the rough plaster scraping through his shirt as he slid down to the floor behind a shelf. The sweater clutched in his fist felt damp with his sweat, the cat design staring up at him as if it were his fault she was there. The mall's quiet pressed in from all sides, the distant jumble of voices from the balcony too far away to reach him. He tried to stand on his shaky legs, but the racks loomed closer. Their metal frames twisted in his vision like the bars of the subway bunker during the blackout. "Mira," he gasped, the word barely forming, lost in the roar building in his head.

The raid replayed sharper now, not just sounds but the feel of it: the door splintering under the soldier's boot, the flashlight beams cutting through the dust like knives. He'd grabbed her then, pulled her through the side exit, but now it blurred with the basement flood, water rushing in cold and fast as she vanished beneath the surface. The Dreamwood surged on, unprovoked. The river's current turned dark, vines from the healing trees coiling tight around his legs, pulling him under the current. No, not vines, soldiers' hands, rough and unyielding, dragging him back to the convoy trucks. His vision of the real world started to blur, the shop's dim corners closing in, the air too thick to breathe.

He clawed at his shirt collar, fingers fumbling, trying to loosen the invisible grip around his neck starving him of air. The helicopter's thump-thumping from the camp joined the roar above the mall's roof, signaling the mall as a target for artillery. Elias rocked forward, forehead to his knees, the sweater pressed to his face, inhaling the faint scent of dust and old fabric as if it could ground him. But the smells twisted too: the metallic tang of blood from his mother's leg wound as he pulled the shrapnel out, the sour rot of the beans she'd eaten to spare them. Why hadn't he stopped her? Why let her go alone for water, just like Theo? The thoughts looped, faster, tighter, his chest heaving as if the basement water was filling his lungs.

The shop's walls seemed to lean in. The racks' metal poles, now dark trees with long whipping branches, pressed closer from every side, their shadows stretching long across the floor like fingers reaching for him. Elias pushed back against the plaster, trying to get away, but it didn't give. His breaths came shallower, each one catching in his throat. The air was turning stale and heavy, like the bunker during the blackout when the lanterns died one by one. He squeezed his eyes shut, trying to block it out, but the images kept coming.

He rocked hard, front to back, the motion giving no relief, just making the dizziness worse. His head spun as if the mall's floor tilted under him. His hands trembled as he clutched the sweater tighter, the cat design blurring through tears he didn't realize were falling. Where was she? The raid's door splintering replayed, the flashlight beams sweeping the seats, finding her doll first, then Mira as they grabbed her while he sat there frozen. He slammed a fist against the floor. Pain shot up his arm, but not enough to cut through the spiral.

Sweat soaked his shirt now, sticking it to his skin, the shop's dim corners growing darker, closing in like the concrete cracks in the bunker widened under the barrage of artillery. Elias crawled forward on his knees, but the door seemed miles away, stretching in front of him, the hall a tunnel with no end. His leg throbbed under the bandage, the old gash from the storm pulling tight as if it were a fresh wound again. Theo's face flashed, unabridged, laughing one second, buried under falling debris the next. Elias's fault for not being there, just like now with Mira. He pressed his forehead to the floor, breaths coming in gasps, the world narrowing to the thump in his chest and the endless loop in his mind.

The racks loomed taller in his mind, their crossbars forming a cage, the ceiling dropping low enough to brush his hair. He couldn't move, couldn't call out, the words stuck behind a knot in his throat. The mall's safety, the group's quiet routines, all crumbled now, exposed as a lie. Soldiers could be anywhere: under the escalator, in the shadows, around the corner, waiting to drag them to the trucks. Elias curled into himself, arms wrapped tight around his middle, rocking as the panic peaked. His body froze in place and vision spotted black at the edges. The basement flood merged fully with the raid. Water poured through the theater door. He was failing. Breaking. The war was winning from inside his sanctuary.

Time stretched thin, lost in the grip, Elias's world reduced to the shop's floor and the roar in his head. No strength left to fight it, just the endless press, and the isolation swallowing him whole.

Mira slid down the alligator's mouth for the third time, the green plastic whooshing under her as she landed with a giggle on the rolling wheels. The play area felt like a secret spot just for her, the big slide's tongue curling just right, the wheels spinning fast when she jumped. She climbed the steps again for her fourth slide down, doll tucked in her jacket pocket. "Your turn, Eli!" she called back toward the shop, expecting Elias to wave from the door. But the hall stretched quiet, racks still in the shadows. She paused at the top, squinting. "Eli?" No answer.

She slid down anyway, the rush making her forget there was a war going on outside, landing with a bounce. The wheels rolled smooth under her feet as she paced back and forth, pretending they were river stones in the Dreamwood, skipping across like the ones Elias had described. But the quiet tugged at her, the escalator opening at the hall's end looking darker now. She climbed up once more, peering over the railing toward the shop door. Empty racks, no Elias poking his head out. "Eli?" Louder this time, her voice carrying down the hall.

Still no response. Mira slid down slower, the fun fading without her brother, and walked back to the shop, peeking inside. "Eli?" She stepped in, checking behind one shelf, then another. The shop felt bigger alone, the corners dim and full of shadows. Panic flickered on her face not knowing where he had gone. "Mom!" she cried out, her feet carrying her back toward the shop where they had left her.

Their mother emerged from the shop, a clean shirt and a pair of sweatpants folded over her arm, turning at Mira's call. "Mira? What is it?" Mira reached her, breathless, grabbing her hand. "Eli's gone! I went to the slide, but he didn't go. I looked everywhere!" Their mother's face sharpened, the folded shirt dropping to the floor as she scanned the hall. "He was with you, where?" Mira nodded fast, tears welling in her eyes as she pointed to the shop they were in. "He was picking shirts and he's not there now!"

She moved quickly, pulling Mira along as she checked the shop; racks pushed aside, corners empty. "Elias!" Her voice was loud and direct, steady but edged. No answer. "He was right there. Did the patrols come?" Their mother shook her head, though doubt flashed in her eyes. "Stay with me." They hurried to the play area, the green alligator now mocking them. "Elias!"

The balcony group stirred at the calls. The scarred man stood up and yelled over, "What's wrong?" Their mother waved him over. "Elias is missing." The clinic woman joined. They split the hall: some checking shops further down, others peering over the edge of the escalator. Mira searched too, calling his name, but the space felt vast, the racks hiding too much.

Their mother pushed open the back shop door where they'd started, the air inside cooler, dimmer. "Elias?" A small shape huddled against the far wall, knees drawn up, head down. He was rocking slightly, breaths coming in sharp hitches, face slick and wet, clothes soaked with a cold sweat. She dropped beside him, hands gentle on his shoulders. "Elias, baby, it's me. It's Mom. Mira's here, too." Mira knelt beside them, eyes wide, not understanding what was going on. "Eli? What happened?"

He lifted his head slow. Their voices cut through the panic, his vision clearing of spots and their faces pulling him back. The raid's echoes faded, the basement's water receding while the shop's walls straightened and the dark trees loosened their clutch on him. "Mom... Mira..." The words rasped out, his hands unclenching from Mira's blue sweater. Their mother pulled him close and wrapped her arms around him tight. "Breathe. Breathe. You're safe. We have you. You're safe." Mira hugged his side, tears still falling down her cheeks. "I looked for you. The slide wasn't fun without you there."

The scarred man appeared at the door with a concerned expression on his weathered face. "Found him?" Their mother nodded, helping Elias stand on unstable legs. "He's okay. Just... got turned around." Elias leaned on her, the air loosening in his chest, though the tremors lingered. The group gave them space as they emerged, speaking in soft and concerned whispers.

Back on the balcony, their mother settled him on a bench and handed him a cup of water. "Sip this down, slow." He drank it, and it started to wash away the fire in his lungs. Mira sat beside him. "I wanted to show you the slide." Elias managed a weak smile. The panic's grip was gone, but it left him raw. Their mother sat close, hand on his. "We can talk when you're ready. Keep breathing, slow, deep breaths."

The afternoon dragged heavy after that. Elias remained on the bench, and Mira chatted softly about the slide to fill the quiet. Their mother watched him close, joining the clinic woman in sorting bandages nearby. She explained what had happened to him, and how she found him sitting there, rocking, alone in the dark room, soaked in sweat and breathing fast and sharp. "Sounds like he had a panic attack," the woman told her. "Not unheard of in people, even adults, who've gone through what that boy has these last months."

The panic's weight sat like a stone, the raid and flood replaying faintly, but Mira's nearness kept it at bay. By evening, the fire crackled and rations were passed around for dinner. Elias ate slowly, the warmth of the fires seeping in. Mira leaned in and placed her head on his shoulder. "I'll never leave you again, Eli. I didn't know it made you feel like that."

The days following blended into the mall's steady pulse, the group's routines weaving Elias back in gradually, at his own pace. He helped with the morning water haul, the stairs less daunting day by day. The scouts brought word of the allies' hold on the city; patrols scattered, and supply drops reached the outer blocks. The clinic woman checked their mother's leg daily and kept her bandage changed, the wound closing clean and stitches ready to come out. Elias joined the talks around the fire bins, his voice quieter but present.

One afternoon, as Mira staged a doll slide on the balcony ledge, pretending it was an alligator slide like the one in the hall, Elias wandered to the halls alone. The escalator's drop caught his eye, but he paused at the top, breathing steady. The view below was just the atrium's scatter, not a flood. He made his way to the play area, climbed the alligator slide, and pictured Mira sliding down. No freeze gripped him. He made his way back, feeling more confident, walking taller and breathing deeper.

Their mother noticed the shift in him and pulled him aside. "You're ok. As long as I'm here, I won't let anything happen to you or your sister." He forced a slight smile, the words landing soft on his mind. The mall held firm. Its multicultural ghosts, faded signs in mixed scripts and murals of linked hands stirred faint optimism. The war pressed outside, but inside, the fractures mended, and the Dreamwood returned to normal. The mall felt like home, fragile but real, healing not just their physical wounds, but also the quiet ones nobody else could see. The shadows waited in the distance, but for now, the mall held them at bay.

Chapter 15
Allies in Imagination

The following week in the mall settled into a rhythm that felt almost normal, the third floor's wide balcony holding the group through days that blurred one into the next. Elias usually woke to the sound of the scarred man stoking the fire bin, the crackle of the wood being enveloped by flame pulling him from his slumber. Mira, usually last to wake, snuggled under a blanket dreaming of the Dreamwood. Their mother was always up and about first, helping the small community however she could, the ache in her leg gone enough that she could now carry crates without pausing.

The scouts headed out at first light, returning midday with whatever they could find. One day it was tins of corn pried from a collapsed storage room, dented but sealed. Next, a coil of rope and a few intact water bottles. The group continued to boil rainwater in the bins as they divided the haul around the flames. Elias helped sort it, stacking them neat in a corner. The clinic woman checked the supplies too, setting aside bandages and anything else she could use when the time came she needed them. "We're making do," she said, tying off a bundle and putting it in a bag. Their mother nodded with a smile, folding a clean cloth and helping her. "Better than the camp, and no fighting for food here."

Mira spent her mornings at the window ledges watching the streets below. Figures moved in small groups, some hauling carts, others just walking with bundles under their arms. "That one's got a dog," she'd say, pointing, her voice carrying over the balcony's edge. Elias joined her sometimes, the view stretching to the distant line of allied vehicles at the edge of the city, trucks still rolling through the outer blocks without trouble. The raids felt far off now, and the war seemed to take a break.

Afternoons brought the children together, the play area in the hall drawing them like a magnet. Mira led the way first, climbing the alligator slide's steps with a grin. Other kids followed: two girls from a new group that arrived recently and a boy with a bandaged arm. "Watch this!" Mira called, sliding down fast, landing on the rolling wheels with a squeak. The girls joined, their laughs combining as they took turns. Elias watched from the balcony edge, the sounds of laughter and fun pulling a faint smile.

By midweek, the adults let the kids roam the halls a bit, sticking to the shops and play area. "Stay where we can see and hear you," their mother said, but Mira darted ahead, the group turning the back stretch of halls into a game of tag. She'd duck behind racks in the clothing shops, popping out with a shout as the other kids chased.

Elias joined sometimes, his longer strides helping him evade being the "it" kid, but he let them catch him sometimes just to keep the game going. The war slipped to the background, the mall's quiet spaces letting them forget the patrols outside.

One afternoon, as the sun slanted low through the windows, Mira pulled Elias to a quiet corner of the balcony in the lounge with its faded murals. "The trees need more," she said, plopping on a cushion pile. He sat beside her. "What else do they need?" Mira closed her eyes. "A slide. Like the alligator, but it's the branches. The wood is slick, with no bark, and the slide goes fast down to soft flowers at the bottom."

Elias let the vision build, the lounge blurring as the healing trees rose around them, trunks thick and steady. "The branches curve smooth and polished like the alligator slide." Mira smiled, her voice gaining speed. "They twist down from high up, leaves brushing your arms as you go. And you land in a pile of flower petals at the bottom, yellow and pink ones." The slide took shape, wood gleaming under the golden sun, the grove's glow lighting the path. Elias felt the rush, the air cool on his skin as he climbed up the tree with Mira to slide down.

They slid together in the Dreamwood, laughter bubbling as they hit the flowers, petals scattering and fluttering in the air. Mira opened her eyes, grinning. "Better than the real one!" Elias chuckled, the vision holding easy with no shadows creeping in. The trees stood taller now, branches linking like the mall's walkways, the slide a new attraction in their world. But as Mira walked away to pick flowers in their dreamscape, stepping away to a nearby bush, Elias's chest tightened faintly. The grove dimmed for a beat, branches darkening at the edges, her form blurring like he was back in the shop's racks alone. He reached out with a sharp, worried voice. "Mira?" She turned quickly, a bundle of stems in hand. "Here! Look, for the bottom of the slide." The light returned, and the darkness faded as she hurried back, flowers bright in hand. "I wouldn't leave you, Eli. Never again." He pulled her close in the vision, the trees steadying and the dark edges retreating as he hugged her, both in the Dreamwood and on the balcony where they sat. The moment passed almost as soon as it had surfaced, but the faint hold over him lingered, like his mind wouldn't let him forget.

The week wound down with the mall feeling more like a shared home. The group's routines were solid, and everyone had something to do or some way to contribute. Elias hauled water without the stairs weighing on him, and Mira's games filled the halls as she kept the other children busy. The scouts' hauls grew steadier, and their mother moved without pain, her leg's wrap gone now. There hadn't been any raid incursions in quite a while, and everyone seemed to forget their presence.

Then the mall's steady calm broke, the sun barely above the horizon when a low rumble built outside one morning, deeper than the usual convoy trucks. Elias woke to it, sitting up on his blanket as Mira stretched and yawned nearby. The scarred man already stood at the balcony windows, hands cupped against the glass. "That's no patrol," he said, voice carrying over the stirring group. Their mother joined him quickly, with Elias pulling Mira along behind.

The rumble grew to a steady growl, vehicles rolling into view along the outer roads of the city, tanks leading a line of armored carriers and trucks packed tight behind. But these moved different, flags snapping in the wind on poles with the linked circles from before. The lead tank halted at the base of the mall. An officer stepped out, gesturing up toward the windows. One of the scouts who'd been collecting supplies broke from the group, sprinting for the entrance below, his boots splashing through puddles left from the week's rains.

The scarred man turned to the rest of the group, face serious. "They're coming up." The clinic woman gathered her bag as the group clustered at the edge of the stairs while the scout escorted the officer and a few soldiers up. Elias held Mira's hand, her grip tightening as the door to the third floor pushed open. The scout entered first. Behind him, three more soldiers, faces weathered but eyes sharp. The leader, a woman with short-cropped blonde hair and a scar across her cheek, stepped forward, scanning the space. "We're with the Summit Alliance. The Summit fleets made it through last night; broke through the gulf line blockade. We've got the outer blocks secured, but enemy units are massing on the city's edge. We need to evacuate everyone here, now."

Whispers rippled through the group. The scarred man crossed his arms. "Evacuate where? The roads are choked, there's nowhere safe to go." The woman nodded, pulling a folded map from her pack, spreading it on a cleared crate. "We have a convoy staged two blocks east. Trucks for civilians, armored personnel carriers for cover. We're pulling out to the secured zone near the old harbor. We have supplies coming in and defenses in place. We need to move fast; their infantry's probing west, and they've got an armor brigade rolling in behind." Elias leaned in, Mira on her toes beside him, the map showing lines marked in red and blue ink, the mall a circled dot near the edge. Their mother stood close, her hand on Elias's shoulder. "How many trucks?"

"Enough," the woman said, folding the map. "We'll load families first. Grab only what you can carry. No more than you can run with if it comes to that." The soldiers moved efficiently, two checking the stairs for stability, the third helping the clinic woman pack her supplies. The group sprang into action, the scarred man directing as if he were their leader. "Water first, then food tins. Blankets for the kids." Elias grabbed their pack, stuffing in the last cans and water bottles, checking its weight on his back to make sure he could move freely. Mira secured her doll, the only thing that really mattered to her. Their mother quickly rolled up blankets and stuffed them into her pack, along with a pair of extra clothes for each of them that they'd retrieved from the mall's shops.

The clinic woman briefly pulled their mother aside. "Your leg, is it good? Can you run on it?" She nodded. "It's solid, I can manage." The woman handed her extra wraps just in case. "I know we took the wrap off, but better safe than sorry. Keep it clean on the road." Mira clutched Elias's arm as the soldiers called out. "Are we leaving the slide?" Elias squeezed her hand. "We still have our slide from the trees, don't worry." The group filed to the stairs, packs slung as they descended, their footsteps echoing off the concrete walls and marble tile as they made their way out of their short-lived community sanctuary.

Outside, the air hung heavy with tank exhaust with the convoy stretched along the road: six trucks idling, carriers flanking, soldiers forming a loose perimeter. The lead tank's engine growled, its main barrel pointed east. The woman officer waved them toward the third truck, canvas sides flapping open. "Women, children, and injured in here. Keep low. Men who don't fit will walk behind with the troops." Elias helped Mira up first, her small frame vanishing into the dim interior. Then their mother. She grabbed his pack as he climbed in last, the canvas slapping shut behind him, plunging them into muffled dark.

The truck had benches along both sides, refugees already packed in from other portions of the city, about twenty or so, packs and bundles in the middle on the floorboard. The clinic woman sat beside them with her medical bag on her lap. Mira squeezed between Elias and their mother. "It's crowded," she whispered. Elias nodded, the press of bodies close a strange comfort after the mall's open spaces. The engine revved, its air brakes disengaging with a loud "kksshhhh", and the truck lurched forward, jolting over cracked pavement pieces and debris. Outside, shouts carried loud as soldiers directed those walking with them.

The woman officer in the cab up front turned around, her voice cutting through the canvas. "We're linking up with the main line to the east. If you hear gunfire, get down, the side walls should protect small arms fire." The truck picked up speed, the road's bumps shaking the benches. Mira pushed into Elias's side, eyes on the canvas flap where light flashed in bursts as the flap bounced. He managed a smile as she looked up at him, though the rumble stirred faint tension, the mall's safety already all but gone.

The convoy snaked through the outskirts, tanks leading, carriers rumbling alongside. Elias peered through a small tear in the canvas, catching glimpses: ruined buildings sliding past, soldiers on foot keeping pace, the city's edge giving way to wider streets. No shots yet, just the steady grind of treads and engines. Their mother checked the pack, passing Mira a strip of dried fruit. The clinic woman muttered something about the ships holding the ports and hopes of the war turning. Elias filled in the rest in his head, hoping this would all end soon.

Half an hour in, the truck slowed at an intersection, voices shouting up front. Elias tensed, Mira's hand finding his in the dark. Through the tear, he saw a carrier halted ahead, and soldiers waving them around a crater. The truck jerked forward again, the group shifting with the motion.

Mira nibbled her fruit as Elias took a drink of water from his pack. "The trees would grow through those holes," Mira chuckled, referencing the craters in the ground. Elias nodded, the words calming as he bounced along on the bench seat.

The miles dragged, the truck's heat building and filling the cramped bed. Outside, the ruins thinned to open stretches of road, the city's border nearing. The woman officer turned around once more, speaking loud through the canvas. "The border is where they'll test us. Infantry likes the cover there. If we get attacked, that's where it will be." Their mother shifted, hand on Elias's knee. "We stay together. No matter what happens, we stay together." The words hung heavy. He'd lost her once from the theater, and Mira in the mall... he wouldn't let it happen again.

About an hour later, the truck braked hard, sliding to a stop. Shouts erupted up front. Elias gripped the bench as he swayed into the person in front of him. Mira buried her face against his chest. Through the tear in the canvas, he saw flashes of soldiers spilling from carriers, rifles up, the road ahead choked with figures in enemy gear. The officer yelled orders. The truck's engine revved high as it swung wide, "Contact front!" Gunfire cracked, sharp pops that made the group duck low. The canvas flapped wild. Elias pulled Mira down onto a heap of packs on the floorboard, their mother's arm around them both as she crouched over them, protecting them with her whole body.

The battle broke loose, the convoy halting in a ragged line as soldiers returned fire, bullets pinging off metal and ricocheting in every direction. Elias pressed against the bench, the truck rocking with a near miss of what sounded like a rocket. Mira whimpered into his shirt. "Stay down," their mother whispered. Shouts and orders mixed with bursts of gunfire and machine guns; Alliance rifles steady, enemy fire wild from cover. The scarred man, who'd been walking on the outside, peered through the flap. "They've got us pinned... their infantry is dug in ahead." The clinic woman clutched her bag, pale-faced.

The truck rocked again, the officer's voice cutting through the chaos: "Hold positions! Carriers covering! They're just probing!" Elias's heart pounded; the gunfire was closer now. A burst ripped through the canvas. Nine holes he counted, right about head level where the clinic woman was sitting. Mira clung tighter, lips quivering, but talking out loud with her eyes closed, "The branches, they're wrapped around us. The branches. They can't get through the branches." The words drew a faint calm, though the shots outside quickly drowned it out. The convoy sat stalled, enemy fire pinning them down.

The gunfire held steady, sharp cracks from the Alliance carriers' machine guns answering the enemy's wild bursts, the truck bed jolting with each near hit as the driver avoided incoming fire. Elias kept his head down and arms around Mira. The canvas covering continued to flap, letting in flashes of the fight: soldiers from the carriers fanning out, rifles talking as they advanced on the rise where enemy infantry crouched behind debris piles. Their mother stayed on top of them. "Breathe. We're okay. This will be over soon."

The scarred man looked in again from outside, ducking as a burst of bullets zipped by. "They're advancing on them! Looks like we might make it out of this one!" The clinic woman pressed against the side, her bag clutched tight. "How long?" He shook his head. "Officer's calling for fire support and the tanks are lining up." Elias peeked quick, the lead tank's barrel swiveling toward the rise, its engine growling deep. Boom! The main gun fired, sending a shockwave through the convoy.

The round impacted on the rise where the enemy infantry was shooting from. The convoy sat exposed, trucks idling in line, refugees hunched low in the dark, overcrowded floorboards at the back of the truck. The tank fire silenced the enemy gunfire momentarily. Mira whimpered, "The slide... can we just go back? There were no soldiers at the mall." Elias squeezed her shoulder. "We're going somewhere better... why don't you go in the cave, with the waterfall over the front." Mira took a deep breath, and calmed almost instantly. She didn't speak, but he pictured her now sitting in the cave on a smooth boulder, turtles at her feet, fireflies lighting the dim area. He relaxed, just a bit. Calm in the eye of the storm.

Up front, the officer shouted into a radio: "Flankers down! Advance the carriers! Infantry's breaking!" The gunfire shifted, Alliance shots gaining ground, enemy bursts thinning as figures retreated from the rise. The truck rocked forward slowly, the line inching ahead, soldiers covering from the sides. Elias felt the tension ease a fraction, though shots still snapped and bounced off the side of their truck. The convoy pushed on. The road cleared gradually, the rise falling behind as the tanks rolled over scattered gear and debris. Elias lifted his head cautiously, the flap showing open stretches now, the fight's smoke trailing. Mira sat up slowly. "Did they win?" Elias shrugged, not knowing what was going on outside their canvas transport. The scarred man grunted as he lifted the flap again, giving an update: "It seems the infantry is pulling back! Looks like we have clear road ahead." The truck picked up speed, the engine's rumble steadying. The group exhaled collectively as they took their seats back on the benches.

But the halt came sudden a mile ahead. The truck braked hard again. Elias gripped the bench, Mira tensing against him again.

Through the tear, enemy figures swarmed from a trench on the side of the road. More infantry, rifles flashing as bullets pinged everywhere, cutting through the convoy's flank. Bullets bounced off the carrier ahead, the convoy stuttering to a stop once more. The officer yelled, "Ambush! Get out, take cover!" The canvas ripped open, Alliance soldiers pulling refugees out, rifles up as they formed ranks behind the trucks.

Elias jumped down with Mira, their mother close behind. The air filled with gunpowder and smoke. The road dipped into a shallow cut where the enemy had fortified a trench, their fire coming from the banks as Alliance soldiers returned fire in bursts from behind the vehicles. Their mother pulled them to a ditch beside the truck, the scarred man and clinic woman dropping in nearby. Gunfire rattled overhead and bullets danced in the dirt around them. Mira buried her face in Elias's shirt, squeezing her doll tight. "The turtles... they're in front of me, they're protecting me," she whispered, voice shaking. Elias squeezed her, the words a thin hold on calm as chaos erupted around them. Just then, the scarred man moved toward the front of the ditch. That's when it happened. As soon as he passed in front of them, a stray round caught him, snapping his head to the side as his body fell flat on the ground. Elias watched it happen, as if in slow motion. The bullet was headed right for him and Mira, but found the scarred man instead as he crouched by. Mira didn't see it, her face on his chest, but his eyes grew big and his jaw dropped open. Their mother noticed, immediately jumping in front of them, both to shield them from any incoming rounds and to shield his eyes from what he just witnessed.

The battle raged on, enemy infantry dug in on the banks, Alliance carriers laying suppressing fire while the tanks swiveled slowly in the cut. Soldiers advanced, crouched, rifles cracking steady. Another enemy burst caught the side of a carrier, sending sparks flying their way. Their mother tried to calm them. "This won't last long. Keep your heads down. I'm right here." Elias saw her lips moving, but couldn't hear any words. All he heard was a single crack of a rifle, a bullet moving fast, but spiraling slow, headed straight for Mira and him. He replayed it over and over in his head, the way the scarred man's head snapped sideways, the way he didn't make a sound. The way he now just lay there in the dirt, lifeless.

Almost as soon as it started, it ended. The gunfire peaked, then subsided all at once. The Summit Alliance had driven the enemy back. The officer waved and shouted from the lead truck. "Mount up! Road's clear! We move out!" Elias helped Mira to her feet, the group scrambling back into the beds, the convoy lurching forward again. The fight's smoke hung behind them, the road opening ahead. Elias moved to the rear of the truck, gazing through a bullet hole in the canvas. The scarred man's body grew smaller in the dirt as the convoy continued forward.

He moved back to his mom and sister, staring blankly as he took a sip of water. His mother placed her arms around him. "This will all be over soon. We just have to keep going." He looked down at Mira, her eyes closed, whispering to herself of flowers and the tree slide. Through the chaos, she didn't let go. He had to be strong. For her. He sat next to her, putting his arm around her shoulders. Mira looked up at him and grinned, "There was a small hole in the slide, but I fixed it, Eli."

Chapter 16
The Core Fracture

Over another deep rut, the truck lurched, its wooden benches groaning under the weight of the packed bodies. Elias gripped the edge to steady himself, splinters digging into his palm. Mira shifted against his side, bumping into him with each bump, squeezing her doll tightly. Their mother sat on her other side, one arm looped around Mira's shoulders, the other braced against the pack wedged between their feet. The air in the canvas-covered bed was thick with the smell of sweat, gunpowder, and the faint metallic tang of blood from a fresh wound sustained on the clinic woman's arm. No one spoke much; the talking that had filled the space right after the ambush had died down to uneasy quiet, broken only by the occasional cough or shift of weight.

Elias wiped sweat from his forehead with the back of his hand, the midday sun baking the metal frame through the canvas. The scarred man's death sat like a heavy stone in his stomach, the image still replaying on loop in his head: the way the man's head had jerked sideways, the way his still form laid there in the dirt as the convoy rolled on. He'd been one of the steady ones, who had shared his last strip of jerky without a word. Elias didn't even know his name. Now he was just a shape left in the ditch, gone in an instant to a stray round that should have taken him, or worse yet, Mira. He glanced at her, her eyes fixed on the canvas flap where slivers of light flashed through with every bump. She hadn't seen it happen, but he had, and the silence in the truck felt heavier because of it.

The convoy stretched out in a ragged line, their truck sandwiched between armored carriers that growled like beasts on either side. Up front, the lead tank chewed up the road, its treads kicking clouds of dust that billowed back toward them. Soldiers marched alongside the carriers, rifles slung low but hands never far from the grips, their boots pounding a steady rhythm that synced with the truck's sway. The fields on either side of the road dipped into shallow craters from old strikes, stubborn weeds pushing up through the cracks. No sign of the enemy, but the air felt charged, like the kind of quiet that came right before a storm unleashed its fury.

Mira tugged at his sleeve, her voice barely louder than the engine noise. "When do we get there? My legs are going numb." Elias squeezed her hand, trying to keep his tone light. "Not long. It's probably right up the road." He didn't know where they were going. The officer had mentioned a secure zone near the old harbor, but the details blurred in his mind, lost amid the ambush's noise. Their mother leaned forward, passing around the near-empty water bottles.

Elias uncapped theirs, the liquid warm and tasting faintly of plastic, then he handed it to Mira. She drank careful, a drop escaping down her chin that she wiped away with her sleeve. "It's almost gone," she said, passing it back. Their mother took a deep gulp, then capped it tight. "We'll refill them when we stop."

The clinic woman across from them dabbed at her arm again, the cut from the ambush still seeping a little under her makeshift bandage. Her medical bag sat open on the bench beside her, vials and cloths spilling out from the jostling uneven of the road. "That was just a probe back there," she said, her voice low, tying off a fresh strip. "I don't think they're done." Elias listened, though the words didn't help his current feeling. The scarred man would have grunted agreement, maybe cracked a rough joke about the enemy's aim. Instead, quiet. Mira noticed the quiet, too, her fingers twisting in Elias's shirt. "The turtles... they kept the bad ones away, right?" He pulled her closer. "Mhmm, and the branches from the trees are wrapping around us, holding us steady like Mom does."

The convoy was anything but steady. The ambush had done real damage, and it showed in the way the line dragged on slowly. Up ahead, one of the carriers belched black smoke from its side, the hit from a rocket leaving a blackened scar on the armor. It limped along, grinding unevenly, forcing the trucks behind to slow and weave around debris kicked up from the road, until it stopped with a grinding halt. Elias caught a few glimpses: a soldier jogging back to check the carrier, his tool kit banging against his leg, sparks flying as he worked the damaged track. The woman officer climbed down from the lead cab, her boots hitting the dirt with purpose. She hurried to the smoking vehicle, barking at the mechanic kneeling by the tread. "Get it moving! The engine's fine, but that tread is dragging the whole line!" The man nodded, wiping grease from his hands, but the fix took time. The convoy crawled to a halt as others bunched up behind.

Elias felt the delay in his bones, the truck idling hot, air inside growing stiller and stuffier. Mira alternated between fanning herself and her doll with her free hand to keep them cool in the heat. Their mother shifted, checking the pack at her feet. "We've still got a few fruit strips." She pulled out a couple, breaking them into pieces and passing them around. Elias chewed his slowly, the dried sweetness sticking to his teeth, a small distraction from the heat and the waiting. As he ate, Elias squinted through a tear in the canvas. The lead tank had pulled off the road slightly, its barrel sweeping the fields. Soldiers standing on top with rifles scanned the area. No movement, but the open stretches felt exposed, the craters on either side like traps waiting to swallow them whole.

The short halt turned into a long halt, minutes turning to what felt like hours. The officer paced between vehicles, radio crackling at her hip as she directed adjustments. "Shut the trucks off before they overheat. Carriers to the flanks." Their driver cut the engine for a beat, the sudden quiet amplifying the distant rumble of the tanks and carriers. Mira sat up straighter. "Is ours broken, too?" Elias shook his head. "Just waiting. The big ones up front are helping." The delay bothered him. What if the enemy came back? What if more bullets flew toward them?

Finally, the carrier lurched forward, smoke still trailing but moving steadier. The officer climbed back into the lead cab, her voice carrying over the radio: "Formation tight, advance on my mark." The engines revved as one as the convoy lurched into motion, the road ahead clear but the fields watchful. Elias exhaled, the motion a small relief providing a slight breeze through the holes in the canvas. But the movement was short-lived. Two spots back, another truck coughed and sputtered as soldiers ran to it, tying down loose panels. The line stretched again, the rear vehicles falling back, forcing the tanks to idle as more fixes were made. Mira leaned her head on his shoulder. "It's like the river after the storm, isn't it? Slow, but still going." He managed a nod, though the comparison felt thin against the heat pressing in.

The rear truck's cough grew worse until it grinded to a standstill entirely. Soldiers piled out again, pushing the truck to the roadside as the line flowed around it. The officer directed from the cab. "Leave it. Transfer the load to the other trucks." Elias watched through the flap as crates shifted between trucks. Mira fidgeted, her foot tapping the bench, "I want to walk with the soldiers." Their mother shushed her gently. "We'll be there soon."

Safety felt far off. The fields opened wider. The road was straight and exposed with no cover. The warehouses were distant. Elias's mind wandered to the mall, the slide's whoosh, Mira's laugh echoing down the hall. It seemed like weeks ago, the routines already fading against the truck's endless sway. The scarred man's rough voice would have cut the tension, cracking something wise about the enemy or how the city used to promise safety and sanctuary. Now the quiet dragged on under the beating sun, broken only by the engine's drone and the occasional radio burst. Mira hummed softly, copying a bird's song sitting in the trees from the Dreamwood, her hand bouncing around his. "I'm going to put my feet in the brook, to cool off," she whispered. It sounded fantastic. Her words drew him in slightly, wishing there was actual flowing water around them.

The warehouses loomed closer, their shadows lengthening in the sun, hinting at relief. The convoy sped up slightly, the damaged vehicles pushing harder, smoke trailing thicker now. Elias felt the shift in speed as the breeze picked up, the road dipping into a shallow cut where the warehouses flanked both sides of the convoy. Soldiers fanned out, rifles up, scanning the gaps between buildings. The lead tank rolled in first, its engine screaming off the walls. The rest of the line followed tight behind.

Inside the truck, tension eased a fraction, the shadows from the larger warehouses offering a break from the sun's relentless beating. "Are we stopping?" Mira asked, sitting up straight, trying to gain a peek through an open flap. "Just passing through it looks like," he told her. The warehouse shadows stretched long across the road, debris piles dotting the gaps. The officer's radio crackled loud: "Slow through here, keep your eyes peeled."

Just then, the first helicopter, flying low and fast, crested the warehouse horizon without warning. Its rotors chopped the air with a deafening thump-thumping that shook the truck. Two more followed, their pure darkness cutting the golden glow of the sun, underbellies loaded with rockets. "Contact!" the officer bellowed. The convoy erupted into motion.

Rockets streaked down, fast and loud, one after another. The first slammed into the carrier ahead, fire blooming orange as metal twisted. The blast wave rocked their truck, the group slamming together violently in the rear. Elias instinctively threw himself over Mira, their mother's arms joining to shield them both. Heavy, continuous gunfire erupted from the helicopter's machine guns, bullets stretching down the road in two straight lines, pinging off the tank's armor. The lead carrier swerved, its gun swiveling up, tracers arcing toward the lead chopper. But the helicopters weaved low, another rocket hitting the rear truck, the explosion lifting it off the ground, screams cutting through the rotor wash and gunfire.

The truck driver gunned the engine, swerving to avoid a crater, but the helicopters banked tight, guns blazing. Bullets tore through the canvas, punching holes that let in flashes of light and the 'snap' of near misses. Elias pressed Mira down, the air filling with screams and shouts. The sharp crack of returned fire from the Alliance soldiers outside began. Their mother covered them both, her body tense and rigid. The assault doubled down, with helicopters circling. A rocket slammed into the side of a warehouse, spraying debris over what was left of their canvas covering.

Then the artillery started, the first shell arcing high before screaming in and cratering the road in front of their truck, erupting in a plume of dirt and fire that shook the ground. The convoy scattered in different directions. The tank fired back at the helicopters as shells walked the line. Elias's ears rang loud, the thump-thumping pounding in his skull. Mira cried out beneath him, squished between him and the hot floorboard. Another shell hit closer, the blast lifting the truck's rear in the air, tires screeching as it fishtailed when it landed.

The final impact came without warning. The shell struck directly next to their bed, the explosion ripping through metal and wood. Heat flashed. Canvas ignited. The floorboard buckled as shrapnel tore through. Elias slammed sideways, Mira slipping from his hold in the other direction amid the screams and loud ringing in his ears, pain exploding in his head. The world spun, blurry, as their mother's arm reached through the fire, her face twisted in the blast's glow... and everything went black.

The black held Elias like quicksand, his body numb and distant, the pain a far-off throb that tugged at the edges of nothing. It sucked him back slow, the world swimming into focus through a haze of gray. His eyelids cracked open, heavy and sticking, the glimpse he saw hitting hard: motion, blurring, bouncing. A soldier's arms clamped around him, the man's uniform chafing his cheek with every step, boots pounding uneven ground. Dirt spraying up, craters smoking nearby, the air sharp with burnt metal and smoking soil. Shouts cut through, "Keep moving!" The words slurred, blending with the blood rushing in his ears. Elias tried to lift his head, to see straight, but the ground blurred below, his head heavy and unmovable. The soldier grunted, shifting his weight, and the dark pulled, dragging Elias into its depths again, the throb sharpening to a spike behind his eyes.

The void stretched longer this time, pain building like pressure in a sealed room, each beat of his pulse pushing against his skull. When awareness clawed back, the Dreamwood flooded in, sudden and unsteady, the grove rising around him like a half-built wall. The big central tree loomed at the path's start, branches heavy and drooping, its trunk marked by a deep split with bark curling away in ragged strips. Elias's feet sank into the moss, softer than it should be, pulling at his boots. "Mira?" The word came out flat, swallowed by the leaves. She stepped from the underbrush behind him, her hand hovering near his. "Over there," she said, her voice thin and shaky, pointing to a bend in the path ahead. No rush of water from her words, no flowers pushing up to light the way, just the suggestion to move. What was this splitting ache he was feeling? Why couldn't he open his eyes?

Elias moved forward, the split in the tree widening with his steps, roots bulging underfoot, ripping through the ground. A shake ran through the ground, distant but growing as it neared where he was standing. The air thickened and the Dreamwood dimmed at the edges, disappearing completely as darkness swallowed everything on its way to him. The pull downward took him under once more.

Consciousness surfaced, jagged and rough. The pain was a thudding hammer now, driving through his temples with every jolt. His eyes opened to dirt and blurry motion: the soldier running hard, his grip bruising Elias's arms. Soldiers fired from low spots, some in craters, rifles yelling in short bursts at dark shapes pushing through the haze ahead. Their mother ran parallel, her pack thumping against her back, face tight with dirt and strain. "Elias! Eyes on me, I'm right here!" she yelled, tears flowing as she saw his eyes open for the first time since they started running. Her hand swung close, fingers brushing his sleeve, but the world smeared. He couldn't hear her. The soldier ducked low, weaving around a smoking wreck of a vehicle. Elias scanned the chaos, struggling for air, the figures blurring together. Where are they? What is happening? Where is Mom? Mira? The questions stuck, sharp, but the ground gave way from a nearby blast. The soldier carrying him stumbled to the ground, and the black rushed back.

The dark pulled deeper, the throb in his skull a constant roar, but the Dreamwood grabbed hold again, stronger, transforming the dark behind his eyes. The grove's paths twisted where they once lay straight. Elias pressed on, Mira's steps matching his a pace behind, her presence light and trailing, the only illumination in the grove overtaken by shadows. "The turn's clear up there," she pushed, voice distant, aligning with where he was running. The central tree dominated the center, its split a raw gash now, bleeding thick sap. Roots snaked up from deep below ground, tripping him as he walked. Shadows gathered at the base, spilling from the gash along the sap. Cold vines brushed his legs like the basement water rising slowly. The theater's raiding door hung at the path's end, half-open, spilling faint light that flickered unsteadily through it. Elias reached back for Mira, grabbing her small hand, dragging her along with him. The ground shook harder, the tree's trunk shuddering as a branch snapped free to crash in front of them. Pain lanced through his head, hot and stabbing. The grove was breaking at the seams. Real shouts bled in: "Push forward! Ridge is ours!" And the Dreamwood faded away completely.

Reality hit in fragments, the pain a vise clamping his skull to his shoulders. Elias's eyes opened to fire. A soldier hauling him behind a low pile of rubble, flames overtaking a nearby wrecked helicopter. Gunpowder and smoke choked his lungs. Soldiers knelt nearby, firing their rifles, muzzles flashing rapidly against the gray, though he couldn't hear them anymore. Enemy figures retreated ahead. Their mother crouched close, pressing a strip of cloth to his head, the fabric warm and sticking to his scalp. "Eli. I'm right here, I'm right here." Her face came in and out of focus, her free hand gripping his shoulder as she attempted to stop the bleeding on his skull. The soldier beside her nodded, his rifle's bolt sliding home with a click. The first thing he'd heard, though he wished he hadn't, as bullets still zipped overhead. He tried to push up. The ground trembled beneath him, his voice broken as he tried to speak: "Mira... she's..." Their mother leaned in, her grip tightening on his shoulder. "With the others. They're going to the safe point. Hold on." Her words blurred at the edges. His vision spotted, the world narrowing, his vision matching the throb in his eyes, and the dark reclaimed him.

The void swirled, fragments of the grove clinging like smoke, the pain as steady as a marching band's drumline. The Dreamwood pulled him in full. The paths were choked with snapped branches, the central tree leaning heavy across the clearing, its gash still oozing dark sap that pooled at the roots below. Elias climbed over the trunk, bark flaking under his palms, Mira's footsteps soft and even behind, following him through. "Around this way," she said, voice hollow, pointing in the direction he was squinting at. No birds stirred the air, no stream cut through to ease the way. The waterfall had dried up, and the flowers' petals all fell to the ground. The roots twisted higher, coiling like ropes across the ground, the gash in the tree widening to show a hollow core. Shadows spilled out, cold and grasping at him. The roots swerved toward him, pulling off the ground as they got closer, reaching toward him. Elias swung at the roots, hands passing straight through. The tree groaned as its lean deepened, another crack splitting at the trunk. Mira's voice came through, calming him momentarily. "There's a gap over there. Should we go through it?" The shaking returned, artillery crashing through the vision. The tree's branches crashed to block the path back, separating him from Mira as she disappeared behind a veil of shadows. Pain gripped, hot in his head. The grove shattered into pieces, shouts from outside pulling through. "The ridge is secured! Get the wounded! Move!"... blackness.

The surface came in waves, now shorter pulls, the pain a constant that wouldn't quit. Elias's eyes opened to more motion: the soldier's steps slowing, the line of fire a distant wink on the horizon. Their mother walked close, half-supporting the clinic woman, her pack low on one shoulder, face drawn tight. The images landed fuzzy. The world steadied around him, but tilted, colors washing out at the corners, blurring red from the blood in his eyes. Soldiers moved around them, hauling stretchers, rifles slung as the advance pushed on. Elias scanned the group, his eyes bouncing as he tried to focus.

Mom? Mira? Where are they? The thoughts hit with every pound in his head, sticking like the pain behind his eyes. The throb peaked again, his vision spotting black, blurring, dark racing in from the edges with a Dreamwood flicker: a toppled tree, Mira trying to help as she flickered like the fireflies. The gash in the tree swallowed all the light, and dark enveloped once more.

The darkness crawled in longer, the fragments sharper, the grove a hollow shell of what it used to be. Elias pushed through the fallen branches, wood splintering into his hands. Mira was a quiet pace behind, her steps matching his. "That split looks open," she said, stuttering a bit. The ground was cluttered with vines, roots, leaves, no clear space ahead. The central tree lay on its side across the clearing, its gash a dark, hollow mouth now, shadows pouring out and pooling at Mira's feet, much as the flood waters did in the basement. The theater's door hung crooked in the trunk's ruin, half-open, spilling in faint cries from outside. Elias grabbed a branch to steady himself, but it cracked in his grip, the tree shuddering as other branches snapped and fell to the ground. Mira stayed back, witnessing the destruction of the world they'd created. The ground began to vanish beneath his feet as falling branches shook everything. Pain flared again. His vision shook from the center outwards. Voices bled through: "Med team's here! Get him on the stretcher!"

Elias blinked, and the dark seized him.

Chapter 17
Unraveling Bonds

The world came back in pieces, sharp and uneven, like shards of glass catching light. Elias's head throbbed with a steady pulse matching his heartbeat, each beat sending a fresh wave of nausea rolling through him. His mouth tasted like dirt and copper. Sounds filtered in slow: low moans from nearby, the snap of bandages being torn, voices calling out names and supplies. He tried to open his eyes, but his lids were heavy, stuck together, the light stabbing when he forced them apart.

Blinking against the blur, he made out shapes: canvas walls sagging around a tent frame, medics moving quickly between stretchers. One knelt close, a woman's face coming into focus, her hands pressing a cool cloth to his forehead. "Easy, kid. You've got a nasty knock on the head and a pretty wicked concussion. Stay still." The words landed fuzzy, her voice cutting through the ringing in his ears. Elias swallowed dry; his throat raw. "Where...?" He couldn't finish. The pain spiked as he shifted.

The medic nodded, mistaking his unfinished question for "where am I?", her fingers working fast to wrap something around his skull. "Outskirts field hospital. Alliance pulled you out after that convoy mess. You're lucky." Lucky. The word didn't fit, not with the ache spreading down his neck.

He scanned the tent, shadows of bodies on cots; some stirring, others still. Their mother sat on a stool nearby, her face pale but set, one hand gripping the edge of his stretcher. In her other hand, the pack, resting at her feet, a small shape peeking from the top flap; her fingers brushed it now and then, as if checking it was still there.

"Mom," he rasped, reaching out. She leaned in, her hand covering his, warm against his cold skin. "Eli, don't move. You're ok, I'm here." Her voice shook just a bit, the lines around her eyes deeper in the tent's dim light. He tried to sit up, but the room spun almost immediately, forcing him back down. "Mira?" The question came urgent through his tightened chest. Their mother glanced at the medic, then back. "She's safe. With the others." The words landed quick, her grip squeezing his hand. Safe. It should have eased him, but the tent's chaos pressed in, moans and calls for water filling the space.

Two soldiers stood at the tent flap, talking low as they watched the medics work. "How's the mom and the boy doing? That round almost directly hit their truck... pulled 'em out just in time." The other nodded, adjusting his rifle sling. "Mom's holding up, boy's just starting to really move now. Tough pair..." Elias heard it through his closed eyes, the words blending with the throb in his head. The soldiers got them out, just in time. The medic finished the wrap, tying it off. "Rest. No moving for a bit. We'll check on you again soon."

Their mother stayed close, her free hand dipping into the pack now and then, fingers lingering on that small figure inside. Elias closed his eyes, the tent's noise fading as exhaustion pulled him away.

Safe.

The word repeated between throbs.

Lucky.

The medic moved to another cot, her voice calling for more bandages. "We've got more incoming, keep the line moving."

The tent felt smaller as time stretched, the air decreasing with each new arrival. Elias lay there, stiff, the bandage pulling tight across his forehead, his thoughts coming in slow and scattered. The medic had given him a sip of water earlier, bitter with some powder mixed in to cut the pain. It only dulled the edges, but left him feeling floaty. He turned his head slightly, spotting their mother talking to another woman across the way, the clinic woman from the mall. She gestured to the pack at her feet, pulling out a bottle to refill from a nearby bucket. The small shape stayed tucked inside, her hand brushing it again as she zipped the flap.

Elias tried to sit up once more, the room steadying a fraction, his eyes unable to fully focus. "How long was I sleeping?" Their mother turned, crossing back to him quickly. "A couple hours. You got a pretty good bump and scratch on your head. How are you feeling?" She sat on the stool, her face showing the strain, tears swelling in her eyes, though he couldn't make it out. Elias nodded, the motion pulling at the bandage. "When is Mira coming back? She needs me..." The question came softer this time. Their mother smiled, thin but real. "She's with the others. They got the kids ahead to a safer spot. I had to get you out of there. You focus on resting right now."

The flap rustled as a soldier ducked in with a crate of supplies, setting it down near the medics. He paused by the cot next to Elias's, speaking low to the man bandaging a leg wound. "Mom and the boy pulled through clean," he said, motioning to Elias. The injured man grunted, flexing his knee. "Kid's got grit."

Elias tried to listen to them, but the pain throbbed a bit. Their mother squeezed his hand again, her other dipping to the pack once more, fingers resting on that small shape inside. She reached in and pulled it out. Mira's doll, a little singed on the backside, but intact. "Here, you can hold this for now. Keep it safe for your sister like you always kept her safe." She placed the doll on the side of his chest, tucked slightly under his arm. The doll soothed him somehow, as if Mira was right there next to him in that moment, not in some other place with a bunch of other kids who didn't know how to protect her.

Outside, the rumble of engines started; the Summit Alliance stirring for the push. The medic returned, checking the wrap on

Elias's head with quick hands and a focused stare. "Stable. You can move soon, but slow, absolutely no running." Elias and their mother both nodded, the world sharpening a bit, the tent's chaos becoming less overwhelming. "We'll come get you when they're ready. For now, rest up, try to take it easy. Get some water in you." Elias laid back, the pain a steady hum now.

The medics worked fast around him. The tent filled with more stretchers as more of the convoy's wounded came in. Elias watched through half-closed eyes, the pain keeping him pinned for the moment, but his mind clearing in fits. A boy on the next cot groaned as they stitched his arm, the needle pulling thread through his skin in long, even strokes. Their mother stayed close, like a steady statue beside the stretcher. She adjusted the pack at her feet and Elias motioned for some water. She glanced down, her smile quick. "Just what you need. Drink what you can, I can fill them here."

A medic called her over after she repacked the full water bottles into the pack to help with the clinic woman's arm, the cut from the ambush flaring under the heat. Their mother went, rolling up her sleeves. Elias watched, the tent's rhythm pulling him along; the snap of scissors, the low talk of doses and wounds. The soldier from earlier passed by again, dropping off more bandages. He paused by the entrance, speaking to a guard outside. "Mom and the boy are set, we're gearing up." The guard acknowledged, rifle slung. "Tough kid. Hope he makes it through." Elias heard it, the words clear but blending seamlessly in his head. He had to make it through, for her sake. The pain dulled further, the powder working its way in, and he let his eyes close. The tent's constant buzz faded out.

A couple hours later, with what felt like a blink to Elias, the tent flap rustled open wide. Sunlight spilled in as the medics called for the stable to move out. Elias pushed up slow, the world tilting but holding. Their mother was at his side quickly, one arm under his to steady him as he swung his legs off the cot. "Take it easy. One step at a time." Her voice came firm, the pack already slung over her other shoulder. "We'll put the doll back in here and keep it safe for when we catch up to Mira." The field hospital sprawled in a cleared lot. Its tents were hastily pitched among ruined sheds, with soldiers directing the flow toward waiting trucks.

Elias leaned on her, the gravel crunching under his boots, each step jarring the throb in his head. "Mira, we're headed out to you," he whispered to himself. He pictured her waiting for them in a tent somewhere else, sliding down the tree slide while she added to the Dreamwood. The thought brought the first smile to his face since the incident, but the throbbing pain quickly removed it from his face.

The line moved steadily, refugees filing out with packs and blankets, the Alliance soldiers waving them to vehicles. A reinforced truck sat idling at the edge, its sides armored with welded plates, canvas tied back to load the wounded first. "Over here," a soldier shouted, guiding them up the step. Their mother climbed in, turning to pull Elias in after, the bench hard under him as he sat. The clinic woman settled across from them, her arm freshly wrapped, nodding to him. "You're looking better already," she whispered to Elias with a slight smile.

The truck filled quick. Bodies pressed in close on the benches, packs wedged between feet. A familiar scene. Elias scanned the faces around him: kids with bandaged heads, a man coughing blood into his sleeve, another with a bag of fluids strung above him on the side rail of the truck. Relief washed over him, glad for a moment Mira wasn't in the truck with them, somewhere safer than another convoy.

Their mother sat beside him, the pack at her feet, her hand resting on it, fingers tapping at the flap now and then. The engine rumbled to life. The truck pulled forward, joining the line of trucks snaking east. "Where are we headed?" one of the men beside him asked a soldier latching up the back of the truck. "Industrial district," he responded. "Alliance is taking it block by block. There's better cover for us there."

The truck bounced hard as it picked up speed through cratered roads. Elias gripped the bench to steady himself, every slight movement inducing a wave of nausea. Fields gave way to the city's fringes, low buildings with walls collapsed from old hits. Soldiers rode on the running boards, rifles out, scanning the sides, ready to defend their cargo. Their mother handed him a strip of damp cloth. "Wipe your face. It'll help with the sick feeling." Elias took it, the coolness cutting the sweat on his skin. The pain eased a notch as the world sharpened outside the window slats. Ruins. He didn't miss these. Mira would like the speed of the convoy this time, he thought, the wind whipping through the open flaps, yet he was still glad she wasn't crammed in the truck.

Half an hour in, the line slowed, the truck braking suddenly. Shouts up front cut the dismal rattle of the trucks quiet. A scout waved from the roadside, rifle pointed to a dip ahead. "Bomb cluster, go wide!" The convoy veered, tires chewing gravel as they skirted the craters. Elias tensed, the bump jarring his head and the pain returning in waves. Their mother gripped his arm. "Breathe through it, it'll get better." The truck hit a pothole. The world blurred, and Elias's vision spotted, darkness pulling at the edges as his vision tunneled.

The medic from the tent had warned him about this, the blackouts coming quick if he pushed too hard. Elias fought it, focusing on the slats in front of him: buildings passing, soldiers jogging, buildings passing, collapsed sign. But the throb built and the road tilted. The Dreamwood took over.

The grove's paths unfolded, narrow and uneven. The central tree still lay in the grove at the start, branches sagging to the ground, the trunk's gash running deep, worse than the one he perceived on his head. Elias's feet sank into the moss, too soft, sucking at his feet the same way his wound sucked at his head. "Mira?" Her name hung flat, searching for her. She stepped out from a boulder nearby, waving him over. "Over there?" she questioned, voice wavering, pointing to a bend ahead. Elias moved, the split widening with his steps, roots bulging underfoot like something straining to break free. A breeze hit him from the truck, and subsequently, a breeze twirled around the Dreamwood. Mira smiled. He knew she'd like the breeze. But the ground shook, distant but building, the branches of the remaining trees creaking above. The path dimmed, and the dark edges of reality tugged, pulling him out.

The truck steadied. The line pushed forward again, the cluster bomb left in the dip behind them, marked with a reflective panel for anyone who might follow. Elias blinked, the grove faded, and the pain returned like a dull hammer. Their mother watched him close. "Are you okay?" He shook his head, the motion careful. "Just in my head, Mira was there." She nodded, rubbing her hand across his forehead with tears in her eyes. He still couldn't focus enough to tell, but he knew she was upset. It had been a rough couple of days. The road curved into the industrial district. Low-sitting factories loomed with walls blown open, their insides gutted like empty shells of what they once were. The convoy slowed and the trucks pulled into covered yards. Soldiers secured the perimeter. "We're holding here for the night," the driver called out. "The Alliance is pushing further at dawn."

They unloaded slow, Elias leaning on their mother as his boots hit the ground, sending a jolt through his bones. The factory yard sprawled wide, rusted machinery scattered like broken toys, the air carrying the old smell of oil and metal. Other refugees gathered in clusters, unloading packs under the watchful eyes of soldiers setting up barricades and concertina wire. Mira. He scanned the groups, expecting her face among the kids, but the yard blurred at the edges. She was here, somewhere, with the others, probably helping unload like she did at the mall. Their mother guided him to a cleared spot near a wall, easing him down onto a crate. "Sit. I'll grab some food." Elias leaned himself down on the ground, back against the crate, the ache settling as he leaned back.

The yard bustled quietly. A pair of soldiers passed nearby, one carrying a med kit. "How's the mom and the boy doing? His head wound looked bad. Check back on them later. It's horrible what happened." The other nodded, slinging a rifle. "Mom's steady, boy's up moving already. Tough kid, they'll make it through." Elias heard them talk between the throbs in his head. It was horrible, he never wanted to go through that again. Their mother returned quickly, never having taken her eyes off him, a tin cup in hand with boiled oats and cool water.

"Better?" she asked as he drank the water. He handed it back. "Yeah. She's around here somewhere? Can we go get her?" "She's not here, we're just stopping here for the night. They're further ahead, we had to stop to get your head fixed," she said with a smile. "This should help." She pulled the doll out, stared at it for a moment, and then tucked it under his right arm. "You can hold this when you're missing her."

The late afternoon wore on in the yard, the sun dropping lower, casting long shadows across the concrete. Elias stayed put, not moving much, the crate at his back rough support to keep his head steady. He watched the Alliance soldiers set up. Soldiers wired barricades from scrap metal, stacking crates high to block the roads in. The convoy's trucks parked in a tight circle, engines cooling with hisses of steam. Refugees moved in small groups, some tending small fires along the sides of the buildings to boil water. Their mother joined the clinic woman at a low table made of crates and cardboard, talking softly. Elias caught her glances his way as she spoke, the clinic woman rubbing her shoulder.

A soldier stopped by the wall, dropping a pack of bandages nearby. He nodded to Elias, then spoke low to another passing by. "The Alliance needs more like that kid, tough as they come." The other grunted and chuckled, checking his rifle. "Mom's got grit too." Elias listened, the words blending with the yard's hum. Mom and the boy. They haven't seen how brave Mira could be. They would, though, when they caught up to the other group.

The sun dipped behind the buildings, the shadows lengthening, and Elias laid down against the wall, the pain a low, constant annoyance. The yard felt secure, the barricades rising steady to stop anyone from getting in. Their mother crossed back and sat beside him with a cup of cooled boiled water. "Drink this down, we're leaving early." He took it, still steaming, though not hot, the words from the soldiers sticking like a quiet promise.

The yard's activity slowed as evening settled, the sun a thin red line on the horizon, the air cooling with the drop. Elias sipped the water slow, the warmth spreading through him, easing the last of the day's ache. A group of soldiers walked by, talking about "taking the district tomorrow, then the whole city back" as they continued past. Elias overheard, but didn't really understand what it meant. He just hoped this would be over soon.

Night fell thick and fast over the factory yard, the last glow of the sun fading behind the buildings. Elias laid against the wall, the concrete hard under his thin blanket. The bandage on his head itched as the swelling went down. Small fires dotted the space, their light flickering on the faces of refugees huddled around, pots bubbling with the last of the day's water. Soldiers stalked the perimeter, rifles catching the flames as they passed. The yard had gone quiet, the earlier bustle turning to low talk and the occasional groan. Elias shifted, the ache in his head manageable right now. He tucked the doll under his arm, a small weight he didn't mind carrying. It felt solid, a piece of Mira waiting here with him while she was away with the others.

Their mother sat nearby, resting her head on the pack. She hadn't said much since the sun dropped, staring at the fires. "Get some sleep," she said, voice soft against the night's hush. "Your head needs rest."

Elias closed his eyes, eased by the yard's sounds: the crackle of wood burning, the distant call of a soldier changing watch. The pounding in his head quieted, the doll pressing against his side like Mira usually did, a small comfort in the dark.

But the night didn't stay quiet.

A low whistle cut the air, high and sharp, followed by a distant boom that shook the air. Elias's eyes snapped open, sitting up quick, the pain flaring instantly. Another whistle, closer, then the explosion rattled the barricades, orange light flashing over the yard. Shouts rose from the perimeter as soldiers scrambled to their positions. "Illumination rounds! They're searching!" Their mother was up fast, one hand on his arm. "Stay low." The third round hit higher, the flare bursting bright overhead, bathing the yard in harsh white light that cast long, eerie shadows between the trucks.

Elias pressed against the wall. The light stung his eyes, and the boom's echo rang in his head. The soldiers called out, scanning the dark beyond the wire. "Hold positions! Eyes up!" The flare hung, drifting slow on its parachute, turning night to day for a long moment. Elias looked around. Refugees ducked low, fires were quickly kicked out with dirt, and the clinic woman gathered her bag. No trucks leaving, no rush to move. The enemy was probing, lighting the area to see what they could find. "Be ready to go," she whispered, pulling her pack close.

The flare died and the dark rushed back. The soldiers' voices steadied. "Clear!" Elias exhaled, the pulse in his head louder now, the light's afterimage burning spots in his vision. Another whistle sounded far off, the boom rolling distant as the enemy searched other spots.

The yard settled uneasy and the fires remained extinguished. The night's quiet was interrupted. Elias laid back, tucking the doll back beside him, thinking of Mira. She's out there with the others. "What if the lights find Mira?" he blurted out, suddenly in a panic. His mother grabbed his shoulder and helped him back down. "They won't find her, she's not in the outer edges anymore like us. Go to sleep, you need to rest your head." The push at dawn would bring them closer to her. Sleep came restless after that, the distant booms pulling him under unevenly as the yard's shadows lingered long in his dreams.

Chapter 18
Shadows Under Siege

Sleep clung to him, heavy with his head wound and concussion weighing down his eyelids. The factory yard's concrete pressed hard against his back, the thin blanket he rested on doing little to soften it. Night had settled thick, the fires from earlier reduced to glowing embers in bins, casting faint orange flickers across the sprawl of bodies and crates. Soldiers moved at the perimeter, rifles ready as they scanned the dark beyond the wire. Mira's face floated in his thoughts, her grin from the mall's slide drawing a faint grin of his own as he slept, clutching her doll as if it were her.

Another whistle cut through the night's quiet, high and thin, slicing through the air. Elias's eyes snapped open, his body tensing before his mind caught up and eyes unblurred. The sound built fast, sharp and urgent, joined by another, then a third. The whistling quickly turned to a raging scream as shells arced overhead. The first impact hit a hundred yards out, the ground jumping with a thud that rattled his teeth. Shouts erupted from the perimeter. "Incoming! Take cover!"

Elias bolted upright and reached for their mother. She was already moving, pack slung over one shoulder, her hand clamping his arm hard enough to leave a bruise. Mira's absence hit him again. She was ahead of them, safe, hopefully nowhere near the bombs going off. The explosions started to chain as another shell slammed closer, a pool of fire erupting across the ground just outside the perimeter. The yard's edge lit up, a burst of bright white and orange from the impact point, flames attacking a stack of crates near the tanks. Elias's head throbbed but he pushed to his feet, legs still unsteady beneath him.

Their mother yanked him toward a low wall of sandbags near the factory's side as gunfire erupted from the dark. "Get down!" She shoved him behind the barrier, dropping beside him, her body shielding his as the next shell whistled in. It struck the yard's center, the explosion ripping through a truck's frame with a horrible screech that briefly drowned out the gunfire. The heat hit them first, then the blast wave, knocking them both backwards. Elias's ears rang. It was all he heard, a high-pitched ringing. Soldiers returned fire into the dark outside the perimeter, muzzle flashes lighting the night like strobes. Bullets were bouncing off of everything as the attack intensified: walls, tanks, the ground, everything.

The yard shook as another shell hit. Refugees scrambled in haste. The clinic woman crouched nearby, her bag clutched tight, calling for anyone hurt. "Over here!" someone yelled, and she moved quickly in that direction. Elias held himself against the sandbags, the rough stitching biting into his hands. His vision started spotting again, the concussion from the impacts messing with his own. The impacts rolled steady. Shells walked the perimeter, each explosion getting closer. Their mother scanned the dark, looking for an escape. As she did, another loud explosion ripped through the sky above. A shell burst high, blooming white light that hung in the night. Flares. They lit the yard, exposing them all.

The flare's glow washed over everything. Alliance soldiers continued to fire from behind crates and vehicles, their shots replying to the enemy's wild bursts from the fields. Elias ducked lower. The harsh light from the flare hurt his eyes. The central tree from the grove flickered in his head, its trunk split wide, releasing more shadows under the white glare. Mira stood at the path's edge, her form flickering as his head pounded, pointing silent toward a bend in the path. "That way." Her lips moved, but he couldn't hear her over the explosions and gunfire. The vision stayed as he held his eyes shut, until the next shattering boom destroyed it. His eyes shot open wide and pain pierced through his skull.

"Keep your head down!" Their mother pressed him flat, her arm across his back as another shell hit the wire's edge, concertina wire snapping like coiled whips. The flare overhead died and the dark rushed back in, but the enemy found their range. A new sound emerged in the sky, different, lower, the shell arcing in fast over the buildings. It struck the far side of the yard, not with the standard explosion, but with a whoosh of fire emerging as it slammed into the ground. Incendiary rounds. They bloomed low and wide, orange fire spreading across the ground. Flames spread quick, catching crates and tarps with heat rolling in waves that singed the air itself. Shouts turned to screams as the fire grew toward where many refugees were taking cover.

Elias lifted his head just enough to see the glow lighting the chaos: soldiers beating at flames with jackets, refugees coughing through the smoke, the clinic woman helping drag a man from a burning pile. The heat pressed close, the sandbags warming under his chest. Another incendiary round hit closer, the explosion a ball of fire that lit the factory's wall. Elias's head felt the brunt of the impact, and the shadows from the fire didn't leave as he closed his eyes, rather, they took over the grove in waves. The clinic woman moved fast, pulling a boy from the edge of the blaze. She turned toward a cluster of others seeking refuge near the main factory door, calling out to them for help.

It was too late, though. The next round came without warning, slamming into the ground not twenty feet from her. The incendiary burst caught her leg first, flames crawling up the fabric quick. She dropped her bag, hands slapping at the fire, but it spread fast, the heat turning her screams raw and primitive. The sound cut through the yard's chaos, sharp and desperate, pulling Elias back to the theater's darkness: the raid's door splintering, soldiers' boots on broken glass,

Mira's hand slipping from his as they ran... that scream that pierced the night. The clinic woman's cry twisted in his head, blending with the memory of it being their mother's scream as she evaded patrols through the alley ruins.

Elias's hand shot out, grabbing their mother's arm hard, fingers digging into her skin. "Mom!" he panicked, pain spiking in his head. She turned fast, eyes wide in the firelight. "Eli, I'm here! It's me! I'm right here with you." Her free hand covered his, prying his fingers loose, gentle but firm. "Breathe. I'm right here. I'm not leaving you." The yard's chaos pressed in, but her voice grounded him as the screams faded. The clinic woman's figure collapsed in flames. Others ran to beat the fire out with whatever they could, but to no avail. Elias's grip loosened, his chest heaving. The memory receded, just as the clinic woman's screams did.

Their mother kept her hand on his, eyes scanning the flames. "We have to move. This place is done." She pulled the pack closer, unzipping it quickly. She grabbed the doll, paused for a moment, then tucked it deep into a side pocket, zipping it shut tight. "Come on, stay with me." Elias nodded, the throb in his head steadying as he pushed up on the sandbags.

The incendiary rounds kept coming with sporadic bursts, lighting the dark. Soldiers herded the group toward the factory's side door. "Inside! Move!" Elias glanced back once. The clinic woman's body laid still in the yard, half covered in jackets and blankets. The image burned into his mind, like the scarred man's body, left lifeless in the dirt as the convoy pulled away. How long until that was them?

Their mother pulled him forward, rushing through the door into the factory's dim interior. Barricades of crates and beams blocked the windows. Soldiers piled more as the shells kept falling outside. The officer's voice carried from the front, her figure directing from a raised platform, "No one out till we call the strike!"

Elias huddled close to his mother, Mira's absence a hollow ache between throbs in his head. The factory shuddered with each impact. Its brick walls did a good job of blocking the fire, but a direct hit would have catastrophic consequences.

Enemy ground troops swarmed next, firing sporadically as they rushed the perimeter of the yard. Alliance soldiers fired back from the barricades. A full-blown battle had unfolded. Elias backed against the wall and slid down, knees to his chest, covering his ears with both hands as the roar from the gunfire intensified the thumping in his head. Their mother crouched beside him, hands over his. "It'll pass. We're getting out of here. Breathe."

The siege tightened, enemy voices yelling closer, the perimeter folding under pressure. Soldiers fell back, step by step, dragging wounded with them as the fires in the yard from the incendiaries spread. The officer's radio crackled loud. "Hold 'em off! Air support inbound! Five minutes!"

The walls trembled as the ground assault poured in, enemy shouts mixing with the bellow of rifles from both sides. Elias pressed tighter against the concrete, the rough surface scraping his back through his shirt, drawing blood to the surface. Outside, the yard's wire gave way and the first enemy soldiers spilled through the gaps as Alliance soldiers targeted the openings.

Their shots were steady, dropping rushing shadows in flare light. One after another. But the enemy pushed hard, numbers swelling from the fields, using the craters for cover as they advanced on the factory's flanks. A grenade arced over the wall, landing short but close enough to pepper the door with gravel. The blast's thud rattled Elias's teeth. "They're through the east side!" a soldier yelled from the barricade, his rifle smoking as he fired over the top. The officer's voice cut through precisely from the platform, directing her soldiers to move and cut off the advancing enemy.

Elias risked a glance around the wall's edge, the yard a battlefield under the fading flare glow. Enemy figures darted from cover to cover, their uniforms dark, matching the night, rifles glinting as they laid down suppressing fire. More poured in, the perimeter buckling, soldiers falling back toward the factory door in a ragged line from all directions. Their mother pulled him back down. "Just look at me. My face. Focus on me." Her grip tightened on his arm as the black started tugging at the edges of his vision. Mira flickered between long blinks; there, then not.

Inside, medics hauled wounded to the rear. Refugees pressed against walls or crouched behind machinery husks and soldiers set up firing positions through missing windows. Outside, the assault intensified. Enemy fire raked the front wall of the factory, bullets slamming into beams and ricocheting off the brick. What was left of a window shattered under a burst of gunfire, glass spraying inward. Near it, a little girl, not much older than Mira, cried out as glass shards cut her arm. "Mira?" Elias questioned, his hazy mind mistaking the girl as he reached out for her. Their mother grabbed him back quickly. He blinked, and Mira disappeared. It wasn't her.

Soldiers returned fire from slits in the walls and windows. "They're massing at the gate!" The officer climbed down from the platform, rifle in hand, directing from the floor. "Pull back to the inner line! Buy us some time!" The fight closed in, grenades detonating at the door, smoke billowing through and filling the entire area. The officer's radio crackled loud: "Strike package confirmed! Danger close! Get out of there!" Soldiers grabbed the wounded, hauling them toward side exits. Everyone else rushed for the rear exit along the back wall.

Elias pushed up, their mother at his side as they pushed toward the rear door. Enemy figures spilled through the front of the building. Alliance's well-placed shots dropped the first few, but more followed. "Go! Rear exit!" The woman officer waved them over between bursts as she covered the retreat with her rifle, bursts of shots behind them.

Elias got his legs working and ran behind his mother as she pulled him along. Out the exit was a loading bay with Alliance trucks waiting. Soldiers loaded the wounded fast, refugees piling in on top of one another.

Elias's vision faded. The back of the truck blended into a cave opening, dark and filled with shadows. Their mother pushed him in, climbing in after. In his mind, he was falling through an endless dark. In reality, he was just standing there. Their mother pulled him onto a bench as the truck's wheels spun and it jolted forward. The final soldiers remaining loaded into the last armored carrier and all the vehicles raced away from the factory.

Enemy soldiers poured through the rear of the factory, standing on the loading dock, firing at the fleeing vehicles. Rounds pierced the rear hatch of the truck, one hitting an already wounded soldier who was laid out on the floor, unseen in the grim dark. "Turn around, Eli. Go back to the grove." Mira. She pulled him back from spiraling in the darkness.

As he opened his eyes, the sky came to life. A line of Alliance planes zoomed in, low, fast, directly above the convoy. As they crested the edge of the factory perimeter, they pulled up into the sky, releasing their payloads. A barrage of bombs, the noise stronger than the world's worst thunderstorm as they detonated all at once. The entire factory lit up in an instant. Debris rained down on the trucks, now hundreds of yards away. And the next moment, silence. Enemy gunfire halted. Screaming and shouts were silenced. The battle was over.

He didn't know his eyes were leaking, his mind fixated on a hundred things at once. "We're out. We're safe. Hold on, baby." Their mother grabbed his hand, pulling him into her side. His pain slowed for a moment as his head came to rest against her chest. "Mira? Are we going to Mira now?" Their mother stroked his hair, her lip quivering, fighting back tears of her own. "Here, hold onto this. It'll help when you're missing her." She reached into the pack and pulled out the doll again, staring into its button eyes for a moment before handing it to Elias.

The doll's singed fabric felt rough against his palm. Elias clutched it tight, the stitches in its arm brushing his fingers like Mira's hand. The truck barreled on, its engine straining beneath the refugees' ragged breaths. Outside, the airstrike's afterglow faded into a pre-dawn haze, the factory's inferno now a distant smudge on the horizon, but the air still carried the bite of smoke and scorched metal seeping through the bullet-riddled flaps.

Their mother shifted beside him, her arm a steady pressure across his shoulders, her free hand rifling the pack for a water bottle. "Sip this," she murmured, pressing it to his lips. The liquid was warm, tasting faintly of the boiled rainwater from the yard mixed with unwashed plastic, but it cut the dryness in his throat. He drank slowly. When he was finished, she put it back in the pack and continued to softly rub his head. The doll tucked under his arm brought thoughts of Mira, appearing in flickers in the Dreamwood as he closed his eyes. The concussion blurred it all, the vision blending into the truck's shadows: the central tree's gash widening with each bump, sap oozing slowly like blood from his bandaged head, roots snaking under the benches like the craters swallowing the road. And Mira remained on the edges, his mind reaching for her but unable to connect.

Dawn crept in, gray and reluctant. Soldiers jogged alongside the convoy, rifles at the ready. Elias peered through a tear in the flap, the world tilting slightly with his head's throb. He saw the skyline, jagged with Nova City's remnants. No enemy fire yet, but the quiet felt brittle, like it could end any moment. The airstrike's victory was a temporary reprieve in the war's endless grip.

Their mother noticed his gaze, her hand squeezing his shoulder. "Rest your eyes." Her voice replayed in his head, even and steady, but Elias caught the strain in it, the way her fingers lingered on the pack's strap, as if weighing its contents against the uncertainty ahead. The doll shifted under his arm, its yarn hair tickling his skin. He couldn't help but wonder what she was doing with the other kids, without him.

The convoy reformed after briefly splitting to clear a mined intersection, pushing deeper into the industrial district. Soldiers fanned out at the flanks, securing crossroads with quick bursts of fire into empty shadows. No major push yet, but the scouts' reports crackled urgent across the officer's radio: "Enemy regrouping to the east. Armor massing."

Chapter 19
Reborn Roots

Elias was tired of riding in these military trucks. "How far?" he asked, longing for his sister. Their mother squeezed his knee. "Not long. The harbor's straight ahead."

The radio up front crackled, the officer's voice cutting through the engine noise. "The main push is underway. Reinforcements hit the gulf line with a coordinated air strike. The enemy armor is decimated. Infantry scattered. We're taking the core block by block." Cheers rippled through the truck; the first time since the mall that anyone was happy or showed excitement. But Elias didn't celebrate. Mira was out there somewhere, with the other kids in the forward group. What if they got caught up in the fighting? He stared at the canvas covering them, playing over every perceived scenario in his head.

Gunfire started in the distance, sharp cracks rolling in from the city ahead, joined by the deeper cough of Alliance tanks returning fire with their main guns. The convoy picked up speed, carriers flanking tighter as they moved. The carriers added to the return fire, their machine guns talking as the convoy raced toward the city.

Elias leaned toward the flap, peering out. Warehouses slid past; their guts exposed to the rising light. A burst of fire lit a side street. Alliance rifles answered with a shower of gunfire. The truck swerved to avoid a crater, jolting Elias's head against the bench frame. He closed his eyes, the world blurring from reality to the Dreamwood: the grove's paths under faint sunlight, trees swaying with the truck's motion. Mira appeared at a distance, her form faint amid the upright trunks, sunlight filtering through the leaves and making her sway with the radio's static bursts. She didn't step forward or shape the scene. She just stood there, hand lifting slowly as if pointing ahead. No words came, just the sense of her presence, like sunlight cast on water without ripples. Elias reached out in the vision, but the trees bent harshly as a distant tank round boomed outside. "Mira?" The name stuck in his throat as the grove dimmed at the edges. She flickered once, her lips moving silently, "Keep going," before the pain yanked him back. His mother was holding him; she watched his head bounce off the truck and immediately grabbed him, but he was already out.

The radio burst again: "Core secured. Enemy falling back to the harbor line. We're pushing in now." Elias's heart skipped a beat. The harbor? That's where they were going. That's where Mira was. He gripped the doll harder, angry and upset. The convoy pushed on, gunfire intensifying outside: tank barrels booming, machine guns rattling from the carriers as they cleared more crossroads. Bullets whined past, one pinging the truck's side, but the line held, weaving through the fringes toward the city proper. Elias's head ached with each shot, the Dreamwood flickering back and forth. Mira remained distant, her form flickering under the swaying trees, as the sunlight danced through them. She pointed again, silent, her presence a quiet nudge toward the path's end.

The truck braked hard at a ruined warehouse lot. The officer shouted from the cab: "Everyone out! We're joining the push. Take this radio; hold here till the harbor's clear." Elias's mother grabbed her pack and helped Elias down as refugees spilled out. Gunfire echoed closer now, the core's battle swelling. A soldier thrust a handheld radio into their mother's hands. "Stay put. We'll signal when it's safe." The convoy roared off, tanks and carriers vanishing around a bend, leaving them in the lot's shadow. Elias leaned against a wall, the ground steady but his head spinning, Mira's distant flicker lingering like a promise in the haze.

The warehouse lot felt too open under the midday sun, its low walls scarred with craters and rusted machinery scattered across the ground. Elias slumped against a concrete pillar, his legs unsteady from the truck's jolts. Their mother scanned the area fast, gunfire cracking from a few blocks away, the sounds carrying clearly over the empty lots. "In here," she said, pointing to a low building at the lot's edge. It was a brick structure with walls mostly standing, roof sagging but solid. She held the radio in one hand, pack in the other, leading him to the door.

Empty shelves lined the walls, some tipped over, their contents spilled: broken crates, loose wires, a few cans here and there. Their mother jammed the door shut with a rod from the debris, then guided Elias to a corner away from the windows. "Sit. You need to eat, you're looking pale." She handed him a dried fruit strip as he lowered himself against the wall and carefully tucked the doll back inside the pack. Elias looked around blankly as he took a bite. "Why are we here?" His mind was losing small stretches of time, and he didn't remember offloading from the convoy. His head wasn't hurting as much as it was diluting his time now. "We're safe, eat your fruit," their mother told him comfortingly, though the look of worry in her eyes when she lightly stroked his head bandage showed anything but comfort.

The radio rested between them. The antenna was bent, but it seemed to be working as static pushed through the speaker. Gunfire swelled outside, closer than before. Short bursts from Alliance rifles answered by enemy gunfire chatter, tank engines turning over in the streets. Elias's head started to hurt more with the noise echoing off the concrete walls, each crack or explosion pushing against his temples. He shut his eyes, trying to shut it out, but the Dreamwood waited inside his eyelids, the grove's paths showing up narrow under the building's low light.

She stood far off, her shape fluid among the standing trees, sunlight coming through the leaves. She stayed in one spot, not moving. Mira just raised her hand slowly, pointing to a turn in the path ahead. No sound, just like she was waiting for him to catch up. Elias stepped toward her, but the trees shook hard as a tank round exploded outside, and she disappeared in the trees. "Mira, where are you?" The words got caught in his throat. She appeared again, and a few words left her lips, "Clean it up a little," before the pain pulled him out.

Their mother turned the radio dial. "Alliance command... refugee holdout...status?" The messages came broken, voices mixing in the back with gunfire between each word: "Core push holding... we took out their armor... Infantry pulling back... holding at the harbor." The words hit Elias like a punch to the stomach. Mira was near the harbor with the other kids. He reached over and pulled the doll from their mother's pack, staring intently into its button eyes, willing Mira to be ok. "It'll be ok, we're going to make it out of here." Their mother tried comforting him, seeing the confusion and worry on his face.

The morning stretched slowly, gunfire coming and going. Their mother walked the small room, checking the door and windows, bracing them where she could. Through the static, sporadic calls gave details of the unfolding battle for the city: tanks pushing through, street by street, carriers clearing side roads, Alliance soldiers cleaning up on foot behind. But the harbor remained a strongpoint for the enemy.

Artillery shells were traded back and forth over the water. As the fire intensified, so did the pain in Elias's head, the sounds mixing into the Dreamwood as his eyes shut. But the sounds were muffled inside, and Mira was waiting for him on the edge of the woods. She pointed once more, "It's a mess in here... Clean it up a little." Elias looked around. The main central tree was half toppled, oozing from the gash. Trees all around laying on their sides, leaves dying off their branches. Mira sparkled a little as the fireflies returned and surrounded her, and in that moment, Elias looked at the first brook they had created, and water started to trickle back down its barren rock bed. The vision stopped with more gunfire outside. He recognized the sounds: machine gun fire from the carriers.

By midday, heat filled the room. Elias's shirt stuck to him as his body was hot with a slight fever, skin moist as his body tried to fight off whatever bacteria made it through his head wound. The pain was steady, but less sharp. More manageable now. Their mother shared the last of the water, taking a small sip before giving him the rest of the bottle. "The city is ours... heading to the harbor," the radio cracked, voices clearer through the static. Elias listened intently, his heart racing faster. Mira. He focused on her name. But the words continued to filter through the static: "Enemy infantry pushing back... big fight at the docks."

He shut his eyes against the words. The grove's paths stretched longer. Mira waited at the end, her color pale in the light coming through the trees. She said it again, "Clean it up a little." No hurry in her, no streams restarting or branches growing back. Just the idea, nimble, suggestive. Elias pushed forward in the vision. He took a dropped branch, pulling it away. As he did, the roots calmed a bit, a few leaves opened slowly. Mira watched from afar, holding still, but the push was enough to keep him going. He pulled a downed branch crossing an empty stream bed, and the water started rising slowly.

The radio buzzed loudly, "Harbor line giving... They're cut off... Hit the flanks!" Elias's eyes popped open. Their mother held the radio, adjusting the dial. "Alliance command, any word of the refugees?" Static buzzed, then a voice, familiar. It was the woman officer: "We dropped them at a warehouse before joining the push. We'll send a unit back to get them." Relief hit hard for Elias, tears dropping off his cheek onto the doll he was squeezing tight.

Hours passed in the heat, the room's walls growing tighter as the battle continued. By late afternoon, the gunfire had dropped to single shots, and the big explosions had ceased. The fear of the unknown was easing, though the darkness in his head remained. Elias took a deep breath as a hail of gunfire made its way through the static, but it was followed up with Alliance voices: "Harbor clear! City is ours.

Move out." Elias let out the air in a big sigh, no more worry for the harbor.

The radio's words remained in his head, replaying over and over. The last static fell silent as their mother put down the radio. "It's done," she said, voice low but sure, pulling Elias close and wrapping her arms around him. Elias's head still hurt, but the pain retreated a little, softened by the good news and his mother's embrace. Mira, safe at the harbor, past the hard part.

"Warehouse, refugees, are you still on this net?" The radio call broke the silence, the officer's voice confident and loud. "We're here! Still in the building you dropped us at," their mother replied. "Hang tight, trucks are enroute to your location. Be ready to move." Their mother packed up quickly, putting the empty bottle and the doll back in safely, pulling it over her shoulder. Elias stood, the floor solid under his feet for the first time since the blast. As they exited the building, they saw other refugees also walking out, the sound of gunfire that they were all now accustomed to absent.

A carrier arrived first, the woman officer leaning from the open top with a smile cutting through the black on her face, followed by a whole line of trucks. "Get in! We're headed to the harbor." The trucks filled fast, people crowded close on the seats, looking out the sides at the smoking wreckage of what used to be their home. Elias joined in looking out of the flap. An Alliance flag waved on the top of an enemy tank, slowly burning and absent any operators. Alliance soldiers waved the trucks past as they hitched rides on the sides of the rear vehicles. No enemy around, just... quiet.

The radio in their mother's lap buzzed with calls: people arriving at the harbor, moving through medical evaluations, reuniting with loved ones they had lost days or weeks ago. Mira. She waited there for them, probably showing the other kids the water, going on about tree slides and turtles. The trucks moved steady, the war's hold on the city finally put to rest.

As evening came, the convoy arrived at the harbor docks. Ships sat in the bay; Alliance boats were unloading boxes under big generator-powered lights, their sides with deep wounds but strong enough to keep floating. The trucks stopped and their mother helped Elias down. A soldier was directing the offload: "People to the middle tents. Assistance teams are waiting."

Elias saw a group of kids near some boxes and a woman in uniform from the front trucks waving them over. But he didn't see Mira. "Where's my sister, Mira?" Elias asked the woman as they neared the tents. The woman looked down, checking a paper on her clipboard. "You all came from the mall? The core move? Say's she was with you on the move."

Their mother's face went pale white, and she swallowed hard before quickly jumping in. "No, she... she went ahead... with another group before... before the factory." She stuttered over her words as she spoke, gripping Elias's shoulder. The woman shook her head as she looked at more papers. "We only got the main group. There's more filling in." "Come on, Eli, we have to get your head looked at. It looks like it was bleeding a little more through the bandage." She pulled him away from the lady into a central tent.

As an Alliance medic placed him onto a cot in the corner of the tent and started to unwrap the bandage from his head, tears fell from his eyes. Not from the pain, but from being so close and still not knowing where she was. "We've gotta clean this. I'll give him something for the pain and some nitrous for the scrubbing," the medic told their mother. She squeezed Elias's hand tight as the medic placed a nitrous mask over his face. "This will only hurt for a second," the medic said as he gave Elias a shot in his arm. He didn't even flinch. His mind was elsewhere. As the nitrous took effect, his eyes fluttered and closed, pulling him under where the Dreamwood waited. "He'll probably be out for a few hours," the medic said as he laid out a bucket of sterile water and began to clean the wound.

Chapter 20

Eternal Canopy

Elias stepped through the Dreamwood like his body didn't weigh anything at all, a floating feeling, brought on by the nitrous. The ground under his feet felt soft, springy, like walking on thick moss that gave just a little with each step. Sunlight poured down through the trees, warm on his skin, turning everything a bright, lively green. Orange and red leaves rustled above him in a breeze, the river ran full and clear off to the side, water sparkling as it rushed over smooth rocks, fish jumping now and then with flashes of silver. Fireflies drifted in groups near the banks, their lights blinking even in the daytime, adding small dots of glow to the air. The cave sat ahead, its entrance draped in vines, the waterfall pouring down steady over the front, sending up a mist that cooled his face as he got closer. Turtles moved along the edge of the pool inside, slow and calm, shells wet and shining.

He took a deep breath. The air smelled like fresh rain on leaves, no smoke, no dust. Just the kind of smell that made you want to stand there with your eyes closed and not move. The path wound through the grove, trees standing tall on both sides, their trunks smooth and strong. Branches reached out high, linking together to make a canopy that let in just enough light. Flowers dotted the grass, yellow and pink ones opening wide, petals catching the breeze. The big central tree rose up in the middle of it all, holding the entire grove together with its solid branches and deep roots.

Elias reached out and touched one of the trunks as he passed. The wood felt warm, alive under his fingers. No cracks. No splinters. Just perfect.

He kept walking, looking around as if it were the first time he'd seen the beauty. The river bubbled louder up ahead, the waterfall's rush pulling him toward the cave. Fireflies floated above the water, their lights dancing on the surface. The vines hung thick over the entrance, green and full, dripping with clean and clear water that clung from the mist.

It all looked right. The way it was supposed to be. Before the bombs and the raids and the running. But something was missing.

He stopped at the cave's edge, the waterfall's spray hitting his shoes. The space inside looked empty. "Mira?" he called out. The waterfall kept pouring. The turtles kept moving. The fireflies kept blinking. No answer.

He turned in a slow circle, scanning the path behind him; the grove, the riverbanks. The Dreamwood stretched out wide and bright, everything in its place. Sun on the leaves, water running steady. But no Mira. His chest tightened, like the air wasn't as easy to pull in anymore. He took a step back toward the path.

The Dreamwood flickered, like the power went out for a split second.

For a moment, the green dropped away. Gray. The river looked like a dry crack in the dirt, no water at all. Fireflies gone. The waterfall just a few drips from cracked rocks. The cave entrance hung with dead vines, brown and brittle. No turtles in sight. The big central tree leaned wrong, half fallen, roots sticking up like broken fingers. A deep gash ran down its trunk, wet sap oozed out, slow and dark.

Elias froze, his breath stuck in his throat.

As he blinked, it snapped back. Green. River rushing. Fireflies. Waterfall pouring full. Everything bright again. He blinked hard, rubbing his eyes. His hands felt shaky, and the ground under him didn't feel as steady now, like it might give out if he stepped wrong.

He turned around again, slower. His body felt light, too light, as if he jumped he might not come back down. Everything looked right. The path looked clear. The grove was bright and the trees swayed in the breeze, birds singing songs on their branches. But that tight feeling in his chest wouldn't go away, like he couldn't get a full breath in.

He took a step towards the river to go wash his face.

The Dreamwood flickered: dark, broken, decayed.

He took another step.

The Dreamwood flickered back: bright, perfect, lively.

The switches came faster now. Broken. Alive. Gray. Green. It was like the Dreamwood couldn't make up its mind, like it was fighting itself. Elias started to panic. He looked around wildly, trying to spot Mira somewhere, anywhere. She could help him fix whatever was wrong; she always added the right thing.

"Mira!" he yelled this time, but the forest didn't answer.

He started running. The path ahead looked open in the green flashes, so he aimed for that. His feet hit the ground, one after another, but it didn't feel like he was getting anywhere. The trees on either side stretched further, the path getting longer the faster he moved his legs, like it was pulling away from him.

Green. Broken. Alive. Gray. The Dreamwood flipped on every step. He ran harder. His legs burned, but the end of the path kept pulling farther away, and the ground began to change beneath his feet. Moss turned to dirt. Dirt turned to cracks. Cracks turned to nothing. Black started creeping in at the edges, swallowing the trees, the river, the light.

He tripped on a root that wasn't there a second ago and fell forward. The path turned black before he hit it, and he just kept falling, nothing to stop him as he descended into the dark.

Elias's eyes snapped open with a gasp of air rushing in.

The world hit him all at once. Dim light, a low ceiling of white canvas, the smell of antiseptic and sweat. His head pounded, but the pain felt farther away than it had before. He blinked, trying to make sense of the shapes around him. Cots lined up in rows, some with people lying still, others empty. A few medics moved between them; their footsteps soft on the dirt floor. No one close.

He pushed up on his elbows, the cot creaking under him. The new bandage felt tighter across his forehead, but the throb was duller, as if it were wrapped in something softer. He swung his legs over the side, feet hitting the ground with a thud. It didn't spin as bad as before. He stood slowly, testing his balance. Steady enough.

"Mom? Mira?" he called out, confused.

The tent remained quiet except for a low groan from a man on a cot across the way.

He shuffled to the entrance, one hand on the bandage like it might slip off, holding the thumping in his head at bay. He pushed the flap aside and the cool night air rushed in, carrying the smell of salt from the harbor. It was dark out, stars scattered above, but a glow pulled his eyes a few tents down. People gathered in an open spot, sitting and standing in a loose circle. Candles dotted the ground, small flames flickering in the breeze, lighting faces from below. Quiet sobs carried on the wind.

Elias stepped out and slowly made his way towards the crowd. As he got closer and his eyes adjusted to the darkness and candlelight, the faces of the people sharpened. A man knelt by a candle, head bowed. Another woman wiped her eyes with a sleeve. And there, in the middle, his mother. She sat on her knees, shoulders shaking, something small in her hands. Mira's doll.

Something was off. He moved faster now, ignoring the pain spiking in his head. The candles formed a rough circle. Items were scattered around them on the ground: a locket on a necklace, a child's shoe, a faded photo, a toy truck. A memorial. For the ones lost in the siege. The ones the war took from them.

He reached their mother, dropping to his knees beside her. "Mom... mom, where is Mira?"

She turned, her face wet with tears, eyes red in the candlelight. For a second, she just stared, like she couldn't believe he was there. Then she pulled him in, arms wrapping tight around him, her body shaking as she sobbed. "Oh, honey... Eli... I'm so sorry..." She held him close, her cheek against his, crying harder now.

Elias froze in her arms. The candles flickered around them, the sobs from others joining hers. He pushed back a little, looking at her face, then at the doll in her hand as tears started to take over his own vision. "Mom... where is she?"

She wiped her eyes, but the tears didn't stop. Her voice broke as she spoke. "Your sister... she... she didn't make it out of the truck, Eli... I... I tried..." She couldn't breathe enough to finish.

The words hit him harder than anything the war hit him with before. He forgot to breathe. The memorial spun around him, the candles blurring into streaks of light. "No... no... she was with us... in the truck... She was right there... You said..."

His mother pulled him close again, crying into his shoulder. "I'm so sorry, I tried... I tried to get her out. The soldiers pulled you away... I just couldn't..." She stopped again, her breaths leaving her lungs faster than she could take them in.

Everything froze.

The world went quiet, except for the pounding in his head which got louder. He shook his head, slow at first, then faster, like if he denied it hard enough the words would change. "No. She's ahead. You said she's with the others. She's waiting for us. She's... she's fine." His voice cracked, rising higher, the pain growing in his chest, building like a wave he couldn't stop. The candles around them seemed to dim. It couldn't be real. She couldn't be gone. Not now. Not after everything they'd been through.

Their mother held his face in her hands, her thumbs wiping at his tears, though her own kept falling. "Eli... I reached for her, but... I couldn't get to her in time." Her words broke apart, cries shaking her entire body. "She's gone, honey. She's with your father... and Theo now..."

The denial shattered.

Flashes of memories came rushing in, pieces his mind had buried so deep they hurt coming up. The truck bed, bodies crammed tight, the rocket's whine cutting the air. The blast hitting. The floor buckling under them. Mira's hand in his, small and warm, slipping away as they were flung apart. Smoke filling everything, choking his lungs, her face disappearing into it. Small. Scared.

Another flash rushed in from the depths of his mind: soldiers grabbing him, pulling him from the wreckage, his arms reaching back into the twisted metal and flames. Their mother's scream the only thing he heard, "Mira! No!" Her hands clawing at the burning frame, skin blistering as another soldier dragged her away.

Then the final memory crept in: the soldier carrying him away on his shoulder, the truck a roaring inferno behind them. Their mother on her knees in the dirt, hands empty except for that doll, screaming her name as the flames erased everything, and everyone, left inside.

Reality crashed in, hard and real. No longer hidden.

Elias broke. A sharp cry ripped out of him, loud and raw. He fell forward into his mother's arms, tears coming fast, his body stuttering as he struggled to breathe. "No... no..." The words choked out between gasps. "Mira... no..." Over and over, as if he said it enough it would change. His chest hurt so bad it felt like it was ripping open. He clawed at her shirt, his whole body heaving with cries he couldn't control. "She was right there... I was holding her hand... I should have held on tighter..." The thoughts spilled out between sobs, guilt stabbing in his stomach like a knife pushing through.

Their mother held him tighter, squeezing and rocking him like he was little again, her own cries mixing with his. "It's not your fault, Eli. It's not your fault. You couldn't... none of us could..." Her voice cracked, her tears soaking into his hair. She kept rocking him, her arms strong around him even as her body shook. "I love you. I love you so, so much." But her words broke apart, turning into sobs that matched his. The cries came in unavoidable waves. Elias felt like he was drowning in them, the hurt so deep it froze him. He couldn't feel anything outside of the pain in his chest.

The candles burned around them slowly. The other people were quiet, giving them space in their grief. He cried harder, the pain in his chest raw and endless. Nothing would ever fill the space she left.

Time blurred, minutes into hours. The sobs slowed eventually, turning to quiet hiccups, his throat raw and sore. Their mother kept holding him, her cheek against his head, whispering words he barely heard. "I'm here... we're still here..." Elias pulled back a little, wiping his face with his sleeve, the skin under his eyes puffy and red. The doll lay between them now, its button eyes staring up blankly.

He stared at it, the yarn singed at the edges, the stitches loose in one arm. It looked small and wrong there on the ground, like it didn't belong without Mira's hand holding it. The hurt swelled again, fresh and sharp, twisting in his chest until he couldn't breathe right. He closed his eyes against it, squeezing them shut, willing the pain to stop. Darkness. Just black, endless and quiet. As he sat there, eyes closed, tears flowing, surrounded by the dark behind his eyelids, a small flicker happened.

In the distance, a glow, small at first, like a firefly waking up for the night. It grew more intense, with more lights joining, floating in clusters that lit the space soft and warm with a lingering glimmer. As the glow neared, he could make out a figure.

Mira.

Surrounded by fireflies swirling around her, their light bright and reflecting off her skin. She looked just like she always had, her tangled hair and that spark in her eyes shining and glimmering in the glow of the fireflies. She walked toward him, steady, slow, her hand reaching out when she got near.

"I wouldn't leave you, Eli," she said, her voice clear and close. "Never again."

She grabbed his hand. It felt real, warm, soft. The dark started to change around them. The Dreamwood rushed back in, piece by piece, overtaking the darkness. Trees pushed up from the ground, trunks straightening tall and strong. Roots sank down into the dirt where they belonged. Leaves unfurled on the branches, green and full, catching the light from the fireflies. The river started flowing again, water bubbling up from the springs, rushing over rocks and filling the streams and brooks. The waterfall over the cave poured steady, mist rising cool and fresh. Turtles lounged near the rocks, shells shining and wet. Fireflies spread out, blinking everywhere, lighting the paths and the pools.

They stood there, hand in hand, watching it all come back. The grove filled in, the grass growing thick under their feet, flowers opening along the banks. The big central tree stood up last, its branches perking high, roots burrowing deep. Elias felt the pull of it, the way the whole place settled like it was breathing again. The air smelled like rain on leaves, the river's rush was steady and strong. Vines draped over the cave entrance again, green and thick. The slide on the branch tree twisted down smooth, ending in a pile of soft flower petals. Birds returned to the branches, their songs starting up, quiet at first, then growing, filling the space with sound.

It was all coming back. The broken pieces mending right in front of him. The decay on the ground returning to fresh grass, leaves floating back up and attaching to branches. Streams that had dried up continued to fill, water sparkling as it flowed. He watched a snapped branch on the ground lift up, twisting back into place on a tree trunk, the bark sealing over like it had never broken off. The colors got brighter, the green deeper, and the flowers more distinct. The whole Dreamwood felt alive again, reassembling itself while they stood there, hand in hand.

They walked together toward the big central tree. Though everything else had seemed to go back to normal, the gash was still there, wide and open, sap oozing out from the edges with shadows lingering inside. It looked raw, like it hurt, like the tree itself was in pain and crying out.

Mira turned toward Elias. "Clean it up a little."

Elias reached out with his free hand, pressing his palm against the bark next to the gash. The sap began to pull back, soaking into the wood and returning to the tree's interior. The edges of the gash drew together, slowly at first, then faster, eventually closing altogether. When it finished, a large scar remained, a thick, jagged line down the trunk where the split had been, a reminder of all that had happened. But the tree stood straight, branches full and green, its roots grounded and stabilizing the entire grove.

The Dreamwood felt whole again. Stronger, even with the scar.

Outside, the sobs still shook his body, but a faint smile pulled at his lips through the tears. He felt it, small and real, cutting through the hurt. He pushed back from his mother a little, looking at her through tear-stained eyes. She stared back at him, her own tears still flowing, confusion mixing with the sadness.

"She's still with us, Mom," he said, voice rough but sure. "In our hearts, and in my head. She'll never leave us, not really."

His mother blinked, fresh tears stirring, but a half-smile broke through. She pulled him back into the hug, holding him tight. "You're right... you're so right, Eli. You're such a good big brother."

She reached down, her hand shaking slightly, and grabbed the doll. She pushed it against her cheek and closed her eyes briefly before she kissed the side of the doll and placed it gently at the base of the candles next to a small stone. "For her," she whispered again, her voice breaking. Elias nodded, the lump in his throat too big to speak. They sat there a while longer, watching the flame dance against the night breeze, the candles around them burning low. The memorial felt quieter now, the sobs from others turning to whispers, people starting to stand and walk away slowly. Elias and his mother got up last, her arms clasped around him.

The doll stayed behind, its button eyes catching the flickering light of the candles one last time before they turned and walked away.

They walked back to the tents slowly, the memorial's light fading behind them. Elias leaned on his mother's arm, each step pulling at the ache in his head, but the salty night air helped clear some of the fog. The harbor smelled stronger now, mixing with the smoke from distant fires that still burned somewhere in the city. The stars looked brighter without the candles competing, but everything felt a bit dimmer inside. She was still there, in his mind, but no longer would he hear her laugh or watch her playful smile light up a room. Their mother kept her arm around him, stepping careful like she was afraid he'd break if she let go.

The tent flap was heavy as they pushed inside. The space felt too big with just the two of them, the cots lined up empty except for his. A lantern hung low from the center pole; its flame turned down to a soft glow that threw long shadows on the canvas walls. Elias sat on his cot with his thin blanket rumpled under him. His mother eased down beside him, her face still wet, eyes red and puffy. She wiped at them with her sleeve, but fresh tears continued, slow and quiet, leaking directly from her injured soul.

Outside, voices carried from a nearby fire, soldiers talking low but clear enough to hear through the thin walls of the tent. Elias listened without meaning to, the words pulling his attention from the hurt. "...they're regrouping fast. Scouts say they're massing just outside the city limits, pulling in reinforcements from all over. Tanks, artillery, the works." Another voice, deeper than the last, spoke next. "They aren't backing down after losing the city. Heard from command they're escalating. Talking nukes if we don't pull out."

The first one grunted. "Nukes? If they drop one of those, it's done for everyone. It'll be their end, too."

The talk faded as the soldiers moved off. Elias stared at the tent flap, the words sinking in like stones in his stomach. Nukes. The kind of thing that erased everything, no hiding from it, no Dreamwood to run to. The war wasn't over. It was just getting bigger, meaner. He looked back at his mother, her face still sad, tears shining in the lantern light. She wiped her eyes again, sniffling quietly.

She reached out, taking his hand in hers, pulling him close. "Tell me about it... the place you and Mira made. The one with the trees and the river. Tell me what it's like."

Elias blinked, the question pulling him out of the soldiers' words. He leaned back against the cot, closing his eyes for a second. The Dreamwood came easy now, its shapes filling his head.

"It's a forest. Big, with trees everywhere. The paths are soft under your feet, like walking on moss that doesn't stick to your shoes. There's a river that runs through it, wide and clear, with fish jumping sometimes. You can hear it all the time, rushing over rocks and filling the streams, making everything feel calm. The cave's there too, with a waterfall over the front, like a door that keeps the bad stuff out. Turtles live in the pool inside the cave, slow ones with shells that shine with patterns on them. Fireflies float around at night, lighting everything up so we don't need lanterns."

He kept going, the words coming easier as he pictured it. "The big tree in the middle has branches that reach out like arms, and we added a slide to one, smooth wood that twists down to a pile of flowers at the bottom. Yellow and pink ones, soft to land on. The vines hang thick around the cave, and there's hidden streams under the bushes. Berries grow along the banks, sweet ones you can pick and eat right there. Birds sit in the branches, singing sometimes, and the air smells like rain on leaves, fresh all the time."

His mother listened, her eyes closing as he talked, tears still slipping down her cheeks. She nodded now and then, like she could see it too. "And there are healing trees in the grove," Elias continued. "Trunks strong, branches that wrap around like a hug. Leaves that catch the light and make everything feel better. Roots go deep, holding it all together. Even after... everything... they stand back up." He paused for a moment, then told her about Theo and their father's trees, and how they could visit them anytime.

She opened her eyes, looking at him with that sad, teary gaze. The lantern light caught the wetness on her face, making it shine. "It sounds beautiful, Eli. Like a place where nothing bad can happen." Her voice trembled a little as she talked. A small smile broke through the tears, though. "All these stories you went on and on about... they remind me of a place. A place I visited as a little girl, no older than Mira... A place where we can hopefully escape this war altogether..."

The words hung there, quiet in the tent. Elias didn't ask what she meant. Not yet. The night outside remained still, the soldiers' talk about regrouping and nuclear threats fading into the background. But her words opened something, a small crack of light in the dark, like a new path emerging in the Dreamwood. He closed his eyes again, and the grove returned.

THE END

About the Author

Brian Ligouri is a veteran of the United States Army and the Global War on Terrorism. His experiences during those years shaped much of the emotional realism and themes found in his writing.

This story reflects the quiet resilience of the human mind and the powerful ways imagination can help us endure life's darkest moments.

Glimpses of the Dreamwood is his debut novel.

The Dreamwood will return.

9 798999 525 4034